# STRANGER DANGER

STEVE RICHER

The cover art for this book makes use of licensed stock photography. All photography is for illustrative purposes only.

This is a work of fiction. Any resemblance of characters to actual persons, living or dead, is purely coincidental.



ISBN-13: 978-1720316916
ISBN-10: 1720316910

Visit the Web Site at http://SteveRicherBooks.com

# SUMMARY

**Don't trust anyone. Especially children.**

After his parents are found murdered, eight-year-old Boyd is sent into foster care. Tori and her husband Lucas believe a child is the one thing that can improve their idyllic suburban life.

They are wrong.

The gifted boy's unstable nature bubbles to the surface, driving a wedge between Tori and Lucas. She's certain they can help Boyd with support and therapy, but Lucas has his doubts.

Meanwhile, Detective Gannon is counting down the days until retirement as he investigates the murders.

What he discovers is the stuff of nightmares.

# CHAPTER 1

Janet Wells was angry and she tightened her grip on the oversized steering wheel. She knew it was a stupid reaction and suffered the consequences. Her arthritis acted up.

Her mood wasn't improved by the fact that she could barely see the road. The entire summer had been cool and now there was a hint of fog in the air, which was accentuated by the headlights of her old Ford.

The road was narrow and serpentine, trees flanking it to the point of claustrophobia. She had driven down this route a million times in her seventy-three years, traveling from her family home to the town. She imagined strangers from the city would get lost or pull to the side to check their doggone GPS devices and newfangled phones.

The trick was to trust the road. When in doubt, look at the ditch and try not to go into it. Her husband, bless his soul, used to say that all the time. You didn't have to see anything. Just follow the path.

Pain flared in her joints and she winced. Her hands were hurting like they hadn't in a long time.

"Goshdarn knitting," she spat at no one in the empty car.

She wasn't sure why she devoted the energy to this god-awful hobby. It was quilting she was into. That was a proper lady's pastime. But like any backwater town in America, hobbies were ruled by politics. Cliques.

Hags!

It was bad enough that she had refused to contribute to the spring potluck at the First Presbyterian. She could still hear the harsh whispers every time she went to town to shop, whispers which were meant to be overheard, obviously. There was no way she could miss those judging glances.

The bloomin' knitting club was her going the extra mile. It was her compromise, not that Betsy Hyden and Augusta Stoops ever made compromises of their own.

Dirty old hags!

They didn't even *like* knitting—and they were terrible at it. It took Betsy four months to make one pair of socks and they didn't even match. No, the whole thing was a sorry excuse to get together to gossip. And drink! Augusta wasn't fooling everyone with her *homemade iced tea*. You could smell the bourbon in that glass from a country mile.

Janet missed her sisters. Cancer had claimed them all. Was that why she loved quilting so much, because that had been a hobby they'd done together? Maybe it was. Nevertheless, that was the one thing she didn't mind doing even if it made her hands ache something fierce.

Her mission in life, she decided, was to find a way to quit knitting club without turning the Blue Hair Brigade against her. That wouldn't be easy. There would be dang gossip, that was inevitable, but maybe she could find a way to make a diplomatic exit.

But I won't be able to miss the next church potluck, she grumbled to herself.

Janet let her mind wander, going through possible outcomes. She used to be good at that. Forty years working for the school district had made her quite adept at improvisation and coming up with solutions to difficult problems. She would think of something to get out of this predicament.

To get away from these fracking' old witches!

She was lost in thought when her headlights illuminated something in the middle of the road.

At first she thought it was a deer and prepared herself to stomp on the brakes and swerve. Back in 1987, her husband had wrecked a perfectly good Chrysler after coming face-to-face with an oversized buck. This had renewed his passion for hunting a few months later. Only the color was wrong now. It wasn't light brown like a typical deer. It was red.

And small.

Fearful of landing into the ditch, she slowed down. It wasn't an animal or even a piece of garbage.

It was a little boy!

What was a child doing in the middle of the road late at night? Her mind went through a thousand hypotheses before she decided on the next course of action. She pulled over and turned off the engine, leaving the headlights on.

Janet forgot the pain in her hands and opened the door. The ding-ding-ding alarm of the keys still being in the ignition pierced the silence, though she barely heard it. Up ahead, the child didn't even flinch. He was looking at her.

A thought crossed her mind. How would the child react? Weren't they told to scream something like "stranger danger!" when someone unknown approached them? Did it matter if it was simply to help? Then again, there was no one else around and she was worried about him.

She stared right back as she came out of the vehicle. Going by her own height, she estimated that he was four feet tall. He was slim but he had a round face, almost cherubic, with soft skin. His face was featureless. Baby fat. His hair was fair and styled in the common bowl cut.

"Hey," she said in a pleasant greeting even though she was filled with anxiety.

He looked at her but didn't reply. He was wearing jeans, a white shirt, and a red windbreaker. It was hanging loose, the wind making it flap gently. Janet shivered in the cool air, but the child didn't react.

"Are you lost?"

No reply.

"What's your name?"

Again, he didn't say anything. He was looking at her and she wondered for an instant if he was blind because it was as if he hadn't even noticed her.

"What are you doing in the middle of the road? Are your parents around?"

Janet took measured steps toward him. She had to do something, right? She could just imagine the knitting club gossip if she didn't. "Did you hear? Janet Wells found a little boy and kept on driving! I always knew she was up to no good."

After a moment, she stopped thinking about those old hags. She was indifferent to them. What mattered was this child. Something was definitely wrong about this situation.

She came even closer and stood three feet away from him. He still hadn't budged, though he was looking at her.

"Are you okay?" she asked.

It occurred to her that she should check his wrist for a tag. Didn't some parents register their children like pets these days? In case they went missing? She had always thought the idea outrageous, more of that millennial snowflake nonsense, yet somehow this would be truly helpful at the moment.

"How old are you, honey?" No answer. "Do you have a phone number I can call to get your mom to come get you?"

Janet considered searching his pockets for some form of identification when she noticed something that didn't belong. It was on the shirt. There were red spots and she knew in her heart that it wasn't some highfalutin modern art pattern.

It was blood.

"Good gravy…"

She had raised four boys and, between football practices and bike spills, she knew what blood looked like. This child seemed in good shape and he sure as heck wasn't returning from football practice.

"Why is there blood on you, honey? You can tell me, you know. Are you hurt?" A darker thought crossed her mind. "Is someone else hurt?"

He once more didn't say anything, but his eyes shifted to meet hers. He understood what she said. It was like he was terrified to tell her the truth.

"Don't move, okay? Stay right there!"

Janet rushed back to the Ford and dipped inside for her purse, rummaging through it as fast as she could. Her youngest had made her vow to keep a cell phone on her at all times. She'd always laughed at the idea—it wasn't as if she was even interested in this Facebook business—but now she made a promise to thank her son for it.

Her hands trembling, the ignition alarm still droning on in the silent night, she called the police.

~ ~ ~ ~

Officer Coffman was on duty tonight, picking up all the overtime and extra shifts he could to afford the wedding he had promised his high school sweetheart. As soon as he left the station, his heart raced.

There were a few old ladies in town who got their rocks off calling the cops for no reason—raccoons knocking down trash cans and "suspicious characters" who turned out to be their own grandkids smoking weed—but Janet Wells had never been a troublemaker. If she called, there had to be a good reason.

He met her five minutes after receiving the call on State Route 7, just off Alcaraz Drive. He stopped the patrol car in the other direction, two wheels off the pavement. He didn't bother putting on his jacket, secretly enjoying people looking at the bulging biceps he worked so hard to maintain.

"Mrs. Wells," he said in greeting.

The elderly woman was crouching in front of her car. She had draped a gray blanket around the shoulders of a child and was holding it in place.

"Evening, Officer."

"This the boy you called about? What is he, lost?"

"I haven't got the foggiest. He won't speak. But…"

"But what?" Coffman asked, coming closer while looking around as if this was some sort of ambush.

"There's blood on his shirt. I know what blood looks like, and this is blood. Fresh, too. Look."

The woman opened the blanket so the police officer could see. His face blanched immediately.

"What's your name, little man? Is somebody hurt?"

"He doesn't speak, Officer."

Coffman fell into a catcher's position in front of the child and smiled. "You have to tell me if someone is hurt, okay? If you tell me, I can help. Do you understand?"

At last, the child nodded. Coffman and Mrs. Wells exchanged a glance pregnant with hope and relief.

"Tell me, where do you live? Can you remember?"

It took several seconds and finally the boy swiveled on his heels. He pointed at a house in the distance on Alcaraz. It was half hidden by trees, but it was recognizable.

“That house, the brick rancher on the corner?”

“The old Wentworth house,” Mrs. Wells remarked.

“New people moved in last week. That would explain why I’ve never seen that kid around.” Coffman looked at the child again. “Did something happen in there?”

The boy nodded faintly.

“Is someone hurt?”

He nodded again.

“Shit,” Coffman muttered. He stood up and instinctively put his hand on his weapon. “Mrs. Wells, stay with him while I check things out, all right?”

Adrenaline taking over, he jogged toward the rancher. Only at the last minute did he remember to radio the station for backup and paramedics. He considered waiting for other officers to show up before going in, yet he couldn’t ignore the fact that someone might be injured inside the house. Every second counted.

He sprinted across the overgrown lawn, drew his pistol, and approached the entrance. His heart was beating a mile a minute when he found the front door ajar.

The house was dark and he fumbled as he pulled out his flashlight. He did what he’d been taught at the police academy six months ago, crossing his wrists so that the beam of light pointed in the same direction as his weapon.

He didn’t know what to do anymore. Should he announce his presence? That would make intruders take off running. On the other hand, there might be people here who needed his help. It was scary how fast you forgot your training when you really needed it, he thought.

"Hello?" he called at last.

He walked into the silent house. His feet echoed and it made him realize that there was little furniture. He saw boxes stacked in what was supposed to be the living room. It smelled like fresh paint.

He followed his beam of light through the dining room, also empty, and then the kitchen. Nausea hit him like a freight train and it was a miracle he didn't puke.

"Mary, mother of God…"

Between the dining set and counter were two corpses, a man and woman. Both were on their backs, mouths open, eyes wide. They were most definitely dead. There was so much blood around them that it was impossible to see the white linoleum underneath.

Coffman finally pitched forward and lost his dinner.

# CHAPTER 2

That first sip of Cherry Coke was pure heaven and Gannon closed his eyes to savor it.

He was well aware that it looked stupid, like some redneck wine connoisseur, but there was nothing as fantastic as feeling those sweet bubbles sparkling on the tongue. He had cut back to two soft drinks a week and tonight he had poured himself a tall glass. There was no ice since he took his time and it only diluted the precious reward.

His feet were on the coffee table and his attention was on HGTV. He had no interest in personally renovating homes, but there was something about watching those twin brothers flipping houses that was riveting. There had to be some sort of psychological reason for it. There always was, as he'd learned from all his years on the job. Humans were complicated creatures.

He took another sip as he watched the brothers pretend to argue about sconces. They clearly didn't have any pride left. Then again, he supposed he could pretend to argue about sconces himself for the amount of money they were raking in.

The phone rang and he groaned. This couldn't be happening. He put down his glass and reached for the phone. Caller ID was a beautiful invention, but it also made it impossible to pretend you didn't know who was calling you.

He reluctantly answered. "Captain Vail, what a pleasant surprise."

"Skip the bullshit, Gannon. I have a case for you."

"No can do, Cap. My shift is over. I have my curlers on, my feet up, a soda in my hand and, after my show, I'm going to bed."

"Why don't you be a team player for once?" his superior spat. "It would go a long way to redeem you in the department."

"Whoever said I need redemption?"

He took a long drag from his glass, anything to make him think of something else. He was too old to be rattled by the young and ambitious captain.

"Gannon, this is important. There's been a double homicide in Hillford."

"Shit."

"Yeah, which is why I need you."

Hillford was half an hour away and local law enforcement was a handful of good ol' boys. They weren't equipped to handle major crimes and that was the reason why the State Police was being called in.

"Send me the address," Gannon said, his words coming out as a sigh.

Aside from having to quickly down the Cherry Coke, his only regret was that he wouldn't find out what sconces the brothers would end up choosing.

~ ~ ~ ~

Gannon arrived on Alcaraz Drive in just over twenty minutes. He remembered to stub out his cigarette before getting out of his car. He didn't want to leave the butt around to confuse forensics. One of their vans was already there, along with the county coroner, and the entire Hillford motor pool.

He flashed his badge and a woman let him past the yellow tape.

"Who was the responding?" he asked her.

"Bucky Coffman. He's over there."

Gannon thanked her and headed toward a young man who was leaning against a squad car. His muscles were intimidating and yet he had the face of a teenager. Even in the relative darkness, his skin was pale.

"Evening, Officer. I'm Detective Gannon, State Police." Coffman looked up and they shook hands. "Word on the street is that you were first on the scene?"

"Yes, sir."

"Why don't you walk me through this?"

The young man straightened up, undoubtedly feeling the importance of the moment. "Yes, sir. Uh, we got a call at the station. Janet Wells said she had found a little kid wandering in the middle of the street. I was dispatched over there on State Route 7. There was blood on his clothing."

"Blood?"

"Yes, sir. A little bit."

The officer pointed to an old Ford on the edge of the perimeter. In the backseat were an elderly woman and a child.

"That's the boy?"

"Yes, sir. CPS has been notified and they're sending somebody to get him. Next to him is Mrs. Wells."

"Okay, so how do we go from wandering child to double homicide?"

"I asked the kid if someone was hurt. He wasn't very talkative, but eventually he pointed out his ho… his dwelling. I made entry and discovered the two deceased bo… uh, subjects."

"You don't have to talk like you're writing a report, Officer. Just use your own words, okay?"

Coffman nodded and rolled his eyes, embarrassed to have made such a basic mistake in front of a senior detective. "Yes, sir."

"Tell me what you saw."

"Two goddamn corpses, sir. It was horrible, blood everywhere."

"You found no intruders on the scene?"

"No, just the bodies on the kitchen floor. They had been slashed open. It was a carnage."

"Yeah…" Gannon muttered, adding this to the long list of eventual nightmares.

"There's something else, Detective."

"What is it?"

"I… I screwed up. It was so awful that… I puked,

sir."

"I've had bad fish before, too, Officer. Nothing to be ashamed of."

"I puked next to the bodies. I contaminated the crime scene, sir. I'm so sorry."

"Don't worry about it. Make sure to tell forensics before you leave, so they can sample your DNA, okay?"

The officer nodded and Gannon walked away. He wasn't in a hurry to see the corpses, so he headed to Janet Wells. He had her meet him ten feet from her car and introduced himself.

"Officer Coffman said you called because you came across a child?"

"That's the craziest doggone situation, isn't it? My word…"

She told her story, corroborating what the cop had already said while adding extra details about knitting clubs and old hags.

"Do you know the boy?" Gannon asked, clutching his notepad.

"I've never seen him before. He wouldn't even tell me his name. I was just keeping him company until somebody comes for him."

"Thank you, ma'am."

Gannon smiled graciously before walking away, though he knew that the effect always looked weird on him, given his wrinkled face and thinning hair. His ex-wife had told him he should keep the smiling to a minimum as to not distress anyone. Just to spite her, he smiled in her presence whenever he could.

He cautiously opened the back door of the Ford, illuminating the interior. He crouched next to the backseat. The kid was expressionless. Gannon had learned years ago that hysterics was rarely the default reaction after gruesome crimes.

"Hey, big guy. My name is Lou. I'm a police detective." The child looked at him. That was a good start. "Can you tell me your name?"

Nothing was said, but Gannon was patient. Silence made people uncomfortable and eventually they always spoke.

"Boyd," the kid said, his voice soft and on the verge of being high-pitched.

"It's nice to meet you, Boyd. Do you have a last name, too? I hear that most people have one."

The joke worked and the child almost smiled. "Begum."

"It's nice to meet you, Boyd Begum. My job here is to find out what happened. Can you help me with that?"

He shrugged.

"Just tell me what you saw, okay? That's all you need to do. That's your house?"

Boyd nodded.

"Okay. Now tell me why you were walking in the middle of the road."

"I was scared."

"What were you scared of, Boyd?"

"The… The man."

"What man?"

He shrugged again. "I didn't see him good."

"What did the man do?" Gannon asked, knowing that he was rushing his questions, but he was curious about the answers.

"I was playing in the laundry room; it's where I make my fort. I heard noises. Mom yelled something. Then dad shouted. There was another man, like they were arguing. I was scared."

"Did you hear what they were saying?"

Boyd shook his head. "I don't remember. There were bad words. Then mommy screamed. I went to look. I saw the blood. Blood everywhere. Mommy and daddy were on the floor, and the man… he ran away. I was scared and I left the house."

"Tell me about this man, Boyd. What did he look like?"

"He had black skin. A beard. He was tall. Are mommy and daddy dead?"

For the first time, the boy showed emotion, fear and sadness morphing together. It broke Gannon's heart.

"I'm sorry, Boyd. Somebody is going to ask you what the black man looks like, okay? He's going to ask you questions so they can draw him. Will you do that for me, Boyd? It would really help me out."

After several seconds, the kid nodded.

*Jesus Christ*, Gannon hated his job sometimes. He hated it more and more. He excused himself and walked further along the perimeter where an ambulance was parked. He knew the paramedic, saw him almost every week somewhere around the county.

"Hey, Lou."

"What's up?"

Gannon leaned against the ambulance and lit a cigarette.

"Those things will kill you, you know."

"So will high cholesterol, diabetes, and getting rammed by a tanker truck on the highway. Get off my case, Bob."

"Fine, whatever. Still going on that fishing trip Labor Day weekend?"

"Absolutely. At least nobody gives me crap about smoking there. How's your wife? Still banging the mailman?"

The paramedic rolled his eyes. "Blow me."

"You know your kids look like the mailman, right?"

"Aren't you supposed to go inside and, you know, do detective work?"

That killed the bantering mood and Gannon took one last drag of his cigarette before crushing it under his foot.

"That kid… Jesus. Can you imagine?"

"Few months back, I saw this little girl," Bob began. "She had witnessed her father getting shot after a carjacking."

"I remember that case. Didn't work it, but I remember."

"She had that same look this kid has. Shell-shocked, probably traumatized for life."

"Hell of a thing to go through," Gannon mumbled.

He felt rage mounting through him. He took a deep breath and headed to the house. It was time to discover what had happened to the child's parents.

# CHAPTER 3

Cadmium Scarlet was probably Tori's favorite color, but it was too red for the sky. She mixed in a little white using the tip of her brush and it promptly yielded the hue she was going for.

"That's better," she whispered with satisfaction.

Before painting the sky—a dusk scene—she took a step back from the easel. The sun was rising outside her workshop and it wasn't the best condition to judge colors. Nevertheless, she felt that having natural light influencing her choice of oils was part of the artistic process. As the sunlight intensified and paled, the image on her canvas changed as well.

Whoever said you had to follow strict rules when creating art anyway?

She moved to her largest brush and swept from side to side, spreading the paint thin to create a gradient across the sky. Then she switched to her palette knife and used Cobalt Blue to outline tall mountains in the distance.

She was in the zone. She switched brushes and colors like a racecar driver switching gears, her eyes barely ever leaving the large canvas. She had a clear vision of what she wanted to paint and she needed to get it her out of her system as fast as possible.

That was why she didn't even hear the door behind her until it slammed shut.

"Morning, baby."

She didn't reply, instead dabbing Yellow Ochre above the mountains to create highlights on the clouds. Lucas finally broke the spell when he came up behind her and kissed her on the cheek, his thick beard scratching her.

She was annoyed by the distraction, but decided not to take it out on her husband. She smiled tightly and said, "Hey."

"Here."

She turned toward Lucas and he handed her a cup of coffee and half a bagel on a paper napkin. There was cream cheese on the bagel. Didn't he know by now that she preferred jam? She kept her mouth shut.

"Thanks."

"I didn't notice you getting out of bed before," he said.

"I woke up before dawn and was inspired. I wanted to come out here while my vision was fresh."

"Geez, what time was it?" He yawned and checked his watch.

"Five something."

"Geez," he repeated as if utterly disgusted.

Tori took a step back so she wouldn't spill coffee or crumbs on her painting. She took a cautious sip of scorching coffee while Lucas observed her canvas.

"Another landscape? Seriously?"

"Thank you so much for the encouragement. I appreciate it."

He winced and lifted his shoulders. "It's fine. It's beautiful."

"But?"

"But… Forget I said anything, baby. It's nice."

She knew he disapproved of her landscapes. It wasn't commercial enough and, if Lucas was anything, it was commercial. He kissed her on the lips this time, a quick peck. Sometimes she wondered if it was more out of habit than out of genuine affection. She hated herself when she had these thoughts.

She put the bagel down half-eaten. "Anyway, I'm planning this series: *Blue Mountains*. Each sky will be a different color, but still realistic, you know? After I have a dozen paintings, I'll pitch them to Savely Artemiev in LA."

"He turned you down last time," Lucas pointed out.

"But this time is different. Please believe in me, all right?"

"Sure thing, baby." He glanced at his watch and groaned. "Shit, I have to get ready."

"Big day?"

"I have to meet with the architect this morning about those changes on the second phase models. The zoning commission is really crawling up my ass about that. Then I'm having lunch at the Steep Gorge Chamber of Commerce."

"Sales pitch?" Tori asked.

"Yeah, it's my moment. If I could get a few of the golden citizens on board, investing in the project, it would really help with the little people and sale-through."

She could tell he was anxious. Lucas had come a long way, from a carpenter to a general contractor. Now was the biggest opportunity of his career as he was trying to become a real estate developer.

"I'm sure you'll do great, Lucas." As she finished her sentence, her phone buzzed in her pocket. She wiped her hands on the bib of her overalls and fished out the phone. "Hello?"

"Mrs. Ramsdale? This is Ruth Zakrzewski from the Department of Children and Families."

Tori's eyes widened. "Of course, Mrs. Zakrzewski! How are you?"

She snapped her fingers so Lucas would stay put. He spun on his heels on his way out.

"Are you and your husband still enthusiastic about becoming foster parents?"

"Absolutely," Tori said without hesitation.

"That's wonderful because we have a little boy here who desperately needs your help."

~ ~ ~ ~

Lucas was irritated and he had trouble hiding it. Or there was also the possibility that he was purposely *not* making an effort to hide it so that Tori would know how he felt about the whole thing. Either was plausible, she knew.

He kept his eyes on the road, not having glanced her way since they'd left home. Tori didn't let that bother her. It wasn't the first time he'd acted this way and she knew from experience it was best to not say anything. She hoped that the ninety-minute drive to Franklin would make him mellow.

In truth, she was doing this for her and she didn't feel remotely guilty. She couldn't have any children and, over six months ago, they had decided to become foster parents. They had been vetted and had taken the mandatory classes.

Tori had started to believe that they would never call her and put a child in their care. Lucas's going theory was that they lived in a shithole town and the government rightly decided not to send a kid to that area.

They had, in fact, moved to Steep Gorge last summer, calling themselves pioneers of sort. It was a perfect plan for what Lucas had in mind, becoming a real estate developer. Land here was cheap and therefore ideal. The town still had that Norman Rockwell feel, Main Street lined up with small shops which could barely stay in business. It was transforming into a commuter town for Franklin even though it was way out on the outskirts.

It was almost an hour before Lucas finally said something. "I don't know if they'll let me do my presentation again."

"Of course, they will," Tori replied.

The meeting with Child Protective Services had been set up for one o'clock and that meant that Lucas had needed to cancel his extremely important lunch.

"You think?" he asked with hope in his voice.

"For once, you have a point about Steep Gorge being a one-horse town. It's not exactly Manhattan, you know? It's not like the Chamber of Commerce has to juggle conferences with Bill Gates and visiting dignitaries from China or anything. They'll let you do your presentation next week."

At that, he relaxed for the first time and smiled faintly. He reached over to his wife and patted her hand, which relieved her. They were a team, she thought. They were in this together. That was required to be great foster parents.

With minutes to spare, they got to the local CPS branch, itself an office in the regional Department of Children and Families building. Built in the late sixties, its blocky form was an insult to the very concept of architecture. They parked the Subaru and went inside. They had to be redirected at three different reception desks before Ruth Zakrzewski came their way.

"Mr. and Mrs. Ramsdale! I'm so happy you could come on such short notice."

Mrs. Zakrzewski was a heavyset woman in her late fifties. She had a round face and an easy smile. Her hair was completely white which accentuated her kind demeanor.

"Of course," Tori answered as they all shook hands. "You said this was an emergency? Is that normal?"

Mrs. Zakrzewski's smile became strained. "Why don't you join me in my office? There are things I need to tell you both."

Tori and Lucas glanced at each other with concern, but followed the older woman through a maze of corridors. They entered a cramped utilitarian office and

Mrs. Zakrzewski sat behind her desk.

"So…" she began with a deep breath. "The little boy who needs help today is called Boyd. He's been under our care for the past few days, in a group home, and now he needs a more permanent solution since he has no family."

Tori was beaming. "That's why we're here."

"I see from your file that this will be your first foster child."

"Yes, and we're very excited."

Lucas nodded as well to echo the sentiment.

"I wish your first time wasn't as complicated," Mrs. Zakrzewski said.

Tori didn't say anything. She was well aware that things had to be quite bad for children to become wards of the state. Abusive homes, absentee parents, orphans, there was no end to the hardships they suffered. Their role as foster parents was to look past that, offering the love and support they had never known.

"The child—Boyd—he's eight years old. He has gone through a very traumatic experience last week in Hillford."

"What sort of experience?" Lucas asked.

Tori herself shifted on her chair. She was expecting anything, though she knew that she was ill-prepared. What would she say to a kid who had been sexually molested or held hostage by a family member? She couldn't guess that the truth was far worse.

"His parents…" Mrs. Zakrzewski cleared her throat. "There was an intruder, some sort of home invasion, and both his parents were killed. He witnessed it."

"Oh my God," Tori whispered.

Mrs. Zakrzewski gave a few lurid details about the murder and what she knew of the police investigation. She also mentioned that the boy's two parents had no next of kin. He was alone in the world.

"Believe it or not, children witnessing violence is not that rare in this business. The good news is that the boy is young enough to be able to recover. I'm not saying it will be easy, especially at first, but we have a good success rate in this kind of situation."

"What does that mean for us?" Lucas asked. "I mean, is he more screwed up than a regular kid?"

"Lucas!"

"It's okay," Mrs. Zakrzewski said patiently. "This is a legitimate concern. What you're facing is a child who will be withdrawn. It may be hard to penetrate his shell, to gain his trust. You can't think about the long-term effects for now. Your role will be to support him in any way you can. Show him a good time. Get him to talk, to act normal again. In time, he will."

Tori looked at her husband and he seemed as worried as she was. Would they be up to the task?

"Is there anything special we need to do?" he inquired. "Pills or treatments or something?"

"He has undergone a medical checkup once he got to our facility," the older woman said, handing a file to Tori. "He was screened for diseases, past surgeries, allergies, that sort of thing. He's physically healthy."

"And psychologically?"

"There's obviously some trauma, as I'm sure you understand. I've taken the liberty of contacting a child psychologist in Steep Gorge, Dr. Talia Curnutt. Do you know her?"

"No," Tori said before Lucas said the same.

"She comes highly recommended. In any case, Boyd's treatments are covered under Medicaid. In addition to the seven hundred dollars monthly rate you get, the state allows for a three hundred dollars trauma allowance."

At that, Lucas perked up and Tori was mortified. This whole foster care thing was an afterthought for him. He was going along with it because it made her happy. But now he was on board because of a thousand bucks a month? It was downright embarrassing, though she decided not to let that bother her. The child had to come first.

Once they had filled out paperwork, Mrs. Zakrzewski led the couple out of office. They ventured into the labyrinth of hallways again until they came upon a playroom. It was small, as if it was a holding pen separate from the actual playroom used by the other children.

Tori's heart stopped beating when she saw the boy. He was small for eight years old. She would've guessed seven. He was kneeling on the carpeted floor, his feet spread sideways and folded as if he was a ragdoll. He was playing with plastic blocks.

"Hi, Boyd," Mrs. Zakrzewski said as she came forward. "You remember when we talked about you going to live with a new family?" He nodded. "Well, this is Tori and Lucas Ramsdale and you're going to stay with them for a while. How does that sound?"

He didn't reply. Tori knelt next to him and smiled broadly.

"You like these blocks? I used to have the same when I was your age. Maybe we can play together sometime."

Boyd shrugged evasively. Tori looked at Lucas who also shrugged, not knowing what to do or say next. Tori realized that she was on her own. The fate of this child was in her hands and she actually welcomed the challenge.

"I promise you two things, Boyd. First, Lucas and I, we'll take great care of you. Second, you'll have the time of your life with us."

# CHAPTER 4

Tori had always known that hosting a foster kid would be difficult, but she had underestimated how hard it would be.

Boyd had been with them several days now. There had been excitement at first as Tori and Lucas purchased clothes and toys, setting him up in his own bedroom. It had already been decorated and filled with furniture months ago for an eventual occupant, but actually having a child here was different from theory.

Today was the fourth day and Tori was coming to the realization that she had to get involved more with him. It was summer, school still a long time away even though she had already signed him up—he was set to start third grade in September. For the time being, she reread a bunch of books on child development.

She had never felt this inadequate.

She envied Lucas who had an excuse to leave the house. He was taking meetings, working at his office downtown, walking through the homes which were still under construction. For her part, she was stuck in the house with Boyd all day long.

No, not *stuck*. It was the wrong word. It wasn't fair to him. She had chosen this situation, unlike him. She refused to let her emotions show. Boyd had to see her as a rock, as someone he could lean on through this ordeal.

She had doted on him since he'd first arrived and yet that yielded little result. He barely spoke and barely ate, picking at his food. It didn't matter if she made macaroni and cheese, hot dogs, or tuna casserole, Boyd took a few bites and then stared into the distance as if he was in a world of his own.

He wasn't interested in books or even video games. *You know that something is wrong when a child refuses to play video games*, she thought. The only time he ever seemed normal was when he was watching cartoons. She figured it was as good a distraction as any, although it made her feel useless. Wasn't she supposed to be doing something?

Actually…

They had given him a tour of the property, but Tori remembered that it hadn't been in depth. And that gave her an idea.

"Hey, Boyd," she said as she found him on the living room floor, flipping idly through one of her fashion magazines. "You want to see something cool? Follow me."

She extended her hand. He didn't take it but he did follow her, which was a start. They left the house through the back door.

"Remember I told you about my workshop? This is it, that building over there. That's where I work."

"You work in there?" he asked, clearly unimpressed by the oversized toolshed.

When they had bought the house last year, this

building had been used as a small chicken coop. It had taken weeks to get the smell out while Lucas had cut in windows and made the place livable.

"I'm a painter and that's where I do it."

"What do you paint? Chairs and tables and walls?"

Tori couldn't help but laugh. "No, I paint on canvases. I do pictures."

"You're an artist?"

"I guess so. You know about art?"

"Mrs. Smith made us finger paint in kindergarten."

They reached the workshop. "Maybe you can paint something for me, then. What do you say?"

Her smile was infectious and he gave her one of his own. This was more progress than she'd seen so far and her heart was suddenly light. They went inside.

The first painting of *Blue Mountains* was still on the easel, having been abandoned since receiving that phone call from Mrs. Zakrzewski. Stacked against the walls were some of her other finished paintings. Two tables were covered with supplies.

"This is what I'm working on at the moment," she said, pointing at the easel. "What do you think?"

"The colors are strange."

"You don't think it's realistic to have a red sky and blue mountains?"

"No. The sky is blue and mountains are green, I guess."

"Okay," Tori began, leaning back against a table. "But

what if it's sunrise? You know what happens at sunrise?"

"The sun goes up. Night is over."

"That's right. And what color is the sun early in the morning?"

"Orange?"

"Exactly! Sometimes it's pink or yellow or purple. It all depends on the clouds, atmospheric pressure, shadows, things like that."

"But…" His voice trailed off and he squinted, looking at the canvas.

"But what?"

"There is no sun in the picture. You didn't paint a sun."

"Just because I didn't paint it, it doesn't mean it's not there. Maybe the sun is right behind the mountain, just below. Maybe it's off to the side, right over here."

She pointed to a spot two feet away to the left of the canvas.

"Oh," Boyd said, grasping what she meant.

"You know what, Boyd? That's the beauty of art. We see things we want to see. But if you keep looking, you'll discover new layers, new elements you never would've guessed."

The hint of a smile appeared across his lips and he took a step closer to the easel, analyzing the painting. "Like… Maybe someone is watching this mountain while wearing sunglasses and that makes everything a different color."

"Yeah!" Tori said, stunned by the idea. "You're a budding art expert, you know that? Sunglasses, I like that."

She realized that this was the most interesting discussion about art she'd had in ages. Even Lucas had never questioned her this way. It's was exhilarating.

"You want to draw something with me, Boyd?"

She didn't give him a chance to answer and produced a couple of sketchbooks. She flipped to blank pages before handing him one of the pads along with a pencil. She helped him up on a stool and he bent over the table as he began to draw.

She stayed on her feet, but remained close enough to watch what he was doing. She herself thought about sketching him. On the other hand, she didn't want to freak him out, so she decided to draw the happy face of a puppy. *Who doesn't like puppies?*

Boyd held his pencil too tight and his strokes were slow as well as imprecise. If he showed an interest, she would teach him how to draw. In the meantime, she just wanted him to have something to do.

She was halfway done with the floppy ears of a beagle when she glanced again at Boyd's page. There were two people in his drawing even though it was difficult to tell who they were or what they were doing. They were glorified stick figures.

"Do you have red crayons?" he asked.

"Uh, sure. I don't have crayons, but I have coloring pencils." She stretched over her table to get the Prismacolor box. "You're thinking about doing a red sky like in my painting? You're wearing sunglasses?"

"No," he said. "It's to draw the blood around my parents."

~ ~ ~ ~

While doing the dishes after dinner, when she recounted the episode to Lucas, he let out a long sigh and stopped moving.

"Fuck…"

"It's not his fault," Tori said. "He's been through so much."

"It's creepy as shit, baby."

"I should have known that making him draw could make some memories come out. It's my fault. We have to find a way for him to enjoy himself without, you know…"

"Creeping us out?" Lucas completed.

"Stop it."

She slapped him playfully on the shoulder, but she was helpless against his disarming smile. Her husband could be insensitive, though never in a mean way.

"You're happy, Tori?"

She nodded. "I am. I think Boyd will be good for me. For us."

"Then I'm happy, too."

"We just need to find something for him to do. There has to be something…" She plunged her hands back into the warm water and washed the last pan, scrubbing it clean. She straightened up and grinned. "I know!"

"What?"

"We have LEGOS! Remember, we bought them just after we were accepted by the Department of Children and Families. I bet he would love playing with those. And you could play with him!"

Lucas snarled. "I don't know, sounds more like art to me."

"It's construction. That's right up your alley, bae."

"Did you just call me *bae*?"

"Why yes, I did!"

"Mrs. Ramsdale, are you trying to seduce me?"

Lucas rushed to her and kissed her neck, exaggerating his movements as if he was nibbling on her. His beard tickled her and she burst into laughter.

Fifteen minutes later, Tori was watching from just outside the living room as Lucas sat on the floor with Boyd. The coffee table had been pushed out of the way and a brand-new set of LEGOS was dumped on the rug.

"You've played with LEGOS before, right?"

"Yes," Boyd replied.

"What do you think we should build? You know that my job is to build houses, yeah? I showed you the pictures yesterday. You think we should build one of our own?"

Before the kid could say anything, Lucas was already snapping blocks together.

"The important thing is to have a strong foundation," he continued. "If the base isn't sturdy, the rest will just collapse, you know?"

"Like the Three Little Pigs?"

"Yeah, exactly. We don't need no huffing and puffing here. I say we double the width at the base. Hand me that wide piece over there."

"Lucas?"

"Yeah, buddy?"

"Can we… Can we build anything we want?"

"Sure! Bungalow, duplex, big ol' castle, anything you want."

Boyd rolled a block between his fingers. "Can we build a prison? It's for the man who hurt my parents."

Lucas looked up at Tori who covered her mouth with her hand. *Poor little guy…*

~ ~ ~ ~

The front porch was wide and covered. Most of all, the large window opened on the living room. Lucas and Tori stood side by side, getting fresh air while looking at Boyd play with the LEGOS by himself. He wasn't building anything specific, mostly just snapping blocks together.

"I still can't believe what he said about the prison," Lucas said before drinking some Wild Turkey.

"Children have no filter. They say what they feel. Pretty amazing, uh?"

She glanced at Lucas who clearly wanted to agree with her, but was too self-conscious to turn sappy. It made her laugh.

"You don't have to pretend not to like him. It's okay to get attached."

"Yeah, yeah, yeah… And what kind of name is that for a kid, anyway?"

"What's wrong with his name?" Tori asked.

"Boyd, seriously? That's the name you give to a long-haul trucker, okay? Boyd chews tobacco. Boyd sleeps around with easy women from smoky honky-tonks and gets in bar fights over burned barbecue. Boyd doesn't play with LEGOS."

Tori was laughing, leaning against her husband. "I think it's cute. Look at him, Lucas. That's the first time he's seemed normal since he got here. He looks at peace."

Indeed, the boy didn't appear to have a care in the world as he built his plastic structure. Tori caught herself imagining that the three of them could be truly happy together.

"There's just one thing that's bothering me," Lucas said.

"What's that?"

"The kid. His parents. They never caught the murderer. He's still out there."

"Lucas…"

"I'm not saying he's gonna come after the kid—after *us*—but, you know. Forget it, it's stupid. I didn't say anything."

He put his arm around Tori's shoulders and drank his whiskey. She pretended to do just that, to act as if he hadn't brought this up, but she couldn't shake it off. There was a killer on the loose.

What if they were in danger?

# CHAPTER 5

I could probably drown a puppy for a cigarette right now, Gannon thought.

The morbid notion made him grin, but it did nothing to remove the urge to smoke. It was like sex and it always happened after he closed a case. Shouldn't he get some sort of reward?

He remembered when the station didn't have any cubicles, only desks pushed together. You could smoke all day long back then and nobody batted an eye. Now they had fancy cubicles—soothingly ergonomic, or some other crap—and you couldn't light one up without it becoming a federal case. Colleagues would look at him funny if they smelled the hint of a Lucky Strike on him.

It was a brave new world and he wasn't sure if he wanted a part of it. How was it possible that life evolved faster than his ability to process it? His ex-wife had called him a dinosaur. Maybe she was right.

Anyway, he was still glad to close this particular case. The son of a state representative had robbed a liquor store to feed his meth addiction and he'd gotten shot for his trouble. What should have been handled by the local cops had quickly turned political and Gannon had been called in as an impartial party. If there was one person in the department who wasn't political, it was Gannon.

The kid was in rehab now, awaiting the trial which would lead to a suspended sentence because daddy had more judicial influence than he had parenting skills. The case was closed as far as Gannon was concerned, and the report was filed.

The aging detective pulled out a cigarette and ran it under his nose as if it was a fine cigar. He closed his eyes, inhaling it, imagining what it would feel like to actually smoke it.

"You're not thinking of lighting that in here, are you?"

Gannon's eyes snapped open and found Captain Vail looking down at him from over the sleek cubicle divider. He was a smug little bastard, which wouldn't be so bad if he didn't actually look like one too. He wasn't even forty-two years old and already was a captain.

He'd attended all the best schools short of the Ivy League, had graduate degrees, and he would probably end up as governor. He made no secret that he was ambitious, although he hid it through the respectable shroud of perfectionism. There was a rumor that the last time he had smiled had been for his school picture. In the sixth grade.

"Good afternoon, Cap," Gannon said as he put the cigarette back in his pocket. "Pull up a chair. We can talk about this fishing boat I have my eye on."

"Where are you on the razor murders?"

Gannon sighed and swiveled his chair to face him. He had been dreading this question. For all his faults, Vail was smart and knew to give his people some leeway in their work. He supervised a team of experienced investigators and it wasn't up to him to tell them how to do their jobs.

It hadn't taken long for the Begum case to be referred to as *the razor murders* by the press. Catchy titles always sold more newspapers. What did they call it online, clickbait? This was clickbait heaven.

"Give me an update, Gannon?"

"I believe *unsolved* is the proper terminology."

"Stop jerking me around, will you?"

Gannon reached for a folder on the corner of his desk and scanned it. The truth of the matter was that he was stumped.

"All right, here's the thing. We have a bunch of elements that amount to nothing. The house had no alarm system. We canvassed three blocks and didn't find a single security camera. We have zero footage. We canvassed *six* blocks, talking to neighbors, and nobody saw nothing."

"Nothing?"

"Bupkis. The Begums had just moved in. Nobody knew them. Now let's switch over to physical evidence," Gannon added, flipping the page in his file. "Nothing again. Autopsy reveals they had their jugulars slashed with razor blades, which we haven't found anywhere. They bled out fast. Toxicology report says they had triple the recommended dosage of Xanax. The lady had a prescription and we found the empty container in the bathroom."

"Fingerprints?"

"Nothing unusual. I mean, the victims, the kid, a bunch of partials we're still sorting through. Most of them will come back unidentified, like the movers or former tenants."

"Don't tell me it's a dead end, Detective."

"You want me to lie instead?"

"The one thing I want is for you to not fabricate evidence," the younger man spat.

Gannon wanted to punch him in the face. He stopped himself just in time. The captain might deserve it, but Gannon deserved the criticism as well. His reputation wasn't stellar around these parts.

"I learned my lesson," Gannon replied with remarkable restraint.

"Are you sure about that? Everything you do reflects upon me, all right? Maybe you're happy ticking down days until your retirement, but I actually have goals I want to meet."

"Ambitions."

"Yes," Vail replied. "Ambition isn't a dirty word. I worked my butt off my entire life to get where I am today and there are still places to go. I sure as hell won't have you screw it up like you did to my predecessor."

Gannon kept his mouth shut, but stared back defiantly. Only ten years ago, he had been a lieutenant and he, himself, had been going places. Insubordination, including punching his superior at the time, had seen him busted down to sergeant after a month-long suspension.

Two years later, he had forged the date on a receipt which was the leading evidence in a gas station homicide. Everybody knew that the man was guilty—he had even confessed, though the confession had been deemed inadmissible on a technicality. Gannon had made sure justice was served even if he'd had to circumvent the law a little bit.

His commanding officer had discovered what he'd done. To avoid risking the reputation of his unit, the incident was swept under the rug. Gannon was once again suspended for a month and lost another rank. It had cost him his marriage and ensured that he stopped caring indefinitely about his job from here on out.

"What have you done so far?" Vail asked.

Obviously, the detective hadn't remained idle since walking away from the crime scene. He'd gone to his trusted sources, but they knew nothing. He had done some of the usual geo-tracking and social media mining. He'd been in contact with the FBI and they had even sent a freelance profiler in case they were dealing with some sort of serial killer. The report was so generic that they might as well have skipped that part altogether.

He told all this to his boss. He had walked the crime scene half a dozen times, trying to get a feel for what had happened. Nothing made sense. There had been no forced entry, which suggested the victims' knew the intruder. But with most of the belongings still in moving boxes and no one knowing the couple, it was hard to say if anything had been stolen.

"I want you to solve this case, Gannon."

"You could always give it to one of the golden boys, Cap."

Vail couldn't assign this case to another detective with a better reputation because everyone around here knew that there was little chance it would ever be solved. As a result, it was better to let a cop with nothing to lose take the blame. There was no sense sullying the name of one of the good guys.

"You keep your eye on the ball. Be a team player, try to blend in."

"Blend in? Captain, haven't you noticed? I've lost my girlish figure a long time ago."

"Make an effort. I saw the latest personnel reports this morning. Your fitness evaluation is poor and you haven't even signed out your electroshock weapon yet. You know that I require all my people to carry them from now on."

Gannon groaned. "I've been on the force twenty-nine years and I've never needed a toy. I've never even fired my weapon in the line of duty. I can go one more year without that thing."

"It's not a request, Detective. Get your Taser, get in good physical shape, and close this case."

The CO shot him one last glare and walked away. The damnedest thing was that Gannon really wanted to solve this case as well. He'd been on cruise control for so long that he wanted to remember what it was like to feel the satisfaction of a high-profile collar.

And that meant he had to pursue every possible lead. That gave him an idea. He stood up, placed the unlit cigarette between his lips, and left the station.

~ ~ ~ ~

The city of Franklin hadn't had a railroad service since the early nineties when hundreds of acres of land had been purchased for ill-fated commercial developments. Nevertheless, everybody still referred to the Northside neighborhood as "the wrong side of the tracks."

The focal point of this downtrodden area was the Tilted Rooster. Officially a bar, in Gannon's experience it was better called a hub of crime. So many of his cases had led to him here over the last three decades that he basically had his own reserved parking spot in front.

It was a long way from Hillford, but a sudden burst of inspiration told him that it was worth a shot. Besides, the detective had exhausted all his other options.

He walked in as people were finishing their shifts at the neighboring businesses. No, that was misleading. Unemployment here was the norm. The patrons didn't need an excuse to drink and hang out. Many of them showed up before lunch and stayed until closing time.

The air smelled of smoke—tobacco and marijuana—as well as skunked beer and sweat. It was dark because half the promotional neon signs were broken and had never been repaired.

There was a crooked pool table nobody ever played except college boys who showed up for the "ghetto experience". Getting cheated out of twenty bucks by pool sharks was apparently a badge of honor on campuses these days. The only thing the Tilted Rooster had going for itself was the amazing selection of music available on the jukebox.

There were two dozen people at the bar and at the few tables scattered around. Every single person turned toward Gannon as he entered. He was used to it by now and even adjusted the badge at his belt to drive his point across. BB King's blues guitar wailed in the distance.

"What's it gonna be?" the toothless, elderly bartender asked as the cop approached.

"Demetrius Godwin. I need to talk to him."

The bartender shook his head and looked away. "Never heard of him."

"Like you never heard of the health code."

"Whatever you say, officer."

"The Rooster is practically his permanent address. Don't make me tear out the walls searching for him, all right?"

That made the old man laugh. "You'd be doing me a favor!"

Without a care in the world, he continued laughing and slid down the bar to refill a customer's glass.

Gannon was mentally calculating how much money he had in his pocket, and how much of it he could spare for bribes, when he saw movement in the back of the room. Someone was coming out of the restrooms, doing a double take.

"Demetrius, buddy!" Gannon said with fake enthusiasm.

Demetrius Godwin was short and scrawny. He was in his early thirties, though he looked twenty years older thanks to decades of drug use. That's how Gannon was able to run to him before he could escape through the back door. The detective put a hand on his neck and pulled him back just as he was going through the emergency exit.

"Not so fast. It's not polite to leave without saying hello."

Gannon led him through the door and they found themselves in the alley, between an overflowing dumpster and brick walls. It almost smelled better inside. Almost.

"Shit, man! Demigod ain't done nothing!"

"Demigod? You're still calling yourself Demigod?"

Demetrius didn't take the bait and simply bristled. His street moniker was supposed to be a portmanteau of his legal name, but he'd always been the only one to use it.

"Whatcha want with Demigod, man? You cramping Demigod's style! Demigod's got a rep to protect."

He made a move to walk away, but Gannon shoved him into the wall. It wasn't hard or meant to hurt him. He got the point.

"I'll leave as soon as you give me a reason to, Demetrius. I'll leave even faster if you stop referring to yourself in the third person."

"Well, hurry, man! It's happy hour."

"Okay, then make me happy. You heard about the double homicide in Hillford?"

Demetrius's eyes widened. "The razor murders? I ain't got nothing to do with that, man!"

"I know, I know." The guy was a lot of things, but he was no killer. That's why Gannon had always liked him as an informant. "Have you heard anything?"

"No, man! You think the Rooster crowd has time to waste slashing yuppies in the middle of nowhere? Get real, man."

Gannon was expecting that answer, but that wasn't why he had come here today.

He said, "Word on the street is that there's new competition in the county, outsiders who want to make a name for themselves. Some guys who like to get real violent."

"Are you talking about the Ohio crew?"

"That's exactly who I'm talking about, Demetrius. People from Cleveland. What do you know?"

"I know nothing, man."

"Demetrius…"

Gannon produced a twenty-dollar bill, although he didn't give it to him. He merely placed it in front of his face, like a juicy steak in front of a St. Bernard.

"Okay, I know they have this enforcer. Real goddamn psycho. Apparently."

"That's also what I'm hearing," Gannon said. "On a scale of Enron to *Friday the 13th*, what kind of psycho is he?"

"Ain't got a clue who Enron is, but he's bad. Works with a blade, surgical and shit."

Gannon felt hope climbing through him. He worked hard not to show it. "He uses razor blades?"

"Nah, not what I hear."

"Then what do you hear, Demetrius?"

"The guy… and I don't know his name, so don't try to threaten me or nothing! The guy is supposedly big into Japanese culture. You know, samurai and shit."

"What does that have to do with anything?" Gannon asked.

"Supposedly, he carries around this butcher knife that looks like a Japanese dagger. The way he makes his point is to cut people's bellies open. You know, like that what-you-call-it suicide…"

"Seppuku."

"Yeah, that's it. Anyway, it's his trademark, know what I'm saying? He never does it any other way. It can't be him or the Ohio boys with that thing in Hillford. Can't be."

In his heart, Gannon knew it made sense. An assassin with a signature wouldn't change his method because the method was part of the message.

"So that's for me, right?"

Demetrius cocked his head to the side and moistened his lips, his eyes riveted to the money in the detective's hand. Gannon could see no way out and gave it to him.

The small man hurried away, no doubt going to his favorite drug dealer, and Gannon remained in place. He was still nowhere near solving this case, which was doubly frustrating since for once he actually was interested in doing something productive with his life.

# CHAPTER 6

"Do I really need to go?"

Tori turned around and looked at Boyd strapped in his booster seat. He had that same lost expression he'd had on the first day he'd come home with them.

"It's for your own good, sweetie. The doctor will help you, okay?"

At that, Lucas rolled his eyes from behind his position at the wheel. Nevertheless, he didn't say a word and they drove halfway across town to the older part of Steep Gorge. The drive wasn't long—nothing was ever far away in Steep Gorge. It was in this area that the first prominent settlers had had their homes.

Most were perched above the river. Lucas was only thinking about land value as they approached their destination. Dr. Curnutt worked out of her own home, a stately Victorian structure which belonged on the official town brochure. Over the years, a garage had been added, connected to the house, and it had been turned into an office.

Mrs. Zakrzewski had said that the therapist came highly recommended. She was supposed to have a way with children who'd suffered intense trauma. Even though Lucas was dubious, Tori was willing to try anything to make Boyd grow up as normal as possible.

There was no receptionist or secretary. The psychologist welcomed them herself and led Boyd to a waiting room designed specifically for children. It resembled a preschool classroom with diminutive furniture and toys strewn around.

He got to his knees and played with a fire truck, making it roll back and forth. Meanwhile, Tori, Lucas, and Dr. Curnutt watched through elegant French doors.

"He's a handsome little man," the woman said.

She was tall and elegant. Her hair was almost completely grey. Some women her age—on the edge of sixty—couldn't pull it off, but she did. She seemed noble, impossible to faze. Tori imagined she looked like the mother of a European monarch during the Renaissance, as if she had remarkable power and wisdom. Her first impression was to trust her implicitly.

"Do you think you can really help him?" Tori asked, biting her fingernails without realizing it.

"The only thing I can do is talk to Boyd. The rest will be up to him."

"Well, that's genuinely reassuring," Lucas shot back, drawing a glare from his wife.

"What I do is open up lines of communication," Dr. Curnutt said, her voice as assured and graceful as her appearance. "You know the saying, children are sponges. They absorb the good with the bad. My job will be to get him to understand that what he went through isn't a reflection of who he is. He needs to be aware that his life doesn't need to be defined by what happened."

The words were oddly soothing for Tori and she began to relax. "Have you ever had a patient who's been through the same thing as Boyd?"

"Witnessing a murder, you mean?"

"Right."

"Yes, too often. I practiced in Baltimore for nearly twenty years, and I have seen children who have suffered in ways that you cannot imagine."

Lucas let out an annoyed sigh. "What's your success rate?"

"There's no scoreboard, Mr. Ramsdale. It doesn't work that way."

"You mean you can't cure him?"

Tori was disconcerted by her husband's reactionary tone, and yet she was curious about the answer herself.

"It's not a question of curing Boyd. He's not sick. He's witnessed his parents being murdered. That means that his feelings, his emotions, they're all jumbled up and impact how he will act in the future. With enough time, communication, and support, he'll eventually emerge from his shell and be as normal as can be without having to rely on defense mechanisms."

"How many sessions will it take?" Lucas asked.

"Lucas!"

"What?" he said, feigning innocence. "It's a legitimate question, right? Look, forgive me, but I think psychiatry is a bunch of crap, okay?"

"Psychology," Dr. Curnutt pointed out.

"Psychiatry, psychology, it's all the same thing. You charge a hundred bucks an hour to talk about feelings and whatnot. I just don't see how that can help."

"Lucas, please!" Tori whispered through clenched teeth.

"It's okay," the older woman said with a kindly smile. "To answer your question, I don't know how many sessions it will take. I've seen children make unbelievable progress after a month. Others require a lifetime of therapy. After a few sessions, I should be able to tell you where Boyd sits on this scale."

"Thank you," Tori said. "I'm just…"

"Yes?"

"The thing that worries me is that you will make Boyd relive these tragic events. I don't want him to be in pain again."

"Mrs. Ramsdale, this child is already in pain. I will do my best to help him remove it. Please, trust me."

Tori didn't have a choice but to nod and smile even though there was nothing to smile about.

~ ~ ~ ~

Dr. Curnutt's office was next to the small playroom. It had a much more adult feel, with beige walls and an earth-tones color scheme. There was a tan couch against one wall with oversized pillows layered on top. The woman's large mahogany desk was at an angle in the corner. Behind it were tall windows which offered a nice view of the river below the house.

The psychologist led Boyd to the couch and he happily sat in the middle of it, the pillows around him becoming a protective fort of sorts. For her part, she sat on a wing chair just off to the side. She crossed her legs, smoothed down her long skirt, and clasped her hands together.

"Are you comfortable, Boyd?"

"Is your name really carrot?"

She smiled. "It's Curnutt, in fact." He chuckled. "It's funny, isn't it?"

"Yes."

"When I was your age they called me Cold Cut. You know, like ham and baloney." Boyd laughed again and she smiled. "You can call me Dr. Talia."

"Okay."

"Can I call you Boyd or should I say Mr. Begum?"

The kid laughed and she smiled along once more. This had been part of her opening routine for at least two decades. Her most important job was to make children at ease with her, and laughter never failed.

"Say, I saw you play with the fire truck in the other room. Was that your favorite toy?"

He shrugged. "I guess."

"Why do you think it was your favorite?"

"Fire trucks are cool."

"You like firemen? Do you want to be a firefighter when you grow up, Boyd?"

"I don't know," he said. "I like fire."

Dr. Curnutt didn't expect that and wished she was taking notes, which she never did during the first session. "You like fire? Why do you think you like fire?"

"It's hot. It's beautiful. I like looking at flames. They always change. They're never the same."

"Do you like watching things burn, Boyd?"

His eyes sharply met hers. "No. I'm not crazy."

This caught her off guard. For an instant, his childhood demeanor was gone and he had looked at her exactly as an adult would have, his eyes shrewd. It destabilized her, but after a moment it was gone. He looked like an eight-year-old again.

"What other toys do you like?" she asked.

"At the house, I have LEGOS."

"Which house, Boyd? At Lucas and Tori's?"

He nodded. "I like playing with the LEGOS."

"Do you build anything beautiful with them? Do you build houses like Lucas?"

"Sometimes."

"And what do you think about Lucas and Tori? Do you like them?"

"I guess."

"Do they treat you well, Boyd?"

There was a long pause before he answered. "I have a lot of toys."

Dr. Curnutt smiled warmly. "That must be fun. What do you prefer, playing with the toys or going to school?"

"Playing!"

"Yeah, it was the same for me. I didn't like going to school too much when I was eight. Probably because the other kids made fun of my name. Cold Cut, remember?"

They shared a soft laugh. Over the next half hour, Dr. Curnutt continued to run through her list of innocent questions. For the most part, she wasn't interested in the answers. She simply wanted to make the child open up, to make him at ease with her.

Of course, she wanted to probe him, to delve deeper into his emotions, except that she wouldn't be able to do that if her patient wasn't comfortable in her presence. He had to know that he could tell her anything.

"I had a great time talking to you, Boyd. How about you? Did you have fun talking with me?"

"It was okay."

"Just okay? I thought I was doing better than okay." They both chuckled. "We have to see each other next week, so I suppose I'll have to make an effort so you think I'm *better than okay*, uh?"

As he smiled, she was pretty confident that she was in a position to help him. It would take some time before they addressed the horrible scene he had witnessed, but they would eventually get there.

She was pushing herself off the chair when Boyd spoke.

"Dr. Talia?"

"Yes?"

"Lucas and Tori… They're my foster parents?"

"That's correct. They explained to you how it works, yes? They're going to take care of you for the time being."

"Are they…" he began with a shaky voice. "Are they going to hurt me?"

Dr. Curnutt sat back down, her body becoming tense. "Have they done anything to you, Boyd? Have they touched you in a way you don't like or believe is inappropriate?"

"No."

"You can tell me anything, you know. I'm here for you. It's my job."

"I was just asking," Boyd said. "Just making sure."

"Did your parents ever hurt you, Boyd?"

The two of them stared at each other for nearly a minute.

"I don't want to talk about it."

Once again, there was that coldness in his eyes which made him seem at least ten years older. He blinked, looked away, and it was gone.

"Boyd…" she began. "I promise you that nothing bad will ever happen to you again. Do you understand me?"

"Can I go now?"

In spite of her eagerness to get to the root of his problems, she knew that she needed to pace herself. She smiled.

"Of course. I'll see you next week, okay?"

He didn't say anything, busy getting off the big couch and walking toward the exit.

~ ~ ~ ~

Tori was waiting outside. She was sitting in the Subaru where she was out of the scorching sun. It wasn't too humid and the windows rolled down offered a nice breeze.

For almost an hour, she had been browsing art galleries on her phone. That very notion gave her nausea. Art galleries going digital? There was simply no way you could appreciate a painting—or a sculpture, for that matter—on a computer screen. There was so much more to art than what it looked like. It was only when you were standing in front of it that you could grasp the importance of a piece.

There was smell, the way it was framed, the way it was lit and presented, it was all designed to let the viewer feel something very specific. The murals of Diego Rivera were of course gorgeous, but it was an entirely different sensation to be dwarfed by the vivid colors when you were standing directly in front of them.

Welcome to the new art world, she told herself.

She didn't have a choice. She didn't make the rules. That's how gallery owners and art dealers operated these days. Conform or get left by the wayside. Only business mattered.

She looked up from her phone when the front door to the house opened. Boyd came out, hurrying down the porch and practically running to the car. Dr. Curnutt observed from the doorframe and waved to her. Tori waved back, simply happy that Boyd wasn't in tears, or worse, catatonic.

Beforehand, the psychologist had told her that she wouldn't meet the foster parents after the session. In the future, yes, but not today because it was a time to build trust and open lines of communication.

Tori was keen to know how things had gone and she swiftly climbed out of the SUV, smiling broadly at the little boy.

"Hey, sweetie! How did it go?"

"Okay." He looked around and frowned. "Lucas isn't here?"

He wasn't. He'd had Tori drive him back home to get his truck so he could go to his office. In fact, Dr. Curnutt had recommended that Tori went home herself, but she had been too curious about Boyd and his progress.

"Where is he?" he asked.

"He had to work." It crushed her to see his disappointed expression. They were already failing him, she decided. "But he's really curious about how it went with Dr. Curnutt. He only wants the best for you. You know that, right? We both do."

"It's okay if he doesn't like me."

Tori was agape. "What?! Of course he likes you! And you know why?"

"Why?"

"Because you're awesome!"

She was reeling from his accusation and it hurt even more because she inferred there was a grain of truth to it. Lucas wasn't the most affectionate person, especially when you didn't know him. There was no way they could let Boyd know that. He was too young to understand.

"And you know what we do to awesome people in this town?" Tori asked, bending down to face him.

"No, what?"

"Promise not to tell?"

"Yes, I promise!"

"Awesome people get ice cream!"

He smiled just like her and she took the opportunity to tickle him. He laughed loudly and she felt relief at last. However, she didn't notice his eyes.

His eyes were darkening and not smiling at all.

# CHAPTER 7

Tori was in pain.

She could barely breathe, her windpipe compressed to the point where she thought it would be torn in two. She jerked back in an effort to get away from this excruciating feeling, yet she couldn't.

Her body trembled, twisting and turning until she had lost all her bearings. Her insides pulled into a ball, leading to searing pain which was nothing compared to the other sharp sensation of her collarbone breaking.

Fighting back did absolutely nothing. It only made the experience more intense. She was powerless. There was nothing she could do to defend herself.

Scream? She tried, sure that her voice would alert someone, that a bystander would come to her rescue. No sound came out.

She was mute, which made the whole thing even worse. It was torture to suffer and not be able to tell anyone. She felt like a child falling into a well in the middle of a forest. She was like a kidnapping victim no one knew was missing.

She went on tumbling until she couldn't discern anything around her. Everything became black and she was aware that something was terribly wrong. She was an artist and she knew that if you mixed all the colors together you got white, not black. Black was the absence of color. The absence of light.

She couldn't see anything now, not even herself. Was she in deep space? That was impossible, right? Her skin wasn't burning.

The pain. Oh the pain…

The whole thing was like coming to the realization that you were going insane and that there was nothing you could do about it. And this made her accept death. Yes, that's what she wanted. As soon as she considered it, it became a ray of hope. There was a way out and that was to let herself go.

She wanted to die, and that was okay if it made the suffering stop.

Tori's eyes snapped open and she sucked in air as if she had just emerged from under water. She wasn't tumbling anymore. She was lying down. Gasping, she glanced around without moving her head. She was in her room, in bed. Lucas was snoring beside her.

It had been a nightmare.

Thunder rolled outside and it did nothing to soothe her. She was still on edge. In the past year, she'd had many similar nightmares, but this one was by far the worst. She kept her eyes wide open while panting, anything to reassure her that it was over.

I'm okay, she told herself. I'm fine. I'm alive.

Heavy rain drummed against the window. There was thunder again, this time closer. She turned her head to the right and that's when lightning struck. It came as a succession of three bolts and, for almost a full second, it cast a white light throughout the entire bedroom.

That's when she noticed that she wasn't alone.

A long, unnatural shadow stretched from the door all the way to the bed. She was terrified once again. Was she still dreaming? She sprung upright, for the first time noticing that she was covered with sweat.

There was somebody in the room and her heart skipped a beat. For years, Lucas had brought up the inevitability of becoming the victims of a home invasion. She had always fought against the idea of getting a security system or a gun. That wasn't the kind of life she'd ever wanted to live. But what if he'd been right all along?

She blinked, doing her best to think rationally, and at long last she made sense of the situation. The next flash of lightning made her relax. It was Boyd. He was standing halfway between the door and the bed, completely immobile.

How long had he been standing there?

"Hey, sweetie," she said in a whisper. "What's wrong?"

"I got scared," he replied.

Before saying another word, she swung her legs out of bed and got up. She didn't bother with slippers or a robe. She was wearing pajama shorts and a tank top. Normally it kept her from getting too hot, but she was sweating again.

"Come with me."

On the way out of the room, she read the thermostat. The air conditioning was set at sixty-eight. And she was still hot? She put a hand on Boyd's shoulders. They were much cooler than her own skin. What was wrong with her?

Instead of leading him back to his room, she opted to go to the kitchen. They padded down the stairs and she switched on the neon under the cabinets.

"Do you want some water?" Tori asked.

He nodded and sat at the counter. She filled two glasses and joined him. He took a sip of his while she drank hers completely. It didn't do much to cool her down. However, it reminded her that she was still alive. The nightmare was over.

They were sitting side by side and it was several moments before she felt confident enough to speak. She watched Boyd drink water and stare into the distance.

"So what's going on, sweetie? Did the thunderstorm scare you?"

"No!"

"It's okay to be afraid. I used to hide under my bed when there was a thunderstorm. Sometimes I ran into my parents' room to sleep with them."

Tori immediately regretted saying this. She didn't want to give him any reminders of his parents since that would only conjure up bad memories. *Damn.*

"But you know that thunderstorms can't hurt you while you're inside, right?" She hoped that putting the conversation back on track would make him forget that she'd mentioned his parents. "We're perfectly safe here."

"I'm not scared of storms," he said.

"Did you have a nightmare?"

At that, he nodded slowly. Maybe it had something to do with meeting with Dr. Curnutt. After all, it was her job to stir the pot. It was meant to make him feel better, but only in the long run. He was bound to go through a rough patch before he got past it. That's what she'd read, anyway.

Tori leaned toward him. "You know what? I had a nightmare, too."

"You did?"

"Yeah. You think it's a coincidence, both of us getting nightmares tonight?" He shrugged. "Actually, you know what I think?"

"What?"

"I think I need to change my shepherd's pie recipe. That has to be it."

They shared a subtle laugh. Tori was pleased with herself, having skirted the issue of his parents. Then she noticed that he'd become serious again.

"It's more than my shepherd's pie, isn't it?"

"I guess."

"Is there something on your mind, Boyd? You know I'm here for you. You can tell me anything."

"It's just…" he whispered.

"It's okay, sweetie. If there's something bothering you, let me know and I'll do everything in my power to fix it. I promise."

Boyd nodded. He took a small sip of water before

putting his glass down. "It's… It's Lucas."

"What about him?" Tori asked, her voice catching in her throat. "Has he done something? Did he say something to you?"

Fright gave away to anger. What the hell had he done now? Her husband was an acquired taste. He was harmless, but you only discovered that after years of marriage.

"It's…" The kid's voice trailed off. "No, forget it."

"Boyd, you can tell me anything. If I can fix it, I will. I swear."

"It's his beard."

"Lucas's beard? You don't like it?"

She was so relieved that she had to restrain herself from bursting into laughter.

"The man who hurt my parents," Boyd muttered. "He had a beard, too."

Tori was no longer in a laughing mood.

~ ~ ~ ~

In the morning, Lucas nearly burned his hand pouring himself a cup of coffee. He spun on his heels toward his wife and had to let go of the mug before everything spilled out.

"He said what?!"

"Lucas, keep your voice down."

"It's my house and I'm pretty sure I can talk as loud as

I want."

"Lucas, please..." Tori said, craning her neck to make sure Boyd was out of earshot.

She somewhat relaxed when she saw that Boyd was still sitting in front of the television in the living room. Meanwhile, Lucas pushed his coffee away and wiped his hands with the dishtowel.

"I'm not cutting off my beard."

"He's scared of it."

"Baby, I've had this beard for ten years. It took time and effort and commitment to grow this."

"It's just hair, Lucas."

He groaned and rolled his eyes. "What if it was you? What if the kid asked you to cut off your hair, Tori? Would you be as Zen about it as you are about me shaving off my beard?"

"It's not the same..."

"Bullshit. It's exactly the same. Your hair is part of who you are and my beard is part of who I am. Nobody knows me without my beard."

Tori leaned against the counter because it felt like the only thing she had on her side these days.

"We knew that we'd have to make sacrifices if we became foster parents, no? This is one of them. It's just a small thing."

"It's not a small thing," Lucas complained. "That's a big deal to me. A big goddamn deal."

"Look," she said, dropping her voice further. "He told

me the man who killed his parents had a beard."

"Shit…"

"What if every time he looks at you, he sees a murderer?"

"Thanks for the guilt trip, baby."

"I'm serious, Lucas. We promised to love and support him in every way we could. If the beard scares him, that's one little thing we can do to ease his pain. Don't you agree?"

He cocked his head to the side, looked away, and pouted. He went to take a sip of coffee before changing his mind. Finally, he turned toward his wife.

"Okay, fine."

"What's fine?"

"I'll do it. I'll shave."

"Oh, thank you!" she exclaimed louder than she'd preferred.

"Don't get too excited. I'm not even sure I have a face underneath this."

Tori smiled and came closer, wrapping her arms around her husband's waist. "I'm fairly confident you do have a face under that rug. I bet it's a really cute face."

"Do you say that to all the guys?"

"Only the ones I'm married to," she added with a wink.

She stretched up and kissed him on the lips. It started as a quick peck and eventually he warmed up to the idea, kissing her back.

"You're going to be the death of me, baby."

"Yeah, but that's why you love me."

She kissed him again, realizing that she had gotten used to that woolly beard and it would be strange to kiss him without one.

"I'm going to stop by the pharmacy on the way back from work. I mean, I get one last day as a real man, don't I?"

"Wait, you were a *real* man?"

He swatted her on the butt, as if to punish her with a spanking, and she tried to get away, collapsing into a laughing fit.

~ ~ ~ ~

Tori was seasoning flounder fillets for her traditional fish burgers when Lucas returned from work. She was in the zone, adding smoked paprika to the fish and not leaving a corner bare. She loved making those because it was easy and it didn't taste like fish, especially with lettuce, tomatoes, and mayonnaise. She hoped Boyd would enjoy.

"Hey," Lucas said as he entered the kitchen.

She finally looked up when he dropped a plastic shopping bag on the counter. "Hi. Had a good day?"

"Pretty much. Did some things. Enjoyed my facial hair for a few hours, stuff like that."

She stuck out her tongue at him as he winked. He greeted her with a kiss.

"Where's the little guy?"

"I'm here."

The two adults turned toward the dining set. Boyd was standing there, motionless.

"I hear you want to see my smooth and beautiful face under all this hair, is that right?" Boyd nodded timidly. "You want to watch me do it?"

The child nodded enthusiastically.

"Awesome. Baby, can you spare your two men for a bit before dinner?"

"Go on, scoot! We eat in a half hour though. Be there or be square."

"Yes, ma'am. Come on, champ."

Boyd followed Lucas upstairs into the master bath. Lucas placed his purchases on the vanity: shaving cream, razor, and a pack of blades. Then he started to unbutton his shirt, removing it completely.

"The thing about shaving off a big, beautiful beard like this is that it gets messy. But if we keep our mouths shut, Tori will never know it's our fault and she'll clean it up without complaining."

He winked and Boyd chuckled.

Lucas was making a Herculean effort to keep this light and fun although it killed him to do this. He had never asked to become a foster dad and this was one hell of a sacrifice. In the end, he told himself that this was the price to pay to get a thousand bucks a month from the government.

"All right, here goes nothing."

He began by using scissors to cut off as much hair as he could. Everything fell into the sink. He did his best not to moan with despair while witnessing his prized beard disappear. After that, he lathered his face with shaving cream, snapped three blades into the razor, and finished the job.

Boyd's gaze wasn't focused on the shaving operation though. No, he was looking at the spare blades placed up in the medicine cabinet.

# CHAPTER 8

"Gannon, are you there?"

The detective recognized his commanding officer's voice. Instead of standing up, prairie dogging above the cubicle wall, he sulked. He lowered his head and stared at his empty mug. He was definitely not caffeinated enough this morning to handle this.

"Gannon," the voice said, much closer this time. "Didn't you hear me?"

The older man spun his chair toward the opening and offered a fake smile to Vail. "Morning, Captain. I was so engrossed in my work that I didn't hear you. Sorry."

Vail was dubious, though he didn't address it. "I want the Begum case off the board ASAP."

"Cap, as I told you…"

"There won't be an unsolved murder case here, not on my watch. I'm assigning you somebody on this one."

"Come on, Cap…" Gannon pleaded, at once seeing fifty reasons why this was a bad idea.

Nevertheless, Vail was already waving over somebody. Within seconds, a young woman was standing by his side.

"Detective Gannon, this is Detective Ghislaine

Mobley. She just transferred from the station in Rusterside County. She's going to be with you until you put this case to bed. Understood?"

"Loud and clear," Gannon said.

"Yes, sir," Mobley added with a decisive nod.

"I'm counting on the both of you."

Vail shot one last look at the older man before leaving. *Christ*, Gannon thought. A year away from his retirement and they were giving him a babysitter?

"It's good to meet you, Detective," she said, taking a step forward and extending her hand.

She was short and slender, but he felt like she was solidly-built, as if she'd once spent a lot of time at the gym. Her blond hair was packed in a tight bun without a single loose strand.

He had no choice but to shake her hand. "Call me Gannon. And your name is Jizz Lane? That doesn't sound right."

"With all due respect, Detective, you seem a little old for these juvenile jokes."

"Sorry. My hearing isn't what it used to be."

"Fair enough," she said. "It's Ghislaine. It's French, named after my grandmother. Mobley will be fine."

"Got it." Gannon motioned for her to put herself at ease, but she remained upright, her hands behind her back. "What's your story? Who did you piss off to get assigned to me?"

"No one that I know of, Detective."

"Gannon."

"Sorry. Gannon."

"You've worked homicide before?"

"Yes, but never as lead. I've been with the State Police for three years."

He was impressed. "And already a detective?"

"I had life experience."

"Look, are you going to make me extract every piece of information one by one? You're aware that we don't actually sleep in this station, yes?"

That finally made her smile and she nodded in understanding. "Fair enough. I graduated from Annapolis. Then I did seven years in the Navy. Naval Intelligence."

"Seven years? That sounds odd. Don't commissions in the Navy last a minimum of eight years?"

"There was an… incident. I'd rather not talk about it. I left the Navy and joined the force."

Gannon was certain that there was a story there but chose not to say anything. He was too busy trying to decipher her. From her ramrod-straight posture and background, he just knew that she was Vail's lackey. She was here to keep him on a leash. She was here to spy on him and report to the captain. He would have to tread lightly.

"So I guess we're stuck together, aren't we?"

"Teamed up together, Detective. Gannon, I mean. We're a team. A burden shared is a burden halved."

"Oh God!" Gannon groaned. "You're not one of those people with motivational posters on the wall, are you? Because if you start spewing fortune cookie wisdom at me all day long, we'll need to set up some sort of punishment system. Fines, hefty."

For the first time, Mobley changed her stance. She stopped with the parade rest crap and bent forward to address the senior detective.

"I'm really not here to report back to the captain about you, Gannon. I know you must be thinking this because some of the others mentioned the two of you don't get along. That's not why I'm here. I asked for a transfer months ago because it's closer to my house. I just want to do the work and solve this case with you, that's all."

Gannon inspected her for a moment and chose to believe her.

"Okay, let's get to work then. Your first mission is to get yourself a chair."

That made her grin. She left the cubicle and returned in record time, pushing a swivel chair. She must have stolen it from a colleague next door and that in itself redeemed her in his eyes.

"Where are you on the investigation?" she asked. "Captain Vail said you don't have anything. He said…"

"What? Go on, you won't offend me."

"Captain Vail said you couldn't find anything."

Gannon snorted. "Let me tell you a little something about our illustrious Captain Vail. He couldn't find a gay man at a Cher concert. He's better off leaving the detective work to the detectives. That means you and me."

"So you have something?" Mobley inquired with renewed optimism.

"Well, no. I don't have anything. But I'm working on it." He grabbed a legal pad from the desk and flipped back several pages. "In terms of physical evidence, it's slim pickings. I was following this theory of a home invasion gone wrong."

"Even with this level of violence?"

"It's a question of statistics. Someone is dead in a house, first you rule out a domestic abuse situation or a fight between friends. After that, your most likely scenario is a home invasion. Everybody likes to think about serial killers and roaming psychopaths because they make sexy headlines, but in reality the odds of that are small."

"Right."

Mobley's tone was serious. Studious. She was taking notes.

"Anyway, after all the time I spent on this, I'm ready to put this theory to bed. It wasn't a home invasion and all my sources have come up dry."

"What's the next move then?"

"As it turns out, the husband—John Begum—he was a CPA. He had just moved to this state and hadn't established his new practice yet. So I had to serve a subpoena to North Carolina, where the victims are from, to get access to his own cases and system. I just got the files and now I'm sifting through them. This is the white collar version of searching for known associates."

Gannon kicked a white box stowed under his desk. The notion of reading through everything gave him a headache.

"That's all there is?" Mobley inquired.

"There are nine other boxes just like this in the conference room."

"Ouch."

"You said it. The plan is to look at Begum's clients and cross-reference them for criminal records or other suspicious activities." He noticed that Mobley wasn't looking at him anymore. Her gaze was riveted to the box on the floor. "Are you thinking of ways to tell Captain Vail to take this job and shove it?"

"No," she replied with a hint of humor. "I'm trying to think of the best system to sort through the files."

"Really?"

"I was Naval Intelligence, remember? I once spent nine months locked in the basement of a Baghdad office building, going through employment and bank records to see who was financing insurgents. These guys had targeted a SEAL team on a recon op off the Bashiqah Mountain. And the documents were in Arabic. It took nine months, but I did root them out."

"I'm officially impressed."

"That wasn't the point."

"Shut up, Mobley. Take the compliment."

She grinned coyly.

They moved the operation to the conference room where Mobley immediately asserted herself. She was in her element and Gannon decided Captain Vail might've had a good idea with partnering them together after all.

The work lasted hours, but they made progress. One would read a client of John Begum's and the other would search the name in the NCIC—the National Crime Information Center—the crime database maintained by the FBI. It was painstaking work. Then again, this was a cornerstone of any investigation. As Gannon's first lieutenant had put it, don't become a detective if you don't like sorting through paperwork.

At two in the afternoon, Gannon went out for a long-overdue cigarette and, when he returned, he found Mobley smiling.

"What is it? You look like you just got a date for the prom."

"I think I have something. There's a client here who appears twice, Timothy Misner. It's not two different people. Same address, same phone number. It's the same man."

"So?"

"So the file is only connected once with the IRS."

"And this is exciting because…"

"Because why would you have two accounts with your accountant? To me, this smells like somebody having two sets of books. Say, these files are all there is?"

"No, there are others. The North Carolina State Bureau of Investigations also sent the contents of Begum's company storage locker. It's in the basement."

"Let's go!"

Gannon was thrilled at finally having a lead, although he wondered if it wasn't just her excitement that was rubbing off. In any case, it felt good and he followed her.

The basement was badly lit, but at least it was cool on this hot summer day. They went past the evidence room and into the larger area which was meant for storage, though more often than not had been used for the annual Christmas party and charity bingo night.

These boxes contained receipts and other documentation Begum's clients would've provided to justify their tax deductions. It took half an hour to locate Timothy Misner.

Mobley winced as she sat on the concrete floor next to the box. Strangely, she didn't seem as solidly-built anymore. He crouched next to her as she went through the contents.

"I have invoices for liquor."

"Funny. I always pay cash myself."

"This is for ten thousand dollars worth of liquor, Gannon. Theatrical accessories. A place called…" She squinted. "Trice Novelties. Hey, look at the billing address. It says VaVoom Adult Bookstore."

Gannon stared into the distance, everything falling into place. "Misner owned a strip club! Booze, porn stuff… It's a strip club."

"I don't understand. Gentlemen's clubs aren't illegal. Why two sets of books?"

"Because somebody was skimming off the top. And…"

"And what?" Mobley asked eagerly. Gannon was lost in thought. "And what, Gannon?"

If you owned a strip club, skimmed off the top, and had the forethought of having your accountant hide everything, it was reasonable to deduce that some level of organization went into it.

This had to be a mob front.

And the mob was known to murder their associates when they skipped town. Was that what had happened to the Begums?

# CHAPTER 9

"How do you like your meat, hun?"

Felicia hid behind her wine glass and leaned toward Tori. "More than just on Tuesday night, personally."

The two women burst into laughter.

"Hun?" Jasper inquired again from his place next to the grill, on the other side of the deck.

"Medium well. Same for Tori." She turned to her friend. "Right?"

"Medium well is great, sure."

It was late afternoon on Saturday and the air was just starting to cool down. They had been invited to the Harbucks' who were their closest friends. Jasper was a plumber and that was how he had met Lucas. They had hit it off and before long they had become a couple they could hang out with. That made the move to Steep Gorge much more tolerable.

Suddenly, their friendship became more strategic to Tori. The Harbucks had a kid, so they could give them pointers in the parenting department.

"I actually like my burger well cooked," Felicia said in a conspiratorial tone. "But after two beers, Jasper is completely useless at the barbecue. He overcooks everything. You're still sure you want medium well? It's going to come out hard and black."

"So almost like Tuesday nights, right?" Tori joked, making them both laugh. "No, really. It's fine. Don't worry about it."

The two women settled into the patio chairs and continued to sip the white Zin. The house was nice, but what really tied it together was the backyard deck. It was large and beautifully stained, with a pergola in a corner. It was also built around an above-ground pool.

Felicia said, "Girl, I can't tell you enough how impressed I am with you."

"Impressed?"

"Totally impressed. Becoming a foster parent, geez…"

Instinctively, they both turned toward the pool. Boyd was frolicking in the shallow end while another boy was swimming farther away. Evan was Felicia and Jasper's son and Tori had never paid much attention to him, until now.

"He's great, isn't he?" Tori commented.

"He's quiet. Quiet is good, believe me. I don't know if I could do that, personally."

"Do what, Felicia?"

"Take in some stranger. I mean, I get wanting to adopt a little baby. At that age, it's a blank slate. It might as well be yours, you know? But Boyd is what, eight? You get him warts and all, as they say. No offense."

Tori gestured that it was fine. "He has been through a lot, that's for sure. I knew that whoever CPS would call us about would come with some issues. We always knew that. We were prepared. But I'm not sure I was ready for the level of trauma he's been through."

"So awful." Felicia was whispering, fascinated.

"He doesn't talk about it."

"That's a good thing."

"You think so?"

"Sure. Besides, you said he's seeing a shrink, right? It's her job to help him get through this. Your job is to take care of him. Your job is to be a mom."

Tori reeled back from that and finished her glass. "Being a mom… That's another thing I'm not sure I'm ready for."

"No one ever is, girl. It's like a hurricane or an earthquake; you deal with it when it comes."

"Did you just compare parenting to managing disaster areas, Felicia?"

"What, there's a difference?" They chuckled and Felicia refilled both their glasses. Listen, I'm not going to blow smoke and tell you that it's easy being a parent. It's not. There are ups and downs and every day brings its load of surprises. But it's worth it."

"It is?" Tori asked.

"Absolutely. Six days out of seven I wouldn't sell Evan on the black market."

"*Six* out of seven?"

"Disaster area, remember? Kids always find new ways to shock you, sometimes by burning their fingers off and sometimes by being awesome. Overall, there's more awesome than ER visits, so it's worth it."

Tori wasn't completely sure her friend was joking about the ER visits, but she believed she was sincere when she said that being a parent was a worthwhile endeavor.

"I'm afraid to be inadequate," she said. "He doesn't deserve for us to fail him, Felicia. He's been through enough."

"Listen, kids are easy. You feed them, clothe them and, when things go bad, you tell them everything will be okay. That's it, that's the big secret. Now drink up, you're going to need it."

"Cheers."

Tori looked at Boyd in the pool. He wasn't really swimming, more like wading around as he played with large foam noodles. He spoke to Evan once in a while.

"Looks like they're getting to be friends, right?"

"Totally. I told you, Tori, he's going to be fine. He'll meet some of Evan's friends, and come September, he'll be all set to go to school. He's young. Kids that age can adapt to anything."

Tori smiled. "Yes, I suppose you're right."

"You bet your butt, I'm right! And you'll see, I'm going to be right about that burned burger, too."

~ ~ ~ ~

"How's your beer?" Jasper asked.

"Mostly cold." Lucas took a quick step back as one beef patty burst into flames. "I think this one is done, man."

"Nah, a few more minutes."

Not exactly confident with the answer, Lucas grabbed the tongs and rolled sausages. He should have insisted on taking the lead on this barbecue. On the other hand, you didn't do that to another man. Grilling was a man's own personal dominion.

"Let me take care of the buns."

Lucas grabbed a handful from a bag nearby. He buttered them while Jasper talked about football and threw them up on the elevated grate in the back.

"This your first time cooking for a kid, Lucas?"

"What, does it show?"

Jasper laughed and took a swig from his beer. "You're making all kinds of changes these days, uh? Jesus, I still can't believe you shaved off your beard. I nearly didn't recognize you."

"Crazy, right? I didn't want to do it, but Tori made me."

"Since when does your wife make you do anything?"

Lucas shrugged. "She said it scared the kid. Apparently, the murderer had a beard."

"Holy shit!" Jasper realized he had been loud enough for the entire neighborhood to hear. He lowered his voice. "Holy shit, dude. That's intense."

"Tell me about it." Lucas turned the buns over. "We're upending our damn lives because of him."

"You don't seem like you approve."

"This whole foster care business was her idea. I only went along with it to make her happy. You know our story. I didn't have much of a choice."

"I don't know, man. If you're not completely on board, you should say something. It's a big deal to raise a kid. You deserve kudos for this."

Lucas nodded and drank. "I just want my beard back, honestly."

Jasper chuckled, prodding some clearly overcooked patties with his spatula.

"Okay, I think these are about done."

"Right," Lucas said with a wince. "I think I'm going to stick with hot dogs tonight."

In silence, the two men opened buns and placed meat between, almost ritualistically.

After a moment, Jasper looked sideways at the pool with an annoyed expression. "Evan, stop splashing around!"

"I'm not, dad!" the kid answered.

"I saw you. Don't jump on Boyd. Play nice."

Lucas also turned to the pool. "You okay, buddy?"

Boyd nodded faintly. It was good enough for Lucas and he returned to preparing dinner.

Jasper then said, "He really saw his parents get butchered?"

"Jesus, man…"

"What, am I being insensitive?"

"I don't really want to know what Boyd saw or didn't see, you know? He has a therapist for all that touchy-feely bullshit."

"Still. I read up on the murders and…"

Lucas was agape. "You what?!"

"After Felicia said you guys were adopting—sorry, foster caring—I went online and read the news. Some major shit went down over there in Hillford. Both his parents were murdered, slashed opened. They don't know if it's some serial killer, or maybe a mob hit. It's scary, dude."

"Like I said, I try to stay out of it."

Jasper leaned closer. "What if the kid saw something?"

"He did see it, Jasper."

"No, I mean… What if the kid saw something he wasn't meant to? If it was some sort of mob thing, maybe he has information about the wrong people. What if…" He lowered his voice even more. "What if the murderer comes back to get rid of the child? To kill all of you?"

For long seconds, neither said anything. That had never occurred to Lucas. The CPS people sure as shit hadn't told them that was a possibility. Then again, if it was, wouldn't Boyd be in protective custody instead? If he was an important witness, they would've put him in the relocation program, no?

Lucas decided it was best to believe that.

"Don't be such a drama queen, Jasper. It's fine. All I'm hoping is that my homes can sell before Christmas.

That way, I can pay back the loans and maybe we can move out of this dump, maybe to Franklin or even Philly or New York. Maybe if we have enough money, I can afford to send Boyd to boarding school."

"Boarding school?"

"Yeah," Lucas said, looking around to make sure Tori couldn't hear. "That way I can send the kid away and not have to deal with him anymore."

~ ~ ~ ~

Evan zoomed by Boyd, practically swimming around him. He was like a shark around a diver, equal measures of curiosity and menace. It had been like that all afternoon and Boyd simply continued to act calmly.

Never tease a shark if you want to remain alive, he decided.

"What's a dead body like?" Evan asked.

There was no answer. Boyd continued to wade around, filling and emptying a plastic bucket.

"Come on, tell me. I'm older than you are, so you have to tell."

"No, I don't."

"You do! It's the law. Are dead bodies really gross? Do they smell funny?"

At last, Boyd followed the edge of the shallow end to get away from him, but Evan kept pace. He ducked in and out of the water, swimming and diving.

"Why don't you answer my questions?"

"Because it's none of your business," Boyd replied.

"Is it because it was your parents? Is that why you don't want to talk about them being dead?"

Boyd stared at him, but again remained impassive.

"You know, you'd better get ready for these questions. In September, when school starts, everybody will want to know. Everybody is going to ask you questions about murders and corpses and stuff."

"They'd better not," Boyd said through clenched teeth.

"Oh yeah? What are you gonna do about it?" Evan thought that was hilarious and laughed before ducking underwater once more. "What's it like being an orphan anyway? I have my parents and you don't. Do you miss them? Do you dream about them at night? Do you have nightmares?"

While Evan was still chuckling at his own wit, Boyd backed up against the far corner, his gaze always riveted to the other kid. The shark.

"I bet it really sucks to be an orphan, uh? I prefer my life way more."

"Evan?" Boyd asked in what could almost pass for a pleasant tone.

"What?"

"Are you a strong swimmer?"

"Yeah. Why?"

"Come closer, Evan." He did and Boyd continued. "It's a lot easier to drown in a swimming pool than out in the ocean."

That was the last thing Evan had expected to hear and he froze in place, frowning. "What?"

"It's science. Since freshwater is a lot like what we have in our bodies, when you breathe it in, it's going to get absorbed by your bloodstream. You think you can escape drowning just by kicking to the surface, right? Well, you can't. When you start to drown, you can't move anymore. You just stay there, bobbing with your head thrown back, breathing water in. The water in your bloodstream I mentioned before? It messes with your cells and your organs begin to fail. In less than three minutes, you're dead."

"What the…"

"I just want you to know the dangers of swimming, Evan. It's always important to be careful."

The two boys stared at each other in silence for a long seconds and Boyd enjoyed the roles being reversed.

"Dinner is ready!" Jasper called.

Felicia stood up with her wine glass. "Come on, kids. Let's eat."

Boyd began climbing up the ladder and Tori was waiting for him with a beach towel, swiftly wrapping him up.

"How was the water, Boyd?"

"It was great. I had a lot of fun."

"Yeah?"

Boyd shot a glance at Evan who was still in the pool. "I think I'm going to like living with you, Tori. I love this place."

# CHAPTER 10

The big Chevrolet pickup stopped in the driveway and honked. Tori would recognize her husband's truck anywhere, but it wasn't his style to blow the horn.

Well, he used to do that when they started going out and she had made him understand that she wasn't a labradoodle at his beck and call. If he wanted her attention, he could call her by name like a normal human being. Besides, this was the twenty-first century. There was this little invention called the cell phone, she'd told him.

In any case, Tori was curious and looked out the window. She found Lucas stepping out of the pickup with a big grin on his face.

"Boyd, come out here!"

She had no idea where the boy was, but she had to find out what was going on. She put away her broom and went outside, getting to the driveway at the same time as Boyd.

"What's going on?" she asked her husband.

"It's a surprise."

"What kind of surprise?"

"A surprise that's not for you," Lucas replied with a

wink. He turned to Boyd. "It's for you."

The kid was shocked and showed more emotion than usual. "Me?"

"Yeah. Come help me out, will you?"

Lucas went around the vehicle and opened the tailgate. He reached in the bed and slid something closer. Tori was standing several feet behind, squinting. She couldn't see anything because whatever the surprise was, it was covered with a tarp. At last, Lucas flung it back and retrieved the thing.

It was a bicycle.

"What do you think?" Lucas asked. "Neat, right?"

Boyd was smiling, coming closer to inspect it, something that looked halfway between a BMX and a mountain bike. It shined in the sunlight, resting on the kickstand.

For her part, Tori approached her husband. "Why did you do that?"

"What? It's a bicycle. What's the big deal?"

"Bikes are dangerous, Lucas."

"Chill out, baby. It's not like I got the kid a chainsaw or a twelve-gauge. It's just a bike. Every kid should have a bike. And it was a floor model, so I got it cheap." He looked at Boyd. "You can ride, can't you?"

"Yes," Boyd answered. "I used to have a Schwinn."

Lucas winked at his wife. "See? Boyd, the man at the store said that this bike is even better than a Schwinn."

"I don't like it," Tori whispered. "What if he gets

hurt?"

"You can't keep him locked up, Tori. Every kid gets hurt on a bike. They fall, they get up, and they learn to toughen up."

Tori wasn't convinced. "But…"

"Look, you wanted me to take an interest? I'm taking an interest. It's going to be good for him. He needs to be a little more independent and not be cooped up in the house all the time. That's reasonable, right?"

"Yes, but…"

"Relax, okay? And I'm not a complete Neanderthal. I got him a helmet."

He winked again at Tori and pulled her into his arms, even if she made it difficult by offering token resistance.

"Boyd," she began. "If you get a bicycle, you need to follow some rules, all right?"

"What rules?"

"No riding after dark, ever. And you stay in the neighborhood."

Lucas groaned faintly next to her. "Baby, what the hell? Boyd, you can ride around town, but you need to stay out of traffic, okay? And never after dark."

Tori was appalled and yet she couldn't have a fight in front of the child. She kept her voice barely above a whisper. "Lucas, he can't go into town! He's eight years old."

"At that age, I was on my bike all day long, going everywhere. It'll be fine. Trust me, baby. For once?"

He kissed her on the forehead, and she knew that she had lost this battle.

~ ~ ~ ~

Boyd quickly made use of his newfound freedom. The bicycle was a smidgen too big for him, but adjusting the seat was a good enough solution. He was able to reach the pedals and ride adequately.

He went down the street, turned the corner, and just kept going. He was starting to get used to the geography of Steep Gorge and before long he reached the heart of town. There wasn't much remarkable about it. All the houses were old. Most of the businesses had last been built in the sixties or seventies, when architecture was on its deathbed.

Still, it was a wonderful summer day and there was nothing like the freedom of riding your bike down an empty street. An old sleepy town meant streets lined with tall, ancient trees. The shade they provided was pleasant.

"Hey, look! It's the weirdo!"

The voice startled Boyd and he glanced over his shoulder. Evan was on his own bike along with a group of boys. They picked up speed and within seconds they were all around Boyd.

"That's him?"

"Hi, Evan," Boyd said. "These are your friends?"

"Alex, Tim, Billy."

None of them acknowledged Boyd. Wordlessly, they kept pace, even going a little faster. Boyd had to keep up so he wouldn't collide with the others.

"Look at his stupid bike!" Alex said.

"Yeah, isn't that the McGoose from the store?" Billy commented, making everybody laugh.

Boyd realized at once that he'd gotten the bicycle no one in town wanted.

"I hope you don't come to school with that bike," Tim added. "Everybody's going to make fun of you."

"Everybody!"

And they weren't making fun of him now? Boyd didn't say anything.

"Did he really see his parents get killed?"

"Yeah, totally!" Evan replied, the absolute authority about everything. "He saw the murderer and the blood and the guts. He knows what it's like to be a psycho."

"Is that true, Boyd? You know what a psycho looks like?" Alex inquired with a sneer.

"Leave me alone."

"Look, he can speak!"

Tim's joke made the others guffaw. Boyd realized that they were riding a lot closer now. He couldn't escape from their little circle without ramming into them.

"But you know what?" Evan began. "I think Boyd is a psycho, too."

"That's no surprise," Billy said, getting appreciative chuckles in return. "I mean, look at him!"

"In the pool yesterday, at my house? He said he would

drown me."

Boyd gently shook his head. "I just explained science to you, Evan."

"Bullshit! You wanted to scare me. Because *you are* a psycho!"

"Look at his haircut," Tim said. "Obviously, he's a psycho."

That was the funniest joke ever as far as they were concerned and they burst into laughter.

Boyd became aware that the street was sloping. It was gentle for now, but it would get steeper soon. At the bottom was the river, although it was far from the road. Then, the street curved to the right.

"This is the best street," Evan said. "We can go really fast. I come here all the time."

The second to last building had a colorful neon sign reading *Candy Shop*. An old man in a white apron was sweeping the steps out in front. He waved.

"Hi, boys!"

"Hey, Mr. Larsen!" Evan replied, waving back.

Tim said, "We should stop. I'm out of gummy bears."

"I don't have money on me," Alex pitched in.

"You never have any money on you." Evan teased, drawing laughter. "Hey, Boyd? Can you lend us money?"

"I don't have any."

"He's useless."

Billy agreed, "So useless!"

They were going fast now, the incline quite pronounced as they careened toward the river. Boyd realized that in addition to the speed, he would have to handle a sharp turn at the bottom. And the other kids were still in a tight formation around him.

Mr. Larsen also noticed that and he stopped sweeping. "You boys be careful! Don't go so fast."

"It's fine, Mr. Larsen!"

"And stop crowding that boy!" the old man shouted. "It's dangerous!"

"Sure, no problem!" Evan lied.

The five of them whooshed by the store. Boyd was trapped in the middle of the circle. He focused his attention on not bumping into the others and remaining upright.

His fingers tightened on the cheap rubber grips of the handlebar. Instinctively, he turned at the same time as the others and they veered around the corner. Boyd looked over his shoulder and could no longer see Mr. Larsen. In fact, the entire street was deserted.

"Let's do it now," Evan said.

"Yeah!"

*Do what?* Boyd wondered, his heart filling with dread.

Before he could give it more thought, Billy slowed down and Alex picked up speed, the two boys getting out of the way on his left flank. At the exact same moment, Tim and Evan turned toward him.

Startled, Boyd didn't have a choice but to swerve to the left so they wouldn't smash into him. In a flash, his wheels skidded off the pavement, onto a thin layer of gravel, and he lost control.

"Oh!" he yelped.

He flew straight down into the two-foot deep ditch. His front wheel crashed hard into the bottom and he was thrown off the bike, landing into the grass and weeds and pebbles. It was painful, sure, but nothing compared to the humiliation of their gleeful cackling.

Boyd was angry though that didn't last long. As soon as he was up on his feet again, he knew what he would do next. Revenge would be amusing.

~ ~ ~ ~

Boyd returned home for a snack, but it was mostly so that Tori wouldn't worry. He understood that she was reluctant to have him ride his bike into town, and by coming back to the house, he was showing her that he was responsible, that it wasn't dangerous for him to be on his own.

"Can I go back on my bike?" he asked softly, glad that he didn't have any bumps or scratches on display. "It won't get dark for a while."

Tori bit her bottom lip, considering the request. "Only if you promise to be careful…"

"Thank you, Tori!"

He gave her a hug, his very first, and it placated her. After leaving the house, making sure she wasn't watching, Boyd entered the garage. He rummaged through it for several minutes until he found what he was looking for.

He returned to town and biked for almost an hour before he saw Evan again. He followed him all afternoon, making sure to keep his distance and remain unseen. He soon got a feel for Evan's patterns. He would go from his house, to the school, and down the sloping street again. As time passed, Tim, Billy, and Alex all went home.

The sun began to go down and Boyd knew that he didn't have much time left to act. He circled back, following the river, and made preparations. He parked behind the building, leaning his bicycle against the wall, and crouched.

Lying in wait.

A few cars went by, yet no one gave him a second glance. After fifteen minutes, Boyd became anxious that he wouldn't succeed. Then he reminded himself that patience was a virtue few people really had. But he did. He peeked around the corner and that's when he saw Evan pedaling down the street.

Boyd retreated to his spot and grabbed the rope he had gotten from Lucas's supplies. Across the street, it was looped around a *Slow Children* sign. On this side, it was loosely coiled around a lamppost.

He waited, his heartrate barely increasing.

Evan let out a cheer as he sped down the hill, his exhilaration the highlight of his day. And that's when Boyd acted.

He pulled on the rope as hard as he could, turning his body and using his shoulder for leverage. He braced against the lamppost. The rope rose twenty inches from the pavement and there was no way Evan could avoid it.

It clotheslined the bicycle just above the front wheel.

Evan cartwheeled, being thrown forward.

"Ah!"

He landed hard on the asphalt and his scream intensified. Boyd could swear he heard bones cracking on impact.

"Aaaahh!" Evan wailed, clutching his arm and wriggling on the ground.

Boyd smirked at the other boy in pain. He reeled the rope to him, got on his bike, and pedaled until he was out of sight, no evidence left behind. However, he remained close enough to see what happened next.

Mr. Larsen was eventually alerted by the cries and came to see what was going on. Jasper, Evan's father, showed up before the ambulance did. Evan never stopped crying, especially when the paramedic suggested that this seemed like a bad break.

It was almost completely dark when Boyd finally headed home. He would most likely get grounded for not returning before dark. Maybe they would take his bicycle away. In any case, it was worth it.

He couldn't help smiling. The revenge was satisfying, yes, but Evan's pain, and knowing how much power Boyd yielded, that was simply pure pleasure.

# CHAPTER 11

The basement wasn't finished. The floor was a concrete slab. The ceiling was nothing but exposed pipes and naked bulbs. The walls were ugly yellowed insulation foam. Tori and Lucas had had grand plans for the space when they had bought the house but, like most things, it took a backseat to more important matters.

Nevertheless, Lucas had insisted on creating himself a personal space. At first, it had been intended as a proverbial man cave, although it had never really gone further than the ambitious drawing board. So he had simply closed a space with studs and drywall, making himself a home office.

The walls had never been painted and were covered with splotches of dried spackle. There was a desk from IKEA, the only thing that had been purchased new. The swivel chair and filing cabinets had been found on Craigslist. There was no decoration and, aside from a table lamp, the only thing remotely personal in the office was the laptop.

It dawned on Lucas how awful the place looked. He felt so alone right now as he sat behind his desk. Without a carpet or wall treatments, his voice echoed through the empty space. Even the small rectangular window near the ceiling was a reminder of how crappy the office was.

This was compounded by the discussion he was having on the phone. Nothing was going as planned.

"Chad, listen…"

"I don't know how I can be more clear, Lucas. We're rethinking our position."

"We had a deal," Lucas reminded him, his voice coming out angrier than he wanted.

"Yes, we did have a deal. The deal was that I would consider your proposal. I did consider it."

"You said you would come on board with me, Chad. Twenty-five percent equity. That was the deal. You promised me!"

There was a pause on the other end of the line. "We never signed the documents."

"So what are you telling me, that you have no word?"

"Now wait a minute…"

Lucas cut him off. "What? You can't stand hearing the truth? Because the truth is that you were supposed to come in on this deal big with me. Now you're telling me that you're weaseling out! Tell me how I'm supposed to react to that? My entire goddamn business plan is falling apart because of you!"

"Lucas, you just used the operative word yourself: business. This isn't personal. It's a *business* decision. I took another look at the figures and I don't think the market is as strong as I thought it was."

"There's a huge potential for real estate in Steep Gorge. I just need this little help from you and then we can make a killing. I know it!"

Lucas was horrified to discover that his hand was shaking and he hadn't taken a breath in nearly a minute. Then he glimpsed a shadow outside the office. Probably the freaking kid snooping around. *Jesus…*

Worst of all, though, was this feeling of helplessness. He hated going up to people hat in hand, which he was essentially doing with this investor. There was nothing worse than not being in control of your own destiny, something that was happening more and more in his life. First, Tori deciding they would become foster parents. Now, his money guy leaving him holding the bag.

"Look, Lucas, if you ever come up with a project you think we could be interested in, give me a call."

"So wait, that's it?" Lucas asked, his voice rising in menace. "You make all these promises and then you cut me loose?"

"Lucas…"

Lucas was already on his feet, ready for a fight. "You invited me to your house. You remember that, Chad? You brought me into your garage, showed me your precious little goddamn Ferrari, and you made me believe that I was only months away from getting one of my own. You remember that, you son of a bitch?"

"Hey! I thought we were being civilized here."

Mortified, Lucas realized what he had just said. Now wasn't time to burn bridges. He sat back down.

"I'm sorry, Chad. Mr. Muhlenburg. I apologize. I'm just under so much pressure. Please reconsider. It's all I'm asking. Half the houses are already up. We're halfway there. With your capital, I can finish the project, sell the homes, and we can all make a bundle."

"Maybe another time, Lucas. On a different development."

"Every single dollar I have is invested in this project, Chad. I could lose everything. I have a wife, a kid…"

"Goodbye, Lucas. And good luck to you."

The line went dead and Lucas slumped in his chair, resisting the urge to throw his phone against the wall. He was about to do it until he realized he couldn't afford to replace it.

~ ~ ~ ~

Felicia said, "It's such an ordeal, girl. You have no idea."

At that, Tori straightened up, remembering that she was in the middle of a phone conversation with her friend. "It's awful."

In truth, she had been somewhat eavesdropping on Lucas's call downstairs. She could only hear his side of it, and his voice was muffled by the distance and the walls between them, but she understood the gist of it. The real estate project was in trouble.

That meant they were all in trouble.

She hadn't found time to paint ever since Boyd had shown up. They were all counting on Lucas finishing the development in order to relax. That was in jeopardy now and Tori felt useless, unable to help.

"I told Evan a million times not to ride his bike down that street," Felicia said. "You heard me tell him, right? I tell him all the time. That hill is dangerous. And with the river at the bottom? I can't believe no one has put up barricades yet. It's so irresponsible."

Tori could swear that Felicia was slurring her words. She had to be on her second bottle of wine. Then again, could she blame her? God knows how she would react if something happened to Boyd.

"How is he now?" Tori asked.

"He's in his room. He's sobbing. I can hear him."

"Poor little guy."

"His arm is broken in two places. Doesn't look like he'll need surgery, at least for now, but you can bet he'll still be in a cast for school portraits."

Tori was about to ask what the big deal was about that, because Felicia sounded more concerned by the less than ideal pictures than Evan's arm, but she kept it to herself.

"His shoulders are bruised. He has scratches on his face. He needed stiches on his head."

"My God!" Tori said.

"They gave him pain meds. I crushed the pill and made him take it with strawberry jam. I should have given him more so he could sleep. His crying breaks my heart."

"And he just fell off the bike?"

There was a gulping sound through the phone as Felicia drank. "Evan says there was an obstacle, just came out of nowhere."

"What kind of obstacle?"

"He doesn't know. Jasper got there and he didn't see

anything. But whatever it was, it had to be big to throw him off like that and hurt him so bad."

"Yeah, I'm sure," Tori said, leaning against the kitchen counter and wishing she was herself drinking wine.

"Jasper wants to sue the city. That's a dangerous hill. There should be warning signs. The road should be better maintained. There shouldn't be obstacles like that to endanger our children." More drinking. "I know what I'll do!"

"What?"

"I'll get the PTA together and I'll start a petition. We need to gather support and show the city council that Steep Gorge is nothing but a death trap, girl."

Tori agreed, although she doubted anything positive would come out of it. Mostly, she let Felicia rant, the alcohol doing most of the talking by now.

She caught movement from the corner of her eye. It was Boyd. He was standing next to the kitchen island, looking at her and trying to make sense of the conversation. She offered him a kind smile while Felicia continued her tirade.

"I'll go to the TV networks if I have to, Tori! The world has to know how dangerous our streets are. Oh, I know; I'll post a video on Facebook! Yes, I'm sure this will work!"

"You do that, Felicia. Don't do it tonight, though. Wait until you're less emotional."

"Right, good idea. I'm going to write down some thoughts."

"Sounds like a plan. Good night."

Tori hung up and almost chuckled at her friend's sudden enthusiasm. Boyd was still there.

"Is Evan going to be okay?" he asked.

"I think so. He hurt his arm pretty bad."

"It's broken?"

"It is, and he has some cuts and bruises. He's going to be fine."

Boyd frowned and nodded. "I hope so. He's my best friend now. I hope nothing bad happens to him."

Tori was touched by that and came forward to pat him on the shoulder, not sure how he would react to an unexpected hug.

"You have a kind heart, sweetie."

Boyd smiled tightly and displayed gratitude as well as something else. Tori could swear it was affection and she knew at once she had made the right decision by welcoming him in their family.

Lucas came up the stairs and appeared in the kitchen, his face ashen. Tori sobered and Boyd took his cue, walking away to the living room where he dropped to the floor with his action figures.

"Everything okay?" Tori inquired.

"Get a picture of what is *okay*. Try to see it in your head. Got it? What's happening is the complete opposite of okay."

Lucas went to the sideboard against the wall separating the dining room and the den, and pulled out a half-empty bottle of Wild Turkey. He returned to the kitchen, fetched a glass, and filled it almost to the top.

Tori kept her voice low. "What happened?"

"Muhlenburg is backing out, that's what's happening."

He avoided looking at her and drank a third of the whiskey.

"But I thought you had an agreement."

"We did have an agreement and first thing in the morning I'm meeting with my lawyer."

"A lawyer? Lawsuits are expensive."

"You don't think I already know that, Tori? I'm getting screwed here, and the worst part is that Muhlenburg is going to get away with it. Without his investment… Christ! I don't know."

He drank another third of the Wild Turkey, leaning against the counter as if it was the only thing keeping him upright.

"Are we in trouble, Lucas?"

"I have to find a way to get enough money to finish the project. If we can finish and sell most of the houses this fall, maybe we can head off the banks. Otherwise…"

"Otherwise what?"

He shrugged, still looking away. "Otherwise, it's bankruptcy. We lose everything."

"What? We can't go bankrupt, Lucas. We have Boyd now. We have to take care of him."

He slammed his glass on the counter and whiskey splashed out. "That was your idea. Remember that."

"Hey! Don't put this on me. We're in this together. We've been in this together for a long time and we've been through a lot. We can get through this, too. Families stick together."

"Well, your little paintings aren't helping the family, are they?"

"Lucas!" she gasped, unable to remember if he'd ever spoken to her that way. It was like getting punched in the face, as if she was being betrayed. "The landscapes I do, they help me express myself."

"And they don't sell for shit! If you were doing modern art, at least, maybe we could get some money out of it. But no! You have to do those Amish landscapes."

"Lucas…"

"If you really want to help this *family*," he spat, the last word coming out sour, "why don't you think about getting a real job, uh?"

He grabbed his glass, the bottle, and stormed back downstairs, leaving Tori unable to process what had just happened between them.

# CHAPTER 12

Gannon felt like he deserved an extra Cherry Coke this week. In fact, he was grinning as if he was under the influence, which unsettled Mobley.

"What?" she asked.

This brought him back to reality and he changed his expression. "Forget it."

"No, what is it?"

"I had forgotten what it's like to be this excited about an investigation, that's all."

She frowned. "That's your excited face?"

"What, do I look constipated instead? Come on, we have a long drive ahead of us."

He was eager to change the subject and, thankfully, she let it go. It didn't change how he felt though. Days of digging through records, cross-referencing phone numbers, bank accounts, and known associates' itineraries had finally paid off.

As hard as Gannon tried to appear aloof and jaded, he couldn't deny that there was a particular rush about making progress on a case. It was something you couldn't get elsewhere. It was pure satisfaction and he was embarrassed that he had let himself forget how that felt as his career drifted into obscurity.

He put on his jacket though he didn't button it because it was snug around the waist. Captain Vail was coming out of a cubicle when he noticed him and Mobley trailing behind.

"Where are you heading?"

"Following up on a lead in Trenton."

That made the commanding officer gasp. "Trenton? We don't have jurisdiction in Trenton. Or is it that you're so old that you're now suffering from dementia and you don't remember little police matters such as jurisdiction?"

"Like I said, it's a lead. I'm not going to arrest anyone. Not today, at least."

Mobley took a step forward and nodded. "It's a good lead, sir."

Her intervention placated Vail and he had no choice but to nod, letting the matter drop.

"All right, fine. As long as you play this by the book. Understood?"

"I wouldn't have it any other way, Cap."

Vail was dubious. "Right. And you still haven't signed out your new equipment. I want you Tasered up by the end of the week. That's an order."

"I'm on it," Gannon replied, making everyone around know that he meant the opposite.

Before the conversation continued, he gave a little wave and left the station. Mobley was following, yet she quickly fell behind. Five minutes later, they were on the road, heading toward the highway.

"I hope you don't think I was being sexist or anything," he said. "I mean, I did ask if you wanted to drive."

"It's fine."

"It's just a habit. I'm used to driving. The first partner I had fell asleep every time he sat in the car, and the last partner I had couldn't drive for shit. But if you want the wheel…"

"It's okay, Gannon. Really."

"If you change your mind, just say so."

He glanced sideways. Mobley nodded, but wasn't looking at him. She nodded vaguely for him to end this conversation. She slumped on her seat and she massaged her temples.

"Everything all right, Mobley?"

"Yeah," she answered curtly.

"Rough night?"

"Personal stuff. Is it okay if I don't talk about it?"

He glanced at her again, gauging her reaction. He decided that they were work colleagues. They weren't relatives and they weren't friends. It wasn't his place to pry. Besides, the last thing he needed was someone else's problems.

"You got it," Gannon said, focusing his gaze on the road.

~ ~ ~ ~

It took hours to reach Trenton and almost as long to

find their destination. Gannon had researched maps before getting here. Apparently, he hadn't researched enough. To add insult to injury, he had been here before, years ago.

*My memory isn't what it used to be*, he thought. He was definitely getting old.

The neighborhood was industrial, with everything that entailed: dirty brick buildings, potholed roads, zero vegetation. It wasn't the kind of place where you took a Sunday drive. Gannon couldn't wait to go back to his own turf. On the other hand, there was a chance he could crack the case today.

"This is it?" Mobley asked as they pulled into the parking lot of a place called Trenton Quality Meats, the sign having faded to practically nothing long ago.

"Yes." She nodded and instinctively checked the pistol at her waist. "You won't need that, Mobley. These people don't do the dirty work in daylight."

They left the car and walked toward the building. They could see the loading docks on the side and it was business as usual, refrigerated trucks being filled with palettes as employees in white smocks came and went.

They walked in and Gannon's memory returned. Getting here had been nothing but trial and error, but now he was in his element. The reception area hadn't changed, still as innocuous as it had been the first time. There was a gray stucco wall behind the reception desk. The smell was commercial air freshener, anything to combat the stench of meat being butchered yards away.

"Good afternoon," the chubby receptionist said without the hint of a smile. "Can I help you?"

"No, I'm good."

Gannon dismissed her with a wave and walked past her, heading to a hallway to her left. Mobley kept up with him.

"Sir, wait a minute! You can't go there!"

Not bothering to reply, Gannon went through the swinging doors on his right. He was faced with another long corridor. From the sound of it, on the right was the processing facility. The saws and conveyors were loud, though muffled by the thick walls.

A door opened on the left and a man wearing a Phillies T-shirt came out, undoubtedly having been alerted by the receptionist.

"Who are you?"

"I'm Detective Gannon."

"You got a warrant?"

"Do I need one?"

The two men stared at each other, sizing each other up. Mobley had unbuttoned her jacket and her right hand was slightly elevated, getting ready to draw if need be. Gannon felt like laughing at her enthusiasm.

He took a step toward the goon and peered into the room behind him. It was like an employee break room, only more stylish. There were couches, a big screen TV, tables and chairs. More importantly, there were four other guys of the same impressive build. They stood up, like they wanted to back up their buddy.

Trenton Quality Meats was a famous mob hangout. It was owned by Gherardo "Gerry" Longo and had been founded by his father before him. Neither of them had ever been indicted of anything since turning to crime sixty years ago, but everyone with a badge on the eastern seaboard knew that many investigations became dead ends at this very address.

"So what's going on?" the Phillies fan asked, coming forward with his head tilted back, probably trying to impress his buddies. "Soliciting funds for the police orphan fund?"

"We're going in to see Gerry."

"No one meets with Mr. Longo unless he personally requests it."

Gannon sighed. These games were made for young people, something he wasn't anymore. "Stop busting my balls, will you? I'm not going away. I drove all the way from Franklin, so if I go back empty handed my captain's going to put me on traffic duty. Ain't no way this is happening."

The Phillies fan took pleasure in this and shook his head, smirking. "Not my problem. Take a hike, you and your pretty little thing over here."

Mobley bristled and her feet shifted. She was getting into a fighting stance.

"It's okay, Mikey."

The voice was older and coming from several yards away. Mikey turned around and the other thugs moved aside, parting like the Red Sea. Gerry Longo came forward. He was roughly Gannon's age, dressed in slacks and a golf shirt. His salt-and-pepper hair was thinning and had been brushed back with enough hairspray to hide the bald spots. It almost worked.

"What do the good people of Franklin want with me, Detective?"

"Just have a little conversation, that's all."

"I've been to Franklin once and, trust me, a *little* conversation is all it warrants."

"I know," Gannon said. "That's where we met the first time."

Longo was genuinely surprised by that. "We met?"

"Twice, some twenty years back. Once there and the second time was here. Asked you some questions about some things you had or hadn't done."

"Looks like I hadn't done these things after all, right?"

The goons shared a laugh with him.

Gannon shrugged. "Officially anyway. Can we talk somewhere private?"

Longo considered that for a few moments, looked at his watch, and exhaled deeply. "Two minutes. I got a meeting soon."

He waved for the cops to follow him and they did. Mobley stayed close to her partner and glanced around suspiciously. They went through the break room and down another hallway. They went past a middle-aged secretary and at last walked into an office.

It was rather small and blandly decorated, nothing to suggest that the occupant was a man who was a millionaire many times over. The air reeked of cigar smoke, making Mobley cough as soon as they entered. The two men ignored her. Longo sat behind his desk while Gannon sat across from him, keeping to the edge of the chair. The young woman did the same.

"So what do you want?"

"Tell me about your relationship with John Begum," Gannon asked, pulling out his notepad.

"John Begum? Doesn't ring a bell with, sorry. You can go now."

"You can do a little better than that, Gerry. Tell me about John Begum. He was killed recently in Hillford. He was slashed to death with his wife."

"Oh, that John Begum! Why didn't you say so? We used to go out together. Gave head like a three-dollar hooker, but really soft hands." He shrugged dramatically. "I got no idea who that guy is, Detective. You're wasting your time and, most of all, you're wasting mine."

"Begum did the books for Timothy Misner."

"Once again, you're talking about somebody I don't know. We gonna go through your whole Rolodex like that?"

Gannon nodded and smiled tightly, keeping his patience in check. "You're going to deny that Misner is operating a string of front companies for you, Gerry?"

"Front companies? That sounds really shady. I'm not shady. I'm an honest businessman. I'm known for the best meat in Trenton."

At that, he winked at Mobley and the subtext gave her goosebumps. Gannon spoke again before she lost her cool.

"You said you have a meeting in a minute, right?"

"Yes, I do," Longo replied, as if this was the most

sensible thing anyone had said so far. "It's a very important meeting. Can't miss it."

"Then we can fast-track this little conversation of ours, Gerry. I'll pretend as if I don't know about all your illegal activities and you'll pretend that you're interested in answering questions, deal?"

"Detective, I've never done anything illegal in my life."

"Right, right. The coal trucks going across Appalachia to smuggle Oxy, that's not you, uh? Or the seven restaurants and bars along I-81 you use to launder money. That's not you either, right?"

Longo shifted in his seat, but he offered no comeback.

"I can do this all day long, Gerry. You think you're wise enough not to get caught? Maybe you are, and I'm going to give you a gift."

"A gift?"

"Call it gesture of good faith. I'll tell you something, and then you'll tell me everything you know about John Begum."

"What?"

"Kurt Kaur. I have it on good authority that the FBI has him."

"Bullshit."

"They've been talking to him seriously for the past four months. He's about to turn state's evidence."

Longo was shooting daggers at the veteran cop sitting across from him. He swallowed with difficulty, his mouth dry. "He wouldn't do that."

There was no conviction in his voice.

"I told you it was a gift. I told you what I know, so now tell me what you know. John Begum. What happened? He get too involved in your business? He was skimming? Is that why you had him whacked?"

"No way!" Longo said, for the first time showing passion. "I didn't kill him and I never wished him harm!"

"A minute ago you said you didn't know him and now you claim that you didn't wish him harm. I'm confused."

"Listen, I knew Begum, by name anyway. Never met the guy. He worked for me, okay? As far as I'm concerned, he was my best accountant. And everything he did was above board!"

"And yet he was knifed to death in his own house, along with his wife, while their kid was in the other room."

"I didn't do that. My people didn't do that. Besides, what kind of sick bastard kills somebody that way? I may be in the meat business, but I ain't no butcher. You got me? There are a lot of easier ways to get rid of a guy. I got nothing to do with this, Detective. I swear."

Obviously, Gannon had never expected Longo to confess a murder, but he wanted to see how he would react. Everything told him that Longo was being sincere. Unfortunately.

Gannon thanked him for his time and a minute later he was sitting in the car again with Mobley.

"We came all the way out here for nothing?" she asked.

"That's the job. It's like a labyrinth. You follow a path

up until you hit a wall. Then you do it again, trying another opening."

Mobley nodded and they drove out of the parking lot. "I can't believe you told them about that Kurt Kaur federal investigation though. Why did you tip him off?"

Gannon started laughing. "I was bluffing about that. I have no idea what the FBI has on Kaur, probably plenty though. He's a lawyer, privately consults for half the mobsters in this country. Whatever happens to him, not many people will weep over his coffin."

"That's harsh," she said.

"It was necessary."

Gannon had no idea what would happen with Kurt Kaur, and he frankly didn't care. All that mattered was this investigation had hit another brick wall in the maze. Worse still, they had run out of leads.

Which meant that the killer was still out there.

# CHAPTER 13

"Boyd, how are you handling it, buddy?"

"It's hard," he replied, shifting his feet on the rocks and holding onto his fishing rod tighter. "I'm not catching anything."

Lucas laughed heartily and Jasper joined in.

"What's so funny?" the boy asked. "Are you making fun of me?"

"No, we're not making fun of you." Lucas cast his line again. "It's just that this is the whole point of fishing. It's not easy."

"Then why are we here? They sell fish at the store."

"The point of fishing is *to fish*, not to catch. Aren't you having fun?"

Boyd shrugged. "I don't know. You two have caught a bunch already, and I'm only wasting my time."

Jasper lost it, practically choking. "You're wasting your time? Did you have somewhere else to be? Are we keeping you from surgery?"

Lucas was laughing just as hard. "You have a dinner reservation?"

"You're making fun of me now," Boyd said, his voice

low but the accusation clear.

"That's also a part of fishing, little buddy. It's where men go to relax and shoot the breeze." Lucas reached between his feet and picked up his beer. He finished it and placed the bottle back into the cooler. "Jasper, you due for a fresh one?"

"Absolutely!"

Jasper finished his just as Lucas tossed him a new one. Then, Lucas changed lures, using Rooster Tails this time, and put another worm on the hook. He cast his line in the river. It wasn't his favorite type of fishing—he preferred sitting in a boat in the middle of a lake—but this place was convenient for last-minute decisions such as today.

Tori had suggested it. After their fight, they both knew that they needed time apart to calm down and, frankly, he didn't want to be at work today anyway. Each minute he spent at the office or on the construction site was another reminder of how he was about to lose everything.

Here under the warm sun, on the banks of the river, he could forget about his problems. The beer helped, too. And Jasper being here took out the awkwardness of being alone with the kid, which had been another one of Tori's suggestions. She'd said that it would be good for Boyd. Male bonding.

The kid had never gone fishing before, so it was moderately cool to show him something. Lucas felt useful for the first time in a long time. The fact that the trout were biting today was a nice bonus.

"I got another one!" he exclaimed.

It was a big one, he knew. It was a strong bastard and

Lucas fought against it, letting the line unspool before yanking back and reeling it in. He had no delusions that he was fighting against a marlin or anything, but it was still sport. Finally, he brought it out of the water.

"Nice," Jasper said, taking a swig of beer to celebrate. "Gotta be what, two pounds?"

"Just about."

Lucas unhooked it and took a few steps back where he dropped the fish in a deep plastic bucket. There were four others at the bottom, still wiggling.

"This sucks," Boyd said.

"You'll catch one, I swear. You just have to be patient, all right?"

"No, I mean that it sucks Evan couldn't come with us."

"Yeah…" Lucas commiserated.

He glanced at Jasper who for a moment looked sheepish. In reality, Evan had refused to come. He'd said that he'd rather stay home and play video games than go fishing with the others.

Boyd pouted. "I don't think he likes me."

"Don't say that, buddy. He just couldn't come, that's all. Maybe some other time."

The kid nodded, though he wasn't convinced. The two men shared another look. Both felt sorry for Boyd. He'd just lost his parents, moved to a different part of the state, and making friends was hard.

Lucas drank some beer before throwing another line. Tori would know what to say to him. He felt completely incompetent at the moment. He hadn't signed up for this, not really. He was just along for the ride. Would it really get better?

His phone rang and he was grateful for having something else to think about.

"You owe me five bucks!" Jasper cheered. "Phone or fish, there can only be one!"

Lucas flipped him the bird and checked his phone. "Shit. I have to take this."

"You still owe me five bucks."

Lucas barely heard him as he put his fishing pole on the ground and took a few steps away for the conversation, trying to figure out who the number belonged to. He knew it was about work, he just didn't remember who it was specifically.

"Hello?"

"Mr. Ramsdale? This is Betty from Ortiz Cabinetry. How are you?"

He was immediately suspicious. "Fine."

"We have a delivery scheduled for next Friday and we still haven't received the second payment. Do you have a moment to talk about this?"

Cursing under his breath, Lucas walked farther away, toward his truck. He didn't want the others to overhear the conversation, to know how much of a failure he was.

~ ~ ~ ~

Boyd looked at Lucas walking away and then shot a

glance at Jasper who was busy juggling fishing and drinking. Boyd had his own glass bottle of Sprite on the ground. He took a sip and winced. It was warm now.

He reeled in his line. Once more, he hadn't caught anything. He crouched and dipped his hand into the bait box. It was filled with dirt and live worms moving about. It was kind of pretty to watch, sort of like harmless little snakes.

He chose a fat brown nightcrawler, turned it between his fingers, admiring it, and then hooked it to his line. He took his time to pierce its body with the sharp point. He folded the worm in half and then pierced it again until it couldn't escape. This was more fun than actual fishing, he decided.

And that gave him an idea.

He put his pole down on the rocks and walked away from the edge. Jasper noticed him, but he kept his eyes on his own fishing.

"Don't worry, kid. You'll catch one."

"I'm taking a break."

Boyd went to the bucket of fish the men had caught. He peered down. Still writhing, the fish reminded him of the worms, only bigger. After a moment, he dipped into it and grabbed the newest one. It was the trout Lucas had caught just a few minutes ago.

It took him three attempts because it was slimy. Also, he couldn't shake the feeling that the fish knew what he was doing. It was like it was trying to get away from him. It made him smile to know that he was the predator now.

He tightened his grip and placed his fingers into the

gills. At last, the trout couldn't get away. He picked up his soda bottle with his other hand and walked away even further. The tree line was thirty feet to the right and he headed in that direction. Lucas was busy on the phone and Jasper didn't even look his way.

Boyd walked around sprawling ferns and went past a couple of pine trees until he reached a little clearing. There was a boulder and a few small rocks below it. A worktable, he thought.

He put the fish on the flattest rock and held it in place. For long seconds, he simply watched the fish thrash. Out of the water, it had very little energy left. Its mouth opened and closed, as if gasping for air.

Was it suffering? Did the fish realize it was about to die? It would be nice if it did, Boyd thought.

He pulled the gills open and the fish squirmed even more. Yes, it had to be in pain somehow!

Without looking away from it—he didn't want to miss a thing—he emptied his soda on the ground and then placed the neck of the bottle against its mouth. The fish was about to die, so he had to act fast. He pried the mouth open until it was wide enough. Next, Boyd rammed the bottle in, impaling the fish almost completely.

Juices and mashed fish guts oozed out along the glass. How did it feel like to be split in two this way? What if the trout was screaming and only the other fish could hear it?

He nestled the bottle into the ground, standing it up. The fish still wasn't dead, which made Boyd happy. He looked at its eye. Was it staring back? Was the fish wondering who he was and why he was doing this to him?

A dark thought occurred to Boyd. The fish was judging him.

In a flash, he held the bottle straight with one hand and, with the other, he plucked the fish's eye out. It was more difficult than he thought it would be, but he pulled and twisted and yanked the thing out.

"So cool," he said to himself as the fish finally died.

He dropped the eye and searched the ground. He found a rock. It was the size of a baseball and it felt comfortable in his hand. He loosened the fish off the bottle and put it back on his makeshift worktable. He grinned, wound his arm back, and crushed the rock against the fish's head. After three blows, nothing remained but pink goo.

"What the hell are you doing?"

Boyd turned around. Jasper was standing two yards back, a shocked expression on his face.

"What's going on, Boyd?"

"Nothing. Just playing."

Jasper nodded, clearly not knowing how to react. "Well, uh, come back to the river. I have Phoebe Minnows for you to try to fish with. Maybe you'll catch something this time."

~ ~ ~ ~

Lucas practically threw the phone inside the truck and returned to the river. Jasper was there, holding his line in the water.

"Everything okay?"

"Yeah," Lucas replied as he picked up his fishing pole, more out of habit than from sheer enthusiasm. "Just one of my suppliers being a bitch."

It was a lot more complicated than that, though he didn't want to talk about it. Jasper was his friend, but they weren't close enough for him to tell him how screwed his business was. Muhlenburg wasn't investing in his company, money was getting tight, and now suppliers were knocking on his door, asking for money.

They stood there side by side for several minutes, fishing quietly. The trout weren't biting anymore. Lucas noticed that Boyd was a little farther than he'd been before. He was slowly rifling through the tackle box.

"Listen…" Jasper said quietly, his voice trailing off.

"What?"

"The kid. I saw him do something before, when you were on the phone. In the woods."

Lucas frowned and chuckled. "He's a little young to beat off, isn't he?"

"No, he was…" Jasper was shaking his head, searching for the right words. "He had a fish, one we caught before. He was smashing it with a rock."

"A rock?"

"He was really bashing it in."

Lucas shrugged it off. "He was just goofing around. Every kid does that, right?"

"No, I mean this was messed up. It was like he was having fun."

"Didn't you make frogs smoke when you were young? My cousin used to put firecrackers on cats' tails. Children do stupid crap."

"Fine, if you think it's normal. Whatever. I just thought you should know. It kinda freaked me out."

Lucas nodded, the complaint registering. He craned his neck toward Boyd and spoke loudly. "How's it going, buddy?"

Boyd turned to face him and smiled brightly. "I think I'll use those little silver spoons. I think I can catch something with it. I'm beginning to love fishing!"

The kid waved as if he didn't have a care in the world and got a lure from the case, enthralled by the activity. Lucas wanted to believe he was happy, yet Jasper's information was jarring.

Was there a difference between goofing around with frogs and torturing a fish? Was something genuinely wrong with Boyd?

# CHAPTER 14

"Did you wash your hands, Boyd?" Tori asked. The child shook his head, almost repentantly. "Well, go do it, okay? We have to leave in just a few minutes."

He nodded and headed upstairs, in no hurry whatsoever. Tori wished he was going faster. She didn't want to be late for his appointment with Dr. Curnutt, although she sensed that he was reluctant to go. Then again, could she blame him? Was anyone ever eager to meet with a shrink?

She sighed and entered the kitchen to look at her grocery list. It was to see if she was missing something for tonight's dinner, but mostly it was to keep herself busy. The psychologist visits made her nervous.

Tori lived in constant fear that Dr. Curnutt would find something wrong with Boyd. She didn't want to have the quiet and happy life she was building here to be disrupted. Her heart was racing at that possibility.

The boy had witnessed something horrible and every time he smiled, which wasn't often, it made her hope that Dr. Curnutt had stepped in just in time to save him from the dangers of PTSD. Still, what if she hadn't? Tori didn't know what she would do if that was her conclusion.

There were footsteps and she turned around. It was

louder than Boyd's feet should've been. Lucas walked into the kitchen.

"Good, you're still here," he said.

"Just waiting for Boyd to come down. What's going on? You want me to pick something up from the store?"

"I'm coming with you."

This gave her pause. "I thought you said you wouldn't be coming anymore."

"I changed my mind."

"But…"

"Are you seriously going to give me the third degree about this, Tori?"

"Uh, no. I think it's great that you want to come. We're in this together, right? A family."

He nodded though there wasn't much conviction in his gesture. "Yeah, sure."

"What's going on, Lucas?"

He opened his mouth to speak and decided not to when Boyd came downstairs.

"I'm ready. I washed my hands."

He lifted his hands for everyone to see that he had complied. Tori smiled to him and turned her attention to her husband.

Lucas shook his head dismissively. "I'll tell you later. Let's go."

~ ~ ~ ~

The older and distinguished woman opened the door and welcomed the family inside her home, smiling broadly.

"Good afternoon," Dr. Talia Curnutt said. "Hello, Boyd. How are you today?"

"Fine."

"Are you ready for us to chat?"

He shrugged. "I guess."

The psychologist laughed gently and invited the three of them further inside. Lucas glanced left and right before leaning toward the woman.

"Can we have a word with you before you start?" he asked.

"Of course. This way."

She led Boyd to the waiting room with all the toys. He went straight for the fire truck. She assured him that she wouldn't be long and closed the French doors so she could speak with the foster parents.

"How has he been, Mr. and Mrs. Ramsdale?"

"He's been great," Tori said at once. "Just great! I feel that he's making a lot of progress, getting to trust us. He's starting to smile more."

"That's wonderful," Dr. Curnutt replied with cautious optimism. "In most cases, it's all about giving the child time to adjust. I'm simply here to help the process."

Tori was beaming and the psychologist didn't do or say anything to affect her mood. Neither of them noticed Lucas becoming tense and jittery.

"Is something wrong with him?" he blurted out.

"Lucas!"

Dr. Curnutt remained even keeled. "What do you mean? What makes you ask that question?"

"Yesterday…"

"Did something happen?"

Lucas hesitated, looking between Boyd and his wife.

"What's going on, Lucas?" Tori asked.

"Look, maybe it's nothing…"

"It's not nothing," Tori said. "Last week you said you didn't want to come here anymore and today you changed your mind. What happened yesterday?"

"It's okay, Mr. Ramsdale," the older woman said quietly, in a tone that worked wonders with her patients. "Anything you say remains between us and I'm only here to help. That's my job."

Lucas took a deep breath. "I took him fishing yesterday. It was his first time. Tori thought it would be good for him. Anyway, I got a phone call and stepped away."

"What happened to him, Lucas?"

"Jasper said… He saw the kid go into the woods and after a while he went after him. He was… He was killing a fish."

"Killing a fish?"

"He was crushing it with a rock. There were fish guts everywhere. He really did a number on it, you know?"

Tori covered her mouth with her hand. "Why didn't you tell me?"

"I'm telling you now!"

"You should've told me, Lucas. This is important and–"

"It's all right," Dr. Curnutt interrupted, putting a hand on Tori's forearm. "I understand you're upset. It's a development, but your husband is sharing it with us now. It's fine."

Lucas avoided his wife's scrutiny, focusing on the psychologist instead. "So what does it mean? Is the kid totally messed up in the head? Did he do that because of what happened to his parents?"

For the first time, Dr. Curnutt wavered. She looked away, lost in thought. "I need to talk to Boyd."

~ ~ ~ ~

"Are you comfortable, Boyd?"

He shifted on the couch, surrounded by pillows. "Yes, Dr. Talia."

She herself crossed her legs, leaning back into her wing chair. A legal pad was balanced on her knee and, with her left hand, she held a digital recorder steady. She hadn't taken notes on their first meeting, but now she would.

"How have you been? Did you have a nice week?"

"I got a bike."

"Good for you! You like riding it?"

He nodded and she made a note.

"Yeah. I get to go around town. It's fun. It's like exploring."

"What about friends? Did you meet anyone so far, Boyd?"

"Yes, Evan."

"Who's Evan?"

"He's the son of Jasper and Felicia. They're friends of my foster parents. We went to their house the other day. They have a pool."

"That sounds exciting. You like swimming?"

"Yes."

"And did you play games in the water with Evan?"

At that, Boyd shrugged. "I like him, but I don't think he likes me back."

"What makes you say that?" Dr. Curnutt asked, clutching her pen.

"We went biking and he was teasing me with his friends."

"And how did that make you feel, Boyd?"

He shrugged and looked down. "I'm used to it."

"Did you get teased a lot at your old school?"

"Sometimes."

Dr. Curnutt wrote this down. She saw way too many cases involving bullying in her day-to-day sessions. "Does that scare you about the new school year? It's coming up soon."

"No, it's okay. I like school."

"What's your favorite subject? Besides phys-ed, I mean," she added with a wink which made him giggle.

"I like English and math and science. Everything. I like to read."

"Oh yeah? What's your favorite book?"

"I read a lot of Wikipedia," he said, looking straight at her.

He enjoyed reading an online encyclopedia? "What do you like about Wikipedia, Boyd?"

"It has all the subjects. I like learning."

"I see..." she said even though she really didn't. He was eight years old. *What kind of eight-year-old reads a reference book?*

"I also like Lewis Carroll."

The psychologist brightened up. "I always loved *Alice in Wonderland*."

"Not me. I prefer *The Game of Logic* and the Euclid book, I forget the name. It's about mathematics. I also like Neil Gaiman and Chuck Palahniuk's early works."

Once again, Dr. Curnutt was baffled. This was advanced literature. He showed intellect beyond his years and she scribbled questions to herself, reminders to investigate. It was too much for now and she decided to drop the matter.

"And how is it going with Tori and Lucas?"

"Good. They're nice."

His smile was sincere and she made a note of that, too. "I heard you went fishing yesterday."

"Yeah."

"Did you have fun?"

"I don't know. Fishing is hard. I didn't catch anything."

Dr. Curnutt's professional instinct was to smile and acquiesce. However, she was still thinking about Lucas Ramsdale's revelation from earlier. She needed to get to that.

"What happened with the fish, Boyd?"

"What fish? What do you mean?"

"You took one of the fish in the bucket and went into the woods with it, didn't you?"

Boyd stared at her as if he was deciding whether to deny it or not. The two of them held each other's gaze for almost a minute.

"So?" he said at last.

"What did you do with the fish, Boyd?"

"Nothing. I just played."

"Did you kill the fish?"

"That's the nature of fishing, isn't it? You catch the fish and they die."

She said, "The fish usually die naturally. People don't use rocks."

"They told you?"

"Why did you do it, Boyd?"

"No reason. It was fun."

"Fun? What kind of fun? How did it make you feel?"

He shrugged. “Normal, I guess. It was easier than I thought to pull its eye out.”

Dr. Curnutt couldn’t write that down. She was frozen. “You plucked the eye out?” He nodded, avoiding her gaze and fidgeting on the couch. “Was it before the fish died?”

“It doesn’t matter.”

“Yes, it does, Boyd.”

“It’s no different from daddy gutting the fish before going home.”

“But the fish is already dead when you gut it. If you pull the eyes out before it’s dead, that’s called torture. And torture is wrong.”

He looked back at her, motionless. “Oh. I didn’t know. I’m sorry.”

The child seemed genuinely contrite and she noted it, realizing that she was already on the third page on her pad. Then a lightbulb went off in her head.

“Boyd, you said *daddy* earlier. I thought you said you had never gone fishing before.”

“That’s right.”

“But you said *daddy gutting the fish*. What did you mean by that?”

“I meant Lucas.”

“Did he tell you to call him daddy?”

He shook his head. “But Tori and Lucas are my new mom and dad, no? They’re my foster parents?”

“They are,” she confirmed.

"Good because I like them, Dr. Talia. I don't want anything to happen to them. We're very happy together."

The psychologist nodded but, for the first time in years, she didn't know how to diagnose her patient. And this was a bad sign.

# CHAPTER 15

"More wine?"

"Oh God yes!" Felicia answered, already thrusting her glass toward her host.

Tori had to smile at her enthusiasm and took the bottle that was on the table between them, topping off both their glasses. Then she sank back into her chair as they drank, staring into the night.

It was a nice evening out on the porch. The humidity had gone down and there was a small breeze as well. At this altitude, evenings were often chilly, even in the summer, but tonight it was perfect. Lucas was working late at the office and Felicia had suggested dropping by, bringing a bottle of Pinot along.

"Can you imagine? Summer's going to be over soon."

Felicia shrugged. "So?"

"The end of summer always depressed me. I never liked what follows."

"Fall? That's the best, girl!"

"I never liked it when it gets cold. I mean, I know many artists love the changing colors—the mountains are always beautiful—but it never really inspired me."

"You're not hearing me, Tori. Fall. September. School." Tori frowned, still not getting it. "When school starts, you're free again!"

"Oh."

"You don't have to be home all day planning activities. You don't have to constantly hear 'Mom, where's my baseball glove?' or 'Mom, I'm hungry!' Best of all, you don't have to hide in the bathroom to sneak in a glass of wine. I used to just put it in my coffee mug, but Evan started asking questions a couple of years ago about why my coffee was purple."

Tori didn't know what to think of that, so she simply nodded. "Right."

"I swear, that boy is strange. One minute you're wondering if he should be taking the short bus to school and the next he's friggin' Columbo. But come September, he'll be at school five days a week and I won't hear any more whining."

Tori smiled in a guarded way and drank so she wouldn't have to say anything.

"Oh God!" Felicia groaned. "I'm a terrible mother, aren't I?"

"Of course, not. There's no one set path for everyone."

"I tried to think about how my mother would do it, but then I remind myself that my mother was pretty much awful. She used to leave my brother and I in the car while she went to drink in this crappy dive near our house. Anyhow, I'm just happy to be here with you."

"Cheers!"

"You know, I don't know what Jasper did, but I'm sure he has something to be forgiven for. That's not like him to volunteer to babysit Evan. Thank God for small mercies."

Felicia raised her glass in a mock toast and drank.

"Maybe going fishing with Lucas yesterday, being with Boyd," Tori offered. "Maybe it reminded him that he didn't spend enough time with his own son."

"Maybe that's it."

Tori felt her stomach tighten into a knot. Talking about the fishing trip made her feel bad as few things had in recent memory.

She said, "If you want to talk about bad mothers, I think I'm in the running."

"What are you talking about, girl?"

"Jasper didn't tell you?"

"Tell me what?"

"About the fishing trip?"

"Girl, I stopped caring about my husband's fishing trips two days after we were married. What? Did something happen?"

Tori opened her mouth to reply, but then changed her mind. Did she really want to talk about this with someone else? On the other hand, everybody else knew already and Felicia was her friend. She would understand. Besides, Tori felt the need to share her burden with someone other than her husband.

"It's…"

"What?" Felicia urged. "Come on, dish."

"Jasper told Lucas that he saw Boyd doing something in the woods."

Felicia snorted. "Boys always do something in the woods."

"No, that's not it." Tori looked over her shoulder to make sure they were alone. Boyd was already in bed but, somehow, she felt as if he could hear them. "He tortured a fish."

"Tortured a fish? How do you torture a fish? He put too much cayenne pepper on it?"

She thought that was hilarious and laughed before drinking wine.

"He played with it. Hurt it while it was still alive. He eventually killed it with a rock."

"Oh shit…"

"We talked about it with his therapist, but she says it's too early for her to know anything about what's going on with him."

Felicia nodded. "Right. She would know these things. I mean, it's her job, no?"

"I guess. I keep thinking that maybe Jasper misinterpreted what he saw. Maybe Boyd really was playing with the fish. Just playing."

"Sure."

"And besides," Tori continued, "Boyd has been through a lot. Maybe whatever he was doing was subconscious because of what he witnessed. There is not a malicious bone in his body. I just know it. He's the sweetest child."

"I'm sure. Everything has been happening so fast. You have to give him time to adjust. He probably just needs to let his guard down and relax."

"You're right. I'm worrying for nothing."

"Totally. You worry way too much for an artist, girl."

They both chuckled.

"You think? I didn't use to be uptight."

"And I didn't used to have a large ass!" Felicia fired back. "That's what ten years of marriage does to you. Listen, I know just the thing to relax you and Boyd. The fair's going to be in town next weekend. We should all go together. The boys will love it."

"I'm sure Evan and Boyd will love it, too."

They burst into laughter again. Tori was grateful for the moral support and that she was allowed to goof off like this. Yet, she had a feeling in the back of her mind which still made her believe something was wrong.

~ ~ ~ ~

It was well past one in the morning and Tori couldn't sleep.

Felicia had left before ten, saying that she wished she could finish the second bottle of wine with her, but she needed to get home. Lucas had himself returned just an hour before, claiming to be drained. He had gone straight to bed after a quick shower. Tori was left tossing and turning.

She wanted to be comforted by Felicia's words. Maybe what Boyd really needed was time to adjust to this new situation. He would turn out like any other boy his age. With time.

She gave herself another twenty minutes to let this reassurance lull her to sleep, but it didn't work. It was strange. Under normal circumstances, drinking the equivalent of a bottle of wine by herself made her doze off. At the moment, she was perfectly awake. She didn't even feel tipsy.

Knowing that she had no choice, Tori got out of bed. Lucas didn't stir even though a part of her wished he had. This way, she'd be able to talk to him about what was bothering her. She had a feeling that he didn't care.

Sure, he had brought it up to the psychologist in the first place, but now he had done his part. It was out of his hands. He had passed on the responsibility to someone else. It was typical and it had taken her years to see that about him.

She remained barefoot, in pajama shorts and tank top, and walked downstairs. Her first instinct was to get a glass of water, but when she opened the refrigerator door, she saw the leftover bottle of wine.

She was pretty certain you weren't supposed to put red wine in the fridge, but she hated drinking anything room temperature. Finishing the bottle seemed like a marvelous idea. Maybe that would finally put her to sleep.

She had only rinsed the wine glasses she had used with Felicia. She hadn't totally cleaned them, figuring it would give her an activity to do in the morning. She took one of them, dried it, and went to the den along with the wine.

There was something particularly crass about bringing the bottle along, as if she was some sort of desperate alcoholic, but who would know?

She sat on the recliner, poured herself a tall glass, and drank with thirst. It was ice cold and delicious. What idiot thought red wine shouldn't be served this way? She enjoyed another sip, hoping that it would make her sleepy faster. Nevertheless, her mind wandered to Boyd again.

To the tortured fish.

Was it a one-time mistake, or a pattern? As Lucas had said, children did stupid things. She herself remembered getting scratched after pulling on the family cat's tail. But what Boyd had done was worse, wasn't it? Hadn't she heard something once about children and animal cruelty?

The best solution was to forget about this entirely. Dr. Curnutt was in the picture exactly for this reason. It was her mission to analyze Boyd's behavior, discover what was going on with him, and pinpoint ways to help him. And yet Tori couldn't get it out of her mind.

She drank more wine to give herself courage and got the iPad from the couch. She returned to her seat, curling into a ball with her legs underneath her, and emptied the bottle into the glass, which she then propped on the arm of the recliner. Once she was convinced it was steady, she began searching on the tablet.

She was appalled at how many search results there were when she typed in "animal torture". Almost seven million hits. She began to scroll down and was overwhelmed by the quantity of information. She refined the search by adding the word "children." Just under three million hits. That was better. The headlines were much more worrisome though.

What drives people to torture animals?

What to do if your child is cruel to animals.

Is childhood cruelty to animals a marker for physical maltreatment?

She scanned through a few of the articles, skimming through them. Much of the phrasing sounded academic and maybe she'd had too much wine after all to make sense of it. She did catch a few buzzwords though: *bullying, punishment, harm, violent acts.*

Serial killers.

"Oh my God…" she whispered.

Her heart racing, she forgot about the wine and started reading with more interest and attention. There was plenty of literature about serial killers and animal abuse. John Wayne Gacy used to set turkeys on fire with gasoline. Jeffrey Dahmer would kill animals, skin them, and mount their heads on spikes in his backyard. As a child, Ted Bundy had mutilated cats and dogs.

As a child?

An article said that animal torture was often the first sign of important psychological problems in children. Yet another offered statistics on school shootings. Out of the last one hundred and fifty-nine events, nearly all perpetrators had previously abused animals.

In the general population, five percent of children were liable to commit animal abuse. With children who had been mistreated in some way, that number jumped up to twenty-five percent.

No, she had this all wrong, Tori told herself. She had no reason to feel scared. She was going down a rabbit hole that had nothing to do with the situation at home. The hair rising on the back of her neck was an irrational reaction.

"You shouldn't do that."

Her heart stopped as terror coursed through her. The voice was cold.

As she swiveled toward it, she knocked her glass off the recliner's armrest. It swiftly crashed to the ground and shattered on impact, sending red wine splashing in all directions.

"Oh!" she cried, dreadfully startled.

She looked up and found Boyd just outside the living room, staring at her. He was wearing his pajamas with the rocket ships on it. His arms hung down alongside his body and his face was an impassive mask.

Tori started laughing out of nervousness, like when you start chuckling after being scared while watching a horror movie. She was angry at herself about the wine on the floor, some of it was already seeping into the gray throw rug, but she didn't want Boyd to feel responsible about that and therefore kept her mouth shut.

"What are you doing up, sweetie?"

"Nothing."

She nodded and glanced at the clock. "It's late. Better go back to bed, okay?"

"Okay."

"Hey Boyd? What did you mean before when you said

I shouldn't do that?"

"Be afraid. You shouldn't be afraid."

"What makes you think I was afraid of anything?" she asked, embarrassed that she had been so transparent.

"I always know when someone is afraid, Tori. Always."

# CHAPTER 16

The music was anachronistic. Just from the sound of it, Gannon could tell the singer was barely out of his teens. Hell, his voice hadn't even broken yet and the lyrics were shit stupid with lots of "baby, baby, baby" variations.

It was a shame because he remembered when this particular bar had had class. Under the former management, Tony Bennett was on rotation every hour. Gannon wasn't longing for all Rat Pack, all the time or anything, but the mood was wrong now. It used to be old school. Classy.

At least the decor hadn't been altered. There was a well-used pool table up a couple of steps, dim lighting, and a bartender who knew how to mix proper drinks which didn't require more than three ingredients. The bar had evolved from a cop hangout to a quasi-sophisticated establishment. Now Gannon wondered when the yuppies would take over.

He swirled the ice cube in his scotch and remembered when portions had been more generous. Prices had gone up, too. He would have to find another place to drink soon.

Something in the music changed. It was acoustical, not anything to do with the sound system or song choice. He glanced over his shoulder and saw the frosted-glass door swinging open. Detective Mobley entered. She took a moment to get her bearings, removing her sunglasses and scanning the area. He waved at her and she joined him at the bar.

"What's going on?" she asked. "Something wrong?"

"Who says anything's wrong?" He waved the bartender over. "Get my partner something to drink, will you?"

"It's three o'clock on a Friday, Gannon."

"Oh, I'm sorry. I thought you were with the State Police, not the drinking police? Sit down and have a drink with me."

The bartender had no other customers to serve at the moment, so he waited dutifully in front of them.

She shook her head. "No, I'm good. Thanks."

"Mobley, this is a bar. People have been known to be thrown out of bars for not drinking. I mean, you're taking up his valuable time and even more valuable counter space. Order something."

She sighed, weighed her options, and shrugged at last. "I'll take some water, please."

The bartender didn't argue and walked away, making Gannon groan.

"That's pathetic," he said.

"What's pathetic is that I thought you had nothing to do with that tired cliché."

"Cliché?"

"Yeah, the over-the-hill burnt out cop who drinks his days away while waiting for retirement. I thought you were better than that."

He raised her glass to her. "Sorry to disappoint you, Mobley. I suppose today is the day I discover you're a Goody Two-Shoes."

"I'm not a Goody Two-Shoes."

"Annapolis, naval officer, morally upright police detective. Yeah, I think you are a Goody Two-Shoes."

"I'm not!"

The bartender returned with bottled water and a glass. "Eight dollars, please."

Gannon reached for his wallet. "You used to be able to take the entire family out for dinner on eight dollars, Jesus…"

"I don't set the prices," the bartender said. "If you're really thirsty, there's a hose out back."

Gannon paid, not hiding his disdain and reluctance, and the employee disappeared to the other end of the bar. Mobley poured some water and took a sip.

"You could have had a martini at that price. So what are you, a Mormon? A Quaker?"

"I just don't drink, that's all. Not anymore."

"Bill W.?" he inquired, referring to Alcoholic Anonymous.

"I'd rather not talk about it, if that's okay."

Gannon showed her the palm of his hands, conceding defeat. "Fine."

"So are you going to tell me why you called me down here?"

"I need a drinking buddy."

"Why? We're still on duty."

"You're going to report me? Look, being a detective isn't exactly a nine-to-five job. Nobody bats an eye if you drop off the radar for a couple of hours. Relax."

He finished his drink and motioned for another.

"Gannon, what's happening?"

"I'm feeling shitty, all right? We've run out of leads in this investigation and that puts me in a bad mood. So I figured I would come to my favorite bar, soon to be ex-favorite bar—I mean, have you heard this music? Feels like Chuck E. Cheese—and I thought we could get to know each other for real. If we're going to be partners, it's the least we can do."

"You should've started with that, Gannon. So?"

"So what?"

"So tell me about you, partner."

The bartender placed a fresh scotch in front of Gannon, making him frown, not only at the price but at the meager quantity. He took a sip after paying.

"I did a hitch in the Army after high school."

That piqued her interest and seemingly changed her opinion of him. "Really?"

"I was young and stupid. Fell in love, got married, and had no choice but to find a stable career. That turned out to be the State Police. Been here almost thirty years.

*Almost.* Along the way I had two kids—both in college right now and costing me a fortune. The rest of said fortune went to the wife who came to her senses about being married to a cop. Must've been divorced nine, ten years now. I stopped counting. All I have left is this job. Gives me a reason to get up in the morning."

"I'm sorry."

"Don't be. The only thing I'm sorry about is that," he raised his voice, "we're not allowed to smoke in bars anymore!"

The bartender overheard, which had been the point, and snorted back a laugh as he returned to wiping glasses.

"So that's my sob story," Gannon continued. "What's yours?"

"You already know mine."

"Beyond your service record, Mobley. Tell me."

She sipped her water without speaking for a long time. "There's no story."

"Everybody has a story," he said.

"Okay, fine. I was in a relationship for many years and he recently dumped me. Happy?"

"No, I'm not happy. Sorry."

"It is what it is, Gannon. I'd rather not talk about it. Some people like to bring their personal lives to the office? Not me. Say, you're not trying to seduce me, are you? Tell me that's not what this is about."

The older man burst into laughter. "I've been out of the game too long, if that's what you think this is about. No, I have no interest in you whatsoever." When he finished laughing, he drank and then his face blanched. "What about Mr. Mobley? Did he beat you up?"

"What? No! Why would you say something like that?"

"That's not why you broke up, Mobley?"

"No," she replied, going for another sip of water, but deciding at the last second she wasn't in the mood for that anymore. "What's with the mood swing?"

"I think we have this all wrong. We instinctively started looking into John Begum as the reason why he and his wife were killed. What if we should've been looking at *Mrs. Begum* from the start?"

She spun toward him on her stool. "Okay…"

"Home invasion was a bust. Organized crime went nowhere. But what about a crime of passion? Think about it. Killed with razor blades, blood everywhere. That sounds like a crime of passion to me, right?"

Mobley shrugged. "I suppose so."

Gannon ignored his scotch, needing his wits about him. He looked beyond his partner, his eyes focusing on a spot on the opposite wall and yet seeing nothing. He mentally went through the entire murder book all over again, cycling through every theory and piece of evidence they had.

"What are you thinking, Detective?"

He remembered the boy, the couple's son. He couldn't remember his name, but he had given him a description of the man who had done this. Bearded African-American man, average height and build. With all the other hypotheses crossed out, a new one jumped up.

"Gannon?" she pressed.

"What if Larissa Begum had a lover? A jealous lover."

~ ~ ~ ~

Gannon sobered up quickly as they made their way back to the station. There was nothing like the excitement of having another lead. He smoked two cigarettes on the way, happy to have Mobley follow in her own car behind, and knowing that he would probably be stuck at his desk for several hours to come.

"What's the plan of attack?" she asked as they both strode into the station.

Captain Vail watched them from the other side of the bullpen, but kept his distance. The determined expression on Gannon's face was enough to inform him that he was making progress at last. Well, maybe.

"You're the former intelligence analyst, Mobley. I want you to analyze."

"Analyze what?"

"We're going through Mrs. Begum's entire history, from the day she was born until the day she died. I want to know everything about her. We have to find out if she was thrashing on mattresses with someone who wasn't her husband."

They went to their respective cubicles and promptly got to work. Being old school, Gannon went through phone records and credit card statements. It was again painstaking work, but there was a chance they could get somewhere.

For her part, Mobley focused on the woman's digital footprint. She dug into her social media accounts, sifting through pictures, tweets, posts, and even double-checking the browsing history to make sure Larissa Begum didn't have secondary accounts through which she could have lived a secret life.

By five o'clock, Mobley reported that she had found no evidence of another man—or woman—in Mrs. Begum's life. She was about to tell the details to her partner when he shushed her.

"You have something?"

"An invoice from seven years ago," he announced. "A place called The Worachek Institute, in Raleigh."

Mobley launched herself toward the computer to make a search. It was a fertility clinic. Five minutes later, they discovered through the IRS that the family had had a nineteen thousand dollars tax deduction with that invoice.

Gannon got busy having Captain Vail procure a warrant while Mobley called the clinic, which of course was deserted at that hour. It was almost another hour until they located a senior nurse at home and got her a copy of the warrant.

The waiting becoming unbearable, Gannon went outside to smoke a cigarette. To him, the nicotine was like a breath of fresh air after spending hours underwater. He was pacing so much along the parking lot that three different cops asked him if he was okay.

Mobley came out of the station. Gannon stopped breathing and crushed his brand-new cigarette under his heel.

"And?"

"Larissa Begum was a patient of The Worachek Institute for over a year. She was treated for acute endometriosis, followed by ART exploration."

"Feel free to switch to English at any point, Mobley."

"Mrs. Begum was infertile. She couldn't have children."

Gannon was speechless. Who was that kid then?

# CHAPTER 17

The road sign was illuminated by the setting sun, turning the green wood engraving mostly orange. It read *Welcome to the Scenic Village of West Gorge.*

"I thought the fair was in town," Boyd asked as the car drove past the sign.

"It is," Tori replied. "On this side of the river, it becomes West Gorge. Everybody treats it as the same town."

"But land is much cheaper over here."

Lucas snorted as he said that, almost mocking his own statement. Boyd picked up on it but didn't say anything. He looked out the windows although there wasn't much to see, generally trees and mountains. Traffic picked up a few minutes later. Out in the distance was a clearing.

"Are we getting close?"

"Almost there, sweetie. Are you excited?"

"Yes," Boyd replied. "I've never been on rides before. Is it as fun as it looks on TV?"

"Even more fun!" Tori turned to her husband. "Maybe we should show him."

"What's the point?" Lucas spat.

"Come on, it's right there."

"Show me what?" Boyd inquired.

Around a bend, a field opened up on the right and there were hundreds of cars parked. Just beyond was a line of trees through which some of the amusement rides were visible, mostly the top part of the Ferris Wheel and other similar thrill rides.

"You see those houses on the left, Boyd?"

Lucas groaned. "Baby, shit…"

"What's the harm in showing him? I'm proud of it."

Boyd perked up. "What?"

"Those houses over there…" Tori pointed ahead, to the left. "That's Lucas's housing development."

The homes came into view. Most were nothing but framework, but the grid was easy to make out. Anyone could tell that they weren't ready to be moved in yet.

"Nice," Boyd said.

"Very nice."

Still, Lucas was shaking his head. "There's nothing to be proud about. The whole project is one big failure. If I don't find a new investor and get funding, the houses will never get built. If they don't get built, they don't get sold and I'm facing bankruptcy."

"Lucas…"

He ignored her. "And that means no one will ever trust me to develop another piece of land ever again. Obviously, forget about being a contractor after that. I'll need to go back to working on somebody else's construction crew. Basically, our lives will be over, but no one cares, right? We're here to have fun."

Tori put her hand on his arm. He shook it off. The evening wasn't off to a great start, she thought bitterly. She had to find a way to make this a positive experience for the kid.

"We're here!" she said, indicating the turnoff.

They drove onto the makeshift parking lot, the ground uneven and the three of them being tossed around, even going at a snail's pace. They parked the Subaru and made their way to the fair entrance. Tori herself bought the tickets because she didn't want to hear Lucas complain about the price.

As they walked onto the fairgrounds—actually Mr. Conley's old farm—they were assaulted by a million sounds and fragrances. The smell of rich buttery popcorn collided with the sweetness of cotton candy. Beyond that was cheap light beer and sweat from the carnival employees who'd been standing in the sun all day.

The whole thing made Tori smile, reminding her of her youth. Her parents would take her every year to the county fair where they spent an entire Saturday. It was the only time her parents made an effort not to fight in front of her, and as such she'd looked forward to that day all year.

"They're over there," Lucas said, pointing with his chin.

Indeed, Jasper and Felicia were standing in line at a concession stand. As they headed toward them, Tori noticed Evan's cast for the first time. It began at his shoulder and encased his entire hand.

"Hi!"

They greeted each other with the usual pleasantries. Felicia joined them out of the line, Lucas taking her place.

"Hey, Evan," Boyd said timidly.

The other kid didn't say anything back.

"Be polite," Felicia scolded, adding a slight tap behind his shoulder.

"Hey."

Boyd looked up at Tori, as if urging her to acknowledge the fact that the other boy didn't like him. She gave him a tight smile in return, in reality not knowing what to do about it.

"We're going to have some fun tonight, right?" she asked him.

He nodded.

Felicia turned to him. "Any ride you're looking forward to in particular, Boyd?"

"I don't know. Do they have a rollercoaster?"

At that, the two women glanced at one another.

"I'm not sure they'll let you on, sweetie. You have to be pretty tall to ride those. It's a safety issue."

"Oh."

"But we'll have lots of fun, okay? Trust me."

Lucas and Jasper came back with a cardboard tray. There were four plastic cups of beer and two sodas for the kids. They started to walk deeper into the fair, Boyd looking around everywhere, clearly overwhelmed by the excitement going on.

They started things easy by going to the game kiosks. Mostly, Tori thought Lucas wanted to impress the kid. He tossed rings at bottles and didn't stop until he'd won a prize, in this case a fluffy carrot with eyes. Then he shot at rows of duck-shaped targets and won nothing.

At another game, they let Boyd handle a water pistol, trying to be the fastest to fill a balloon. A loudmouth middle-aged man next to him beat him. Then they got popcorn for the kids, Evan grumbling that he needed someone to hold the box up for him.

Tori detected a smile on Boyd's lips and it made her happy. This was exactly what he needed. It was a distraction from their mundane lives, yes, but mostly from his terrifying past.

Waiting to ride the Tea Cups, Evan grew tired of having to pick popcorn from the box his mother was holding, especially since he had to hold his soda between his chest and his cast.

"Mom, can I go off by myself? Alex is here with his family tonight."

"I don't know…"

"He's with his parents. He said they were going to hang out by the Centrifuge. Please, mom!"

Jasper glanced at Felicia and she rolled her eyes.

"Okay, fine. But just for a little bit. Meet us next to the bumper cars in twenty minutes, okay?"

"Thanks, mom!" Evan shouted, already running away.

At that, Boyd looked at Tori. "Can I go too?"

"I don't think so, sweetie."

"Please? I'll just hang out with Evan and Alex."

Lucas shrugged and leaned toward his wife. "You can't keep the kid in a cocoon, baby."

"He's eight years old," she pointed out, doing her best not to be overheard.

"Look around. There are cops everywhere." Sure enough, several Sheriff's deputies and security people were milling about, keeping an eye out for suspicious behavior. "Nothing's going to happen to the kid."

Felicia jumped in. "He'll be fine, girl. Let him have fun."

Tori felt betrayed. She would've thought that at least Felicia would have backed her up. Then again, Felicia had been a mother much longer than she had. Maybe she knew that being overprotective wasn't the way to go. Maybe Tori was worried for nothing.

With no more argument aside from appearing like a shrew in front of everyone, she fell into a crouch in front of Boyd.

"Same rules apply to you, okay? You meet us by the bumper cars in twenty minutes. Deal?"

"Deal."

"You remember where the bumper cars are, yes?"

"Yes, next to the restrooms."

Tori hesitated once more and then nodded with a sigh. "Okay. Have fun and be safe."

Boyd smiled and walked away, still eating his popcorn

even though he had nothing left to drink.

Tori found it difficult to enjoy herself over the next twenty minutes. How could the three other adults laugh and joke and continue to drink beer while Boyd was away? Why was she the only one agonizing over his safety?

Lucas and Jasper insisted on riding the Pirate, the giant pendulum designed to look like a pirate ship. Tori was perfectly happy to remain on the sidelines.

In fact, she looked around to spy on Boyd. She saw him at first as he was hanging around Evan and his friend, although she didn't have the best vantage point. There were simply too many people walking in one direction and then the other. It was like looking at something through trees from a passing car. Eventually, she lost track of him completely.

Nevertheless, twenty minutes later he showed up at the bumper cars, just as promised. Evan was a good five minutes late and Felicia only gave him a token reprimand.

"Where'd you go?" Tori asked Boyd.

"Just walking around."

"Did you have fun?"

At that, Boyd nodded enthusiastically which made her feel somewhat better about leaving him on his own. Perhaps a little freedom wasn't so bad.

"You remember the Tunnel of Love?" Jasper asked.

Felicia groaned. "You are so gross!"

"No, not that! The fair that used to come to town when I was in high school, they had this thing called the

Tunnel of Love. You sat in the cart, went slowly through a cave, and that gave you a few minutes to make out with your date."

This time it was Evan who said, "Gross!"

Lucas chuckled. "In my hometown, we used to do that in the haunted house."

"They have a funhouse that way," Jasper said. "Feeling up to reliving the glory days?"

"Hell yeah!" Lucas replied, giving him a high-five.

"The two of you are going to make out with each other?" Felicia snarked.

"Come on, you know you want it."

Felicia was still unconvinced though she was warming up to the idea. "What about the kids?"

"They can go on the Ferris Wheel. Look, almost no lineup. What do you say, boys?"

"No," Evan said. "I'm not going on the Ferris Wheel with him."

"Come on! It'll be fun."

Lucas was getting tipsy and his arm was around Tori's waist. "It could be very fun," he whispered in her ear.

"Let's do it," Jasper added eagerly.

Tori didn't want to make a scene, especially since Felicia appeared to be willing to do it. She turned to Boyd.

"You want to go on the Ferris Wheel with Evan?"

"Sure."

Evan was shaking his head vehemently, arguing in hushed tones with his mother.

Ultimately, Jasper raised his voice. "You're going on the Ferris Wheel with him, and that's final. Do we have a problem?"

"Fine…"

The four parents ushered the kids all the way to the operator of the Ferris Wheel, handing him tickets, and then they went their own way.

"This is retarded," Evan said as he dropped into his seat.

Boyd sat next to him and the safety bar was lowered across them. Soon they began moving up.

"Why do you hate me so much?" Boyd asked.

"Because you're a psycho."

"No, I'm not."

"You look like one anyway."

"Do you know the difference between a psychopath and a sociopath, Evan?"

"No."

"Maybe you should keep quiet then."

Evan was taken aback as they rose even higher.

"When school starts, you'll see what we do to you. Alex, Billy, Tim, and me, we'll beat you up bad. You'll see."

"You'll break my arm?" Boyd asked.

"Totally!"

"Like you broke your arm on your bike? Does it hurt?"

Evan squinted at him. The boy was such a freak. "Yeah, it hurts."

"Then you should look where you're going when you speed down the hill. Sometimes there are ropes across the street and it can be dangerous. You have to be careful, Evan."

It took a few seconds, but Evan gasped. "You did this?! You made me get into an accident?"

Boyd leaned forward and looked down. Everyone was so tiny. Since it was dark now, they might as well have been alone in the sky.

"I'm so gonna tell my dad you did this to me!"

"How high do you think we are, Evan? Ninety feet? A hundred feet?"

"You psycho…"

"Did you know that, according to the Consumer Product Safety Commission, fourteen hundred people are injured on carnival rides each year? In this state alone, twenty-two people have died in the past five years. Even Ferris Wheels are dangerous."

Evan's bluster vanished. He retreated in his corner, holding the safety bar as if it was a lifeline.

"Are you saying you want to throw me off?"

Boyd straightened up and spun toward him. "I'm telling you that accidents happen all the time, especially when people call others psychos. I hurt you once, Evan. I have no problem doing it again."

# CHAPTER 18

Someone knocking on your door in the middle of the night is never a good sign.

Tori's eyes snapped open, unsure whether she was dreaming or not. But as she stared at the black ceiling above her, she realized that the knocking sound was still going on. If anything, it was growing louder. More insistent.

Something bad was happening.

"Lucas," she whispered. "There's someone at the door."

He barely stirred, grunting unintelligibly, and didn't wake up. The knocking continued. Whoever this was, they weren't going away. Had there been an accident? *Oh God*, was Boyd all right?

That woke her up completely. She swung her legs out of bed and didn't bother rummaging through the closet for a robe. She hurried out of her room and headed to Boyd's room.

She opened his door and peeked inside. He had told her that he was a big boy, that he didn't need a nightlight, but there was just enough moonlight for her to see that he was snugly in bed. The rapping on the front door didn't stop.

She bounded down the stairs two by two, only realizing how dangerous it was when she reached the last step, and at last got to the foyer. She glimpsed a shadow through the frosted glass of the door. That wasn't what made her stop breathing.

Beyond the shadow were red and blue flashing lights.

She opened the door and found a police officer on the doorstep. He was young and vaguely familiar. She must have seen him here and there over the past year.

"Mrs. Ramsdale?" he began tentatively.

"Yes, Tori Ramsdale. What's going on?"

"Ma'am, I'm Deputy Gonzalez. I…"

Right then, Tori felt a presence behind her. She turned, finding a disheveled Lucas joining her. He was yawning without even trying to cover his mouth. She had woken him up after all, even though he had been borderline drunk when they had returned from the fair. In fact, she had insisted on taking the wheel for the drive home.

"What's happening?" he asked.

"You're Mr. Ramsdale?"

"Yeah."

Lucas yawned again and rubbed his eyes.

"Are you the owner of the West Gorge Estates project?"

"Yeah. What's the deal?"

"I'm sorry to have to tell you this, sir, but there's been a fire."

~ ~ ~ ~

The deputy offered to drive Lucas, but he would have none of it. He left on his own, his mission accomplished. For her part, Tori was mindful of Boyd being sound asleep.

"I have to stay here with him," she said. "You should've left with the deputy. You had a lot to drink."

"I'm fine," Lucas replied curtly as he got dressed in record time.

"Now's not the time to get into an accident."

"Damn it, baby. I'm a grown man. Let me act like one. I'm not drunk. Shit, I can't believe this is happening…"

He put on old white sneakers, grabbed his keys, and jogged to his truck. He had driven a thousand times from the house to the development project, but never this fast. He just couldn't wait to get there and assess the damage.

A fire, really? Who had he pissed off in a former life for all this crap to be falling on him lately? He had been diligent. He had paid his dues. This project was supposed to go flawlessly. He had planned every little detail. There was no way he would ever end up a failure like his dad.

The longer he drove, the faster he went. Going to the fair was supposed to have been a rest stop in this crazy summer. Despite his grumbling, he had been looking forward to today. But as he approached the fairgrounds—and his land across the road—his mood changed.

He had never considered suicide until right this instant.

While the fair was closed for the night, only a few lights were being kept on for security reasons, the action was on the other side. The fire was still raging, turning the dark night into a spectacle of shimmering shades of yellow and orange. Before he had even reached his property, he knew that it was a disaster area.

The town had a small fire department and both trucks were on the scene. Police cars were blocking one of the lanes up ahead and barricades had been set up. There were bystanders gawking at the inferno, some filming with their phones.

Lucas was on autopilot. He didn't really know what he was doing and his body acted on its own accord. He pulled over and got out. Deputy Gonzalez was there again and noticed him.

"This way!"

He waved him over and lifted the yellow tape, inviting him within the perimeter. Some of the onlookers grumbled, asking why he got to come closer while they were stuck behind the barricades. They shut up when they realized who he was.

"God no…" Lucas whispered, truly seeing for the first time the state of his houses.

Every single one was on fire. He knew that it oftentimes looked worse than it really was. Smoke damage was usually superficial. This was different. The flames were strong and some of the structures were already crumbling.

Not a single building was salvageable, that much he could tell.

The firefighters were keeping their distance. They

weren't wasting their water putting out the fire. Instead, the hoses were turned toward the wooded areas beyond. This was August and they couldn't risk a forest fire.

"Lucas Ramsdale, right?"

Startled, he turned around as an older fireman headed his way. He had a white helmet and it wasn't particularly clean. He had been here for a while. He recognized him, Fire Chief Dugan. He was in his early sixties though his plump cheeks concealed any wrinkle he could have had.

"Hey, Chief. What…" Lucas's voice trailed off. "What the hell happened? I've been in construction my whole adult life. I take safety very seriously."

"I understand."

"The power was off. Most employees had taken their tools with them," Lucas added, not bothering to mention that he had laid everybody off until he could figure out how to afford their next paycheck. "There's no way there could've been a fire. You think it's somebody from the fair?"

Chief Dugan was surprised by the question. "How do you mean?"

"It's right across the road. One of the employees comes over, has a cigarette, and the thing goes up in flames? All because one of those sons of bitches is being irresponsible?"

Lucas looked over his shoulder at the fairgrounds. That had to be the explanation. He couldn't think of anything else.

While his head was still turned, he saw someone else walk over. It was Sheriff McKenzie, his bald head reflecting the police lights and flames like a disco ball.

"Evening, Mr. Ramsdale."

Lucas acknowledged him with a glance, but otherwise didn't say anything. He ran both hands through his hair and turned his attention back to the fire. His life's work was going up in flames, literally.

"Sheriff," Chief Dugan began. "I was about to tell Mr. Ramsdale the bad news."

Lucas's mouth went dry. "What bad news?"

What could possibly be worse than this?

"I'm very confident we're dealing with arson here."

"What?!"

Chief Dugan pointed forward. "You see the color of the flames? You see the dark smoke? That doesn't happen unless accelerants have been used. Before taking the job here, I spent twenty years in the Chicago Fire Department. I did two years in the Office of Fire Investigation. I've seen my share of deliberate jobs and I would stake my career that what we're dealing with here is arson."

"No, that can't be…"

"What are your thoughts on this, Mr. Ramsdale?" Sheriff McKenzie asked.

"My thoughts?"

"Can you think of anyone who could have done this? Any enemies? Guy with a grudge?"

Lucas shook his head, trying to make sense of this. The only thing he could think of was that maybe a carpenter had been pissed about being laid off. Still, that didn't make any sense. All the people had been paid so far and you would have to be rather stupid to risk jail for setting your job site on fire.

He was about to share his theory when something occurred to him. If he mentioned laying off employees, the Sheriff would assume he was hard up for cash.

What if that made *him* a suspect for this arson case?

"No," Lucas finally said, shaking his head. "I can't think of anyone."

~ ~ ~ ~

Devastated, Lucas remained on the scene another hour before returning home. It was as if he wanted to make sure this wasn't a dream. A nightmare. But it wasn't. As time passed, more structures crumbled.

He drove back slowly, no longer in a hurry. Tori would question him, and answering her would make this situation final. It would be real. He wasn't sure if he was ready for that. He felt like a zombie in one of those TV shows.

He parked and entered the house. His heart sank when he realized that there would be no avoiding his wife. Tori was sitting at the kitchen table with a glass of water.

She quickly stood up as he approached. "And? What happened? Why didn't you answer when I called?"

"Because this is the worst day of my life, okay? Excuse me for not being chatty."

"How bad was the fire?"

"How bad?" he shot back derisively. "It's gone, Tori."

"What do you mean?"

"It's all gone."

"It can't be all gone. I don't understand..."

"You want me to draw you a picture? Every single house has burned down! There's nothing left."

Tori covered her mouth as she gasped. "That can't be."

"Chief Dugan says it's arson. The Sheriff asked me questions."

"But... You have nothing to do with that, do you?"

Lucas was horrified. "Are you seriously asking me this right now? Of course, I don't have anything to do with that!"

"I'm so sorry," Tori said, coming closer still. "We'll find a way to get through this."

Just as she was wrapping her arms around him, he shoved her back.

"Don't touch me!"

"Lucas," she cried, stunned by his action.

"My entire goddamn life is over now! Are you happy?"

Without warning, he swept the glass of water off the table. It flew through the air for two yards before hitting the wall and shattering in a hundred pieces.

While she was reeling from his outburst, Lucas fetched his bottle of Wild Turkey, along with a glass, and went downstairs to his office.

"Is everything okay?"

Tori snapped out of her reverie at the voice. It was Boyd. She had utterly forgotten about him and now felt ashamed that he had witnessed this row between her and Lucas.

"You should go back to bed, sweetie."

"You had a fight?"

She forced a smile. "It was just a discussion between grown-ups."

"I heard about the fire."

"You were down here all this time?"

"I'm sorry. I just came down to see what was going on. It's sad about the fire."

Tori nodded, her gaze locked on the broken glass and water on the floor. She knew she should clean it up, but she didn't have the energy.

"Yes…"

"But the insurance money will fix everything, right?" Boyd said with a hopeful smile.

"What did you say?"

"That's what insurance is for, isn't it? Contractors always get insurance. So now you and Lucas won't have any more problems or worries."

Tori didn't reply. She was suddenly troubled. How could a child possibly know about insurance and, worst of all, why was he so calm?

# CHAPTER 19

Tori held her palette knife delicately. She felt like she was conducting an orchestra. That was how her first art teacher had taught her to hold the instrument anyway. She wiped the pointy blade on a rag, making sure it was clean, and then picked up some Prussian Blue.

She needed to paint something. It was a desire to express herself, yes, but also guilt. What Lucas had said the other day about her not contributing to the family still hurt.

She knew that he had said it in a moment of passion, he couldn't possibly have meant it the way it had come out. And yet, every time she thought about those words, it twisted her insides and made her nauseated.

She looked at the canvas, holding her knife in midair, and realized she had no inspiration. She couldn't think of anything original to paint. She had done a million landscapes and, after a while, they all started to blend in together.

This in itself was stupid. She was an artist, she had never thought along those lines before. She could make anything old seem fresh and original again. She always had been able to do this. That was the essence of art, wasn't it?

Be that as it may, she had no idea what direction to go in with this painting. It was like she was empty. And she was tired, oh so tired. Her brain was fried, which wasn't conducive to creativity.

But the guilt was still there.

She had to contribute in some way, didn't she? Maybe her husband had been right. She was wasting her time painting pictures no one wanted. Worst of all, she wasn't bringing in any income. With Lucas's project collapsing, they needed money like never before.

It was difficult, but Tori knew that she wouldn't have a choice but to look for a real job soon. She shuddered at the thought. She wasn't qualified for anything. She had a feeling that even working a cash register at the supermarket would be challenging. She hadn't worked in retail since college.

Maybe she could be a waitress? She would be terrible at it, she was convinced. What she knew for certain though was that any job she'd be able to get would pay minimum wage and it would do little to save the family, especially since they had to take care of Boyd now.

She stared at the canvas, but was still immobile. She thought about her husband. She wasn't angry that he had brought up the subject of her getting a job. No, what made her blood boil was how he had said it. He had said "your little paintings aren't helping". It had been mean. Malicious.

What kind of man was mean to his wife? She couldn't ignore how much he had changed since they'd gotten married. He had been so supportive at first. She had told him from the start that art was her chosen career path and that it would be tough.

He had been on board, never bringing up the fact that it wasn't lucrative. After she'd sold her first painting—for two hundred dollars—he had bought a bottle of champagne as if Sotheby's had just closed on a two hundred million-dollar deal. What had changed?

She snorted. Of course, she knew what had changed. The turning point had been *The Incident.* A little over a year ago, their whole lives had been transformed. That was when the nightmares had started. Was she still in denial about this? Had it been a mistake to come here for a fresh start?

She seriously didn't know anymore. As days went by, she trusted her judgment less and less. Was she going insane? It felt as if her life was slipping out of her grasp.

She blinked a few times to clear her head and focused on the canvas. The trick to creativity was to stop thinking. That's what she did. She attacked the blank space and at once painted the outline of blue mountains.

She was getting into it, still not sure what the final picture would look like, when the door creaked open behind her. She glanced over her shoulder and saw Boyd come in.

"Hey, sweetie. Come to see me work?"

He came closer while she continued to add oils to the canvas, changing shades of blue.

"Why are you painting with a spatula?" he asked, making her chuckle.

"It's not a spatula. It's called a palette knife."

"Aren't you supposed to paint with a brush?"

"There are many techniques. You went to preschool, no?"

"Yes."

"Didn't they make you paint with your fingers?" He nodded. "You see? You can paint lots of different ways."

She decided not to tell him about her college roommate who had once covered herself in paint before tossing and turning on the canvas, essentially using her naked body as a tool. She had gotten a C, the professor commenting that at least two students did that every semester and it hadn't been original in decades.

"You want to try, Boyd?"

He nodded and she motioned for him to come closer. She moved out of the way, standing behind him. She decided that he could do anything on her canvas; it wasn't as if he was going to ruin it.

"Careful, okay? It's sharp. Hold the handle firmly, but keep it loose between your fingers."

He did as instructed and she made him dip the blade into Permanent Mauve.

"The cool thing about using a palette knife is that you can create different textures." She guided his wrist as he made a purple swath. "You see how thick it is?"

"It's like a three-D painting," he said.

"Pretty much, yes. Then you imagine this is frosting on the cake. You spread it thinner, creating the effect you're looking for."

He got the gist and she helped him make little swirls. After a moment, she let go of his wrist and he continued on his own. He wasn't painting anything specific, that she could tell anyway, but it was oddly beautiful. What began as a huge, formless blob soon took form. He added another layer, Bismuth Yellow this time, and the texture gave it an impressionist's charm.

"You're doing great, sweetie. You're a natural."

"Thank you."

"I have a spare easel. You want me to set it up next to mine and we can paint together?"

"Actually, I came here to ask you a question. Can I go on a bike ride?"

"By yourself?"

He spun around and nodded. "I really like it. It helps me to forget all the bad things. Can I go?"

Lucas would have said yes right away, but her first instinct was to turn him down. Surely, she had to loosen up, yes? He had to know what was good for him.

"Okay," she said. "But just for a little bit, okay?"

"Thanks."

"And don't go too far. Stay around the block."

"Okay," he agreed, walking out of the shed.

"And be careful!"

He didn't reply. He was already gone.

~ ~ ~ ~

Boyd didn't stay around the block.

He went to the end of the street, then turned on to another, and before long he was going into town. He had no set plan. He enjoyed the freedom of being on the bicycle and felt the need to explore further. Information was power.

He came across three flat buildings arranged in a semicircle around an open space. Those were the schools. Just beyond the biggest of the three, on the other side, was a soccer field. There were a few clusters of kids, some of whom were actually practicing—they had colorful uniforms—but others were just goofing around with a ball.

He recognized the closest kid. It was Billy. He slowed his bike, not exactly sure why, and that brought attention to himself. Billy recognized him. He said something and the two others turned his way. They were Alex and Tim. They approached the fence and Boyd did the same.

"Hello," he greeted.

"What do you want?" Billy asked.

"Yeah, what are you doing here?"

Tim added, "Freak."

"Why are you being mean to me? Did I do something?"

"Yeah, you're a freak!"

This was the funniest thing ever and they started laughing. Boyd held onto the fence to keep himself stable. Alex grabbed his ball and threw it at Boyd's hand.

"Ouch!" he yelped, letting go of the fence and losing his balance.

He caught himself just in time before falling off his bike, which made the boys laugh once more.

"Look, he doesn't even know how to stay upright on a bike!"

"He's such a loser."

Boyd nodded. "I guess I'm no worse than Evan, uh? He's not really good with bikes."

This sobered up the kids. They no doubt could picture their friend with his arm in a cast.

"You have to be careful, you know," Boyd continued. "It would be a shame if the same thing happened to you. Accidents happen so fast. Well, I guess that's why they call them *accidents*."

He was proud of himself for shutting them up. He placed his feet on the pedals and sped away. They didn't jeer him as he left.

The mention of Evan made him want to see him. He had been so scared last night on the Ferris Wheel that Boyd wanted to see if he still was today. That expression on someone, the fear in their eyes, it was something so beautiful. To know that he was responsible for that was exhilarating.

He picked up speed and stayed out of traffic even though it was fun sometimes to dodge cars. He found himself in a residential area again and he had no trouble finding the Harbuck house.

Boyd came closer, slowing down. The living room had large windows and, once his eyes adjusted, he saw Evan inside. He was playing a video game. Boyd stopped, putting his feet on the ground, and simply stared at him.

He imagined it was how grown-ups hunted. They crouched in their blind, searching for defenseless little animals through their scope. Then they waited until the right moment to strike, to pull the trigger. To kill.

It was nearly five minutes before Evan noticed him outside. He was startled at first and then stared back. The bravado was gone. Before the weekend, Boyd imagined that he would have flipped him off or shouted insults. Not anymore. They were past that now. Evan was on his own. He was powerless.

"What are you doing here?"

The voice scared Boyd, but not as much as being yanked back by a strong grip. It was Jasper.

"What the hell's the matter with you, kid?"

"What?" Boyd asked, the bicycle falling from between his legs. "What did I do?"

"Evan told me what you said to him. Did you hurt him?"

"No."

Jasper bent forward, bringing his face right above the child's. "Did you make him fall off his bike? Did you break his arm?"

"Of course not! He's lying because he doesn't like me. He's a bully."

"I want you to stay away from my son. If you don't, I'll tell Lucas. He's going to punish you. He's going to spank you hard, you hear me? Stay away from Evan."

The man was so angry that spittle flew into Boyd's face.

"Come closer, Jasper. I want to tell you something."

Boyd's tone was so calm and commanding for an eight-year-old that Jasper could only comply. He leaned in, his hands still holding the kid by the shoulders.

"What?"

"I have advice for you, Jasper. You keep your mouth shut."

"What the hell did you say?"

Boyd snarled. "You don't want to fuck with me."

The harshness of his tone took Jasper by surprise and he let go of him. Boyd picked up his bike, got up on it, and pedaled until he disappeared at the end of the street.

# CHAPTER 20

Gannon couldn't say anything and it was maddening. Captain Vail was looking at him with disappointment and a small measure of repugnance, as if he had just learned that his twelve-year-old son was sucking his thumb. In class.

"I don't like it, Detective."

Gannon glanced at Mobley who was sitting in a borrowed swivel chair next to him. Her head was down, avoiding this conflict at all costs.

"The big white board out there is moving along at a nice clip. Everybody else's cases are getting solved, except for yours."

"Sorry, Captain," Mobley said, finally making eye contact.

"Sorry doesn't get cases solved."

Gannon straightened up. "Don't snap at her, Cap. None of this is her fault."

"So it's your fault then, Gannon?"

"I guess so," the older man replied with a shrug. "Or I could use one of those ancient police methods. You know, taking a lowlife and pinning the crime on him. What do you think, Cap? Would that make your perfect record nice and shiny?"

Vail bristled. "You watch your mouth!"

"Which is it, solve the case or watch my mouth? It's hard to keep up."

"Get this done, Gannon. My patience has limits."

He glared at the two detectives a few more seconds and then left the cubicle. Mobley let out an audible sigh of relief.

"Thanks for standing up for me," she said.

"Are you kidding, telling that asshole off is always the highlight of my day."

She gave him a soft smile to express her gratefulness and he nodded back. He wasn't the chivalrous type, but compliments were always welcome. He leaned back in his chair, opening a folder, while she scooted forward to research on her computer.

They were still looking into Larissa Begum although they had very little to go on. She was an only child and they still hadn't found any trace of her having had an affair, which was the most likely scenario for the double murder.

"According to these documents," Gannon began, "this woman was the most boring human being on the planet. No hobbies, no lover, and apparently no life."

Mobley didn't answer right away and he took offense to that. She was engrossed in what she was reading, leaning forward and squinting at the screen.

"A thrilling read, partner?"

"I think I got something," she whispered, not taking

her eyes off what she was reading.

"And it's about…"

She didn't answer his question and he considered going out for a cigarette, or at the very least coffee. When he decided to make his move, standing up, she held up her hand.

"Wait."

"I *have* been waiting."

Mobley finally turned to him with the hint of smile. "I have somebody."

"Good for you. I hope he makes you very happy."

"No, it's about Mrs. Begum. I was digging through her social media interactions. She had a bunch of friends but, you know, most of them were just Internet friends. It doesn't mean anything. But there's this woman, Roxanne Pinedo, with whom she's had many conversations. They seem to have been school friends. In fact, I'd say that she's her best friend."

"Why haven't we interviewed her before?" Gannon asked.

"She lives in Swayze County. It was far enough out of our way not to bother. Besides, we weren't looking into Mrs. Begum before."

"Fair point. How do you feel about a field trip?"

~ ~ ~ ~

Swayze County was a two-hour drive away. They didn't bother asking Captain Vail permission to go, especially since it was out of the state. Gannon figured that the man would agree to anything that would get them closer to solving the case anyway.

At first, Mobley had called Roxanne Pinedo. She was at work and was also scheduled to work a second shift. She couldn't talk on the phone. Waiting was also out of the question. Coming to her was therefore a no-brainer and she'd accepted to meet the police officers for a few minutes at the hospital where she worked.

Throughout the ride, Gannon pestered his partner for a chance to have a cigarette. Mobley stood her ground, even when he offered to hang his head out the window like a golden retriever as he smoked. She would have none of it. He was considerably cranky when they reached the hospital. They texted Roxanne and she promised to meet them soon in the cafeteria.

"I hate hospitals," Gannon said as they took one long corridor after another.

"Does anyone ever enjoy hospitals?"

"Well, I'm sure surgeons do. And their spouses." Mobley rolled her eyes at his joke. "Mostly, I hate that everything tastes bad in a hospital."

"It's called healthy food."

They sat down at a long table near the window, as instructed by their witness.

"Healthy food has never made anybody healthy, Mobley. No, they should make patients comfortable, you know? Chips, chicken wings, Cherry Coke. Booze. Hospitals definitely need booze."

"Ugh," his partner groaned.

"That's right, I forgot that you're on the wagon."

That took her by surprise. "I'm not *on the wagon*," she replied, making finger quotes.

"You said you didn't drink anymore. I figured you were in AA."

"No, it's just…"

"What? Come on, you can talk to me. We're partners, remember?"

She raised her head and met his eyes. "I have MS."

"Oh shit."

"Yeah, that's what I said."

Gannon audibly exhaled, the wind knocked out of him. He had expected some sob story about how drinking had ruined her life. He hadn't expected anything related to a deadly, degenerative disease.

"How… When did you get diagnosed with multiple sclerosis?"

"It was a little while back during a Navy physical. I was at Diego Garcia, in the middle of the Pacific Ocean. I truly felt alone in the world when the test results came back."

"Jesus… So that's why you left the Navy after seven years. Medical discharge?"

"I got a separation without benefits. Some desk jockey on the PEB argued that it was a pre-existing condition. Anyway, joining the State Police was the only way I could see to get stable income, especially after my boyfriend scampered. With MS, you have good days and bad days. I was lucky to have some good days while I got through the physical tests. And the disease wasn't as advanced back then."

Gannon nodded, understanding that she must've had some help to forge paperwork. There was no way they would've missed her condition during the application process.

"Good for you," he said, meaning it.

"I'm not looking for a handout. I don't want anyone to make it easy for me. I'm not trying to defraud the system. But I need this job, Gannon. I need the money, yes, but it's the only thing keeping me from going insane, you know? I'm too young to be considered an invalid. I don't want to get sent home and wait to die."

"Your secret is safe with me, partner. You have my word."

She gave him one of her rare smiles and he nodded to her. They were in this together.

Gannon stood up to get himself coffee, and perhaps sneak off for a cigarette, but a nurse entered the cafeteria. She was tall, in her thirties. Her hair was a mass of brass-colored curls. Her head pivoted back and forth as if she was looking for someone. Her eyes locked on him and she came forward.

"Are you the police officers?"

"That's right. That must make you Roxanne Pinedo."

"Yes."

"I'm Detective Gannon. She's Detective Mobley who you talked on the phone with before. We'd be grateful if you could answer some questions."

"Okay. I'm on my break."

Gannon motioned for her to sit down across the table. "Can I get anyone some coffee?"

That nurse shook her head. "I don't have much time."

That was just his luck, Gannon thought, sitting down. Coffeeless. He pulled his notebook out and they exchanged a few banalities.

"So you came down here to ask me about Larissa?"

"That's right. You wouldn't know who's responsible for what happened to her and John, do you?"

"Of course not," Roxanne replied.

Gannon grinned. "Just thought I'd ask the obvious. You never know, right? How long have you been friends?"

"All our lives," she said, her southern drawl coming through thicker. "We grew up together, from preschool to college. Then we remained close until recently."

"What happened recently?" Mobley asked.

"I got a good job offer here in Swayze County. I was happy when Larissa moved to Hillford. It's not next door, but I thought we'd get to see each other often again. And then this horrible thing happened…"

The nurse sulked and looked away. She reached into her pocket for a tissue. She dabbed her eyes and struggled not to sniffle.

"You talked a lot, didn't you?"

"Sure. We called each other all the time, texted. Emails and Facebook. But lately, not as much. In the last few weeks, they were busy with the move and all."

Mobley perked up. "And why did they move here anyhow?"

"John was looking into some new tax incentives, apparently. That was him, all right. Always thinking about ways to save a buck. They got a good price on their house and found a cheaper one up here."

"And Mr. and Mrs. Begum were happy together?"

"Yes, in a disgusting way."

"Disgusting?" Gannon repeated.

"Well, you know. They were one of those couples who are together fifteen years and are always holding hands, kissing in public. That's disgusting. I'm thirty-four and I was married three miserable times."

"So they really were happy together?"

"As happy as can be. They had the odd argument here and there, like anybody, I guess, but they were together for the long haul."

"Did Mrs. Begum ever sleep around?"

Roxanne looked up sharply at the old man. "No, never!"

"She didn't have a lover?"

"No."

"Are you sure? Maybe some man she met one day at the country club? Maybe… a woman?"

"No way," Roxanne said without hesitation. "Sometimes I joked about it because I sure as hell wasn't experiencing marital bliss, but Larissa always said she would never cheat on John. They loved each other."

Mobley made a note. "But sometimes having a child can put a strain on a marriage."

"They did go through a little bit of a rough patch when Larissa found out she couldn't have kids. But it only lasted a few weeks. They made their peace with that and John was very supportive."

"As I understand it, adopting a child can open up wounds again. Did that happen with them?"

"What do you mean?"

"Adopting Boyd. Their kid."

"I don't know what you mean," Roxanne said, looking back and forth between the two detectives. She was confused. "Larissa and John didn't have any children."

"Are you sure?" Gannon asked. "You said yourself that you weren't really in contact during the last few weeks."

"Adopting a kid is not something you do in a few weeks, Detective. It takes months. Years. Besides, Larissa told me that they'd decided they would never adopt. They were okay with not having any kids. They were happy just having each other."

~ ~ ~ ~

Gannon practically sprinted back to his car.

He was lost in thought and promptly forgot about Mobley struggling to follow. His mind was jumbled. How could he have missed this?

The kid had told him that his parents were dead. He had assumed this was the truth. He had never thought to check records beyond finding out that there were no next of kin.

He glanced behind his shoulder as he reached the parking lot. Mobley was walking slower with the phone clutched to her ear. She was already thinking along the same lines and making inquiries.

Gannon planted a cigarette between his lips. It took four tries to light it because he was so frazzled. He could hear her calmly explain the situation to a government employee. He followed the conversation as best as he could and it lasted an eternity.

"Okay, thank you," she said before hanging up.

"And? Talk to me, Mobley."

"There are no records of the Begums ever adopting a child!"

"What?!"

She shook her head, as puzzled as he was. "The state has nothing on the Begums. Same with North Carolina."

Unable to breathe, Gannon threw his cigarette away half finished. Things weren't adding up.

Who the hell was this kid?

# CHAPTER 21

It was a summer of contrasts and mood swings. The stifling heat had given way to a cold front which was being led by heavy showers. Rain drummed against the windows.

Dr. Curnutt tightened the cardigan around her shoulders, a shiver running up her spine. Her first instinct was to turn off the air conditioning, but in her opinion it was best to keep it on for the patients. Sharing feelings was often a trying experience and discussions sometimes heated up, literally.

She steadied the legal pad on her thigh and gripped her pen. The digital recorder was on. She could see the LCD seconds ticking by. Several had gone by without her patient having said a word. In truth, she liked to test them after a few sessions. Were they able to initiate conversations or did they still need prodding?

Young Boyd was sitting on the overstuffed couch before her. He was wringing his hands, not looking at her. She had a list of questions ready. She decided to ease into them though.

"I hear that you went to the fair last weekend."

"Yes."

"How did you enjoy it, Boyd?" He shrugged. "It was

your first time, yes? That must have been exciting. I remember the first time I went to a fair. I was about your age and I won a stuffed giraffe at Skee-Ball. I kept that giraffe up until I left for college. Did you win any stuffed animals?"

"Stuffed animals are for babies," he said.

"There are some places where prizes include goldfish."

Boyd looked up at her, his head still tilted forward. "Goldfish. That could have been fun."

"Really?" she asked, knowing what he meant though wishing he explained anyway. "What kind of fun are we talking about?"

"Doesn't matter. I didn't win anything, Dr. Talia. Lucas played the games and won."

"Lucas? I thought you had started to call him daddy?"

"I changed my mind."

"That's okay," she said with a comforting smile. "It's always up to you. I bet you can't wait to go back to the fair again next year, uh?"

Boyd shook his head. "Not really. It wasn't my first fair."

"I don't understand," Dr. Curnutt replied. "Tori said it was."

"It wasn't. She lied to you."

"Why would she do that? Why would she lie about this, Boyd?

"Why do people do anything? Because they're untrustworthy or they have an agenda. They have something to hide. Maybe she wanted to make herself appear more interesting to you. Who knows? Doesn't matter. I hate fairs."

The psychologist made a note. "And why do you hate fairs exactly?"

"Because it's fake. Everything is fake. People pretend to smile, pretend to be happy. They give away stuffed animals as if they're prized possessions, but they're just cheap toys. They're trash. They're things people wouldn't want if they hadn't won them. Carnival employees give trash to people who pretend to be happy about it. It's nothing but salesmanship."

"But there are other fun things, aren't there? There are rides. Those can be fun, no?"

Boyd looked into the distance, still wringing his hands. Dr. Curnutt felt as if there was something he wanted to say and she was determined to keep her mouth shut until he did. It took over four minutes.

"The first time I went to a fair, I wanted to go on the rollercoaster. They had a big one. It was upside down with your legs dangling off. It looked amazing. My dad said I was too small to ride it, so I started crying. It was natural for me to do that, right? I was just a little boy, not like now."

"And what happened, Boyd?"

He looked at her, staring straight into her eyes without blinking. "He slapped me. In front of everyone, he slapped me in the face. If that's what family fun is about, I'd rather have a goldfish."

"What happened after that?" she asked. "How did it make you feel?"

"I'm hungry."

"Excuse me?"

"I'm hungry. Do you have any cookies, Dr. Talia? I feel like chocolate chip cookies. Or Oreos."

She frowned. Where was this coming from? It was out of character for him.

"I can get you something to eat a little later, okay? Tell me about your parents, Boyd?"

"I don't want to talk about them."

"Why is that?"

"I didn't like them."

"Oh?" Dr. Curnutt whispered. "Why didn't you like your parents?"

"Because they hated me."

"Parents rarely hate their children, Boyd. There may be some…" She caught herself before using technical terms like *family dynamics* and *behavioral patterns*. "Some families act differently. No one is the same. That doesn't mean they hated you."

"They didn't love me, then. I always came second. They never picked me up from school. I had to walk all the time. My mother sold my toys at a pawn shop once. She needed money for vodka and cigarettes."

She had heard a million tragic stories involving children and they never failed to make her sad. This time was no different.

"Did you ever tell this to anyone?" she inquired.

"What's the point?"

"The point is that not everyone is like that. Some adults are eager to help."

He shrugged. "One time, my father saw that I was going to tell Mrs. Bingaman, my teacher. He slapped me in the face. He said if I talked, he would get his belt."

"I'm sorry, Boyd. But you're safe now."

"Aside from the abandonment issues and difficulty with relating to my peers?"

She frowned, startled by the little boy suddenly sounding like a grad student. "Where did you hear these words, Boyd?"

"I told you that I like to read. It's probably somewhere in your notebook."

"It is. It's because I need to understand you."

"Why? Because you're getting paid to?"

She offered a kind smile. "Because I want to help you, Boyd. That's my job, yes, but it's also my mission in life. I don't sleep well if I don't know for a fact that I have helped someone get better."

"So if I need to get better, then that means I'm sick, Dr. Talia."

"I don't know. Do you feel sick?"

"I'm hungry," he shot back.

She waited a few minutes before continuing, flipping a page on her pad.

"Now I'd like to talk about what happened after the fair. There was a fire at your foster dad's work."

"There's nothing left now."

"Did you see the damage, Boyd?"

"No, but I can picture it."

"Do you know what happened? How it started?"

"Are you asking me if I'm involved?"

She paused, gauging him. He was unreadable. "Are you?"

"I'm eight years old, Dr. Talia. I was at the fair. I didn't do anything."

"The other day when we met, you said that you enjoy fire."

"Fire cleanses. Did you know that it's the best way to get rid of diseases? Microbes? Fire is powerful."

"During our meeting, you said that you like watching things burn."

"I also enjoy eating; that doesn't mean I like to cook."

"Boyd…"

"Can I have a cookie now?"

He was looking at her defiantly now. She sensed that he was shutting her out. She'd gotten everything she would out of him today.

~ ~ ~ ~

It had been nearly twelve years since Tori had chewed her fingernails. Well, that wasn't true. She had done it the day they had picked up Boyd, the stress getting to her. She thought she had kicked the habit, but here she was doing it again.

She was watching Boyd through the French doors. He was on the playroom floor, tentatively playing with a fire truck, but mostly nibbling on a chocolate chip cookie. A glass of milk was on the table next to him.

She turned to Dr. Curnutt who sported an expression she hadn't seen on her before. Until now, she had always been utterly confident. Unshakable. It was as if she had never met a patient she couldn't handle and, even if she didn't hold the key to solving whatever ailed them right now, she would soon.

At the moment, the psychologist's expression was the opposite. It was dismay, bafflement. Maybe even apprehension.

"Something is wrong, isn't it?" Tori began. "I can tell."

"No, everything is fine."

"I can see that it's not. Is something going on with Boyd, Doctor?"

"He's… a peculiar case."

Tori immediately saw something worrisome in that and covered her mouth to avoid chewing her nails again.

"Peculiar how?"

Dr. Curnutt considered that for several seconds before speaking. Neither of them looked at the child on the other side of the door, yet neither of them could ignore him. For his part, Boyd seemed blissfully unaware.

"He enjoys reading rather dense material. He has quite the advanced vocabulary, too."

Tori nodded. "He does. Yesterday I caught him reading on my iPad. I thought it was kids' stuff, you know? Turns out he was reading an article in *The Atlantic* about the social implications of urban development, or some such thing. For a while, I thought he was kidding, but he really was reading that."

"I see. Have you noticed that sometimes he acts older than his years?"

"I have," Tori admitted. "I never had kids or been around them much. I just thought he was smart."

"He is smart. At some point, I'd like to have him take an IQ test, even if in some circles they aren't believed to be reliable. I would stake my reputation that Boyd would score near one forty, which would qualify his intelligence as genius."

Tori was stunned. "That's a good thing, no?"

"It is, but it can also be indicative of other pathologies. I have a feeling lying comes easy to him. And then there was that event with the fish out in the woods. I wonder if he's having trouble differentiating between right and wrong."

"What… What are you saying?"

Dr. Curnutt winced, as if wondering how much she should actually say. "On the one hand, he's showing signs of ASPD."

"What is that?"

"I'm sorry, antisocial personality disorder. It's what people commonly refer to sociopaths."

"Oh God!"

"Please don't be alarmed. It's a perfectly natural medical term. People with this condition generally present symptoms during childhood, but it's not until later that they can be officially diagnosed. It would take at least ten years to be able to put this label on Boyd."

"What are those symptoms?" Tori asked, simultaneously not eager to hear the answer.

"Having trouble dealing with the outside world, being antisocial."

"Boyd isn't antisocial."

The therapist ignored her. "They can be impulsive, break laws, lie. They tend to have a conscience—a sense of right and wrong—but it's usually very faint. They always look out for themselves, first and foremost."

Tori was shaking her head. "That doesn't mean anything. He's been through so much."

"Of course, Mrs. Ramsdale. As I said before, it's not well-defined in him. He's also presenting with symptoms of psychopathy."

"Psychopathy… Wait, you mean like psychopath? You think Boyd is a…" Tori lowered her voice. "You think he's a psychopath?"

"In my opinion, the child is deficient in empathy and remorse. People with this condition can be very manipulative because they don't have a moral compass like we do. He's also quite charming which can catch friends and relatives off guard. They are experts at perceiving social cues and mimicking them, anything so they appear normal to those around them. I'm sorry to say that psychology isn't an exact science. Nevertheless, I'm worried."

"Can he be fixed?"

"There are treatments. Mostly therapy. Support groups for family members. It's a process, as I'm sure you understand."

"Boyd isn't a psycho. He can't be."

"And perhaps he isn't. There are some academic papers which suggests that their brain is different from other people's, chemically and physiologically. I think he should consult with someone more knowledgeable about this than me. There's an excellent neuropsychiatrist at Johns Hopkins, I could make an introduction."

"I don't know," Tori said half-heartedly.

*Excellent neuropsychiatrist at Johns Hopkins* was a synonym for expensive. Moreover, a part of her didn't want to admit that something was wrong with Boyd. If he got brain scans and became a lab rat, it could bring the confirmation that the poor boy was beyond salvation, and she wasn't ready for that.

"Mrs. Ramsdale, you don't have to decide right away. Take your time. Meanwhile, I'll continue my sessions with Boyd. I promise, it will help."

Tori smiled with gratefulness, but one question was spinning in her mind. If Boyd was a sociopath, or worse, a psychopath, would therapy actually help?

She wasn't certain she wanted to know the real answer.

# CHAPTER 22

Tori skipped past the dishwasher. It was there, staring at her in the face, but she wanted the distraction of doing the dishes the old-fashioned way. She had always focused better while doing something with her hands. It probably explained her career as an artist.

She snorted at the thought. Artist. She was ashamed to call herself that lately. She hadn't sold a painting in months. Landscapes weren't a hot commodity at the moment. Maybe she would be better off if she stopped deluding herself. It was time to face the real world.

Thunder rolled in the distance. The rain had picked up, and so had the wind. They were in for a powerful August storm. The wind was already howling outside.

"Boyd, go upstairs and play. Okay, sweetie? Then I'll be up for your bath before going to bed."

He got down from his chair, nodded, and disappeared. Lucas was still at the table with no hint that he was about to help her clean up.

"Come here," she said. "I need to talk to you."

It was only after several seconds of reluctance that her husband joined her at the sink, which she was filling up, rinsing plates at the same time.

"What is it?"

"Boyd's therapy session today… It was…"

"What?

"Upsetting."

Lucas rolled his eyes. "That's the whole point of therapy, no?"

"It isn't like that. Dr. Curnutt, she said some things." Tori took a deep breath, unable to believe this was really happening. "She thinks something is wrong with Boyd."

"We don't need a hundred bucks an hour shrink to tell us that, do we?"

"This is serious, Lucas. He's unnaturally smart and he's showing… tendencies."

"Tendencies?" he repeated, looking at the stack of dishes while not moving a muscle to help with them. "Like he's a fag? Isn't he a little young for that?"

"No, that's not what I'm talking about. Dr. Curnutt thinks he might be a sociopath. Maybe a psychopath."

"Holy shit!"

"Therapy is what he needs right now. She also says that a specialist at Johns Hopkins could help him recover."

Lucas frowned. "You don't recover if you're a psycho. Anyone who tells you that is after your money. Jesus Christ…"

Methodically, Tori began scrubbing the plates under the surface. The hot water was soothing.

"He's a troubled little boy. We just need to help him."

"No shit, he's troubled! You understand what that means, right? He probably had something to do with the fire."

"Oh please! He was at the fair, with us."

"Not all the time, he wasn't. And the fair was right across the street from my land. A one-legged retard in a pink dress could have gone over there and no one would've seen him. I'm telling you, he rigged something. You said so yourself, he's smart. He could have done that."

Tori shook her head. "No way. He never could have done that. He's eight."

"And a psychopath! Your precious doctor told you as much, Tori. Open your goddamn eyes already. All kinds of spooky shit has been happening since he's come into our lives. I don't want him here anymore."

"What?!" she exclaimed, turning toward him yet leaving her hands in the water. "You can't say that!"

"Look, maybe he did something, maybe he didn't. In any case, I can't trust him, okay? And if I can't trust him, then I can't love him."

"What are you saying, Lucas?"

"I'm saying that I can't be his foster dad anymore. That means that, by definition, this relationship isn't working out. If I can't stand to be around the kid, then it can't possibly work out with me being his foster dad."

"Lucas…"

"I want him gone, Tori. I want him out of my house and out of our lives."

She couldn't believe they were having this conversation. "It's our job to care for him. We knew from the start it was going to be hard. We have to look past that and do our best. We have to give him a peaceful environment so he can get better. We always knew that the child we would take in would be troubled."

"This is way worse, Tori. Can't you see that? Anyway, I can't stand being in this house. I'm going out."

He propelled himself from the counter and Tori glared at him.

"Who are you going to see?" she asked between clenched teeth.

"Since when do you care? It's none of your business."

"Are you going to see a woman? Are you having an affair, Lucas?"

He spun around. "Why are you being such a little bitch suddenly? Why don't you trust me? That's a wife's job, to trust her husband."

"A wife loses trust in her husband after he already had an affair."

He shrugged theatrically, looking at the ceiling, and groaned. "Oh, here we go again! Do you get Brownie points for bringing up ancient history? Is that it, uh?"

"It would explain a lot of things," Tori said, turning back toward the dishes which she washed compulsively. "For months, you've been going out. There've been long absences."

She could see from the corner of her eye that he was snarling, trying to be bold, but his male pride was clearly hurt.

"I've been working, okay? In case you haven't noticed, I've been trying to build a business. For us! I've been busting my ass putting this project together."

"I've seen lipstick on you, Lucas. I tried to make myself believe it was nothing, but it's not. I don't think you're being faithful."

He rushed forward and pulled her hands out of the water, making it dribble everywhere.

"Goddamn it! I'm not having an affair! Get that shit out of your head!"

He reached for one of the clean plates on the rack. He threw it on the ground where it exploded.

"I don't believe you," she said.

"You don't trust me? You don't believe me? What the hell's your problem?"

He shoved her back and she lost her footing. Her heart lurched and she put her hands behind her, catching herself against the stove at the last second. Meanwhile, Lucas cocked his arm back, his hand balling into a fist.

"Go ahead," she whispered. "Do it if it's going to make you feel better."

He was snarling again, saliva dripping from a corner of his mouth. He lowered his arm and grabbed another plate from the rack. He launched it sideways against the wall.

Tori didn't jump when it shattered. Her eyes were riveted to her husband who was storming out of the kitchen. A second later, she heard him grab his keys and slam the door as he left.

# CHAPTER 23

The storm had blown past the area. Flashes of lightning were still visible in the distance, but they were going in the opposite direction, growing dimmer. The same applied to the thunder, which was now nothing but a soft purr. The rain continued to fall although it was no longer threatening.

Tori was sitting on the front porch by herself. She stared into the darkness, not trying to discern anything. She had thought that by coming here and doing this, it would clear her mind. It didn't. It only gave her a better opportunity to think about Lucas and their marriage, which was obviously in shambles.

But at least the rain trickling out of the gutters drowned out her sobbing. She had always been self-conscious about crying. The way she had grown up, it was better if no one knew that you were vulnerable. Most of the time, she held back. Tonight, she couldn't.

She suddenly felt a deep aversion to Steep Gorge. They had left San Francisco to live here, not because she had ever wanted to, but because her husband had made her. She had seen this as a fair trade, in fact.

He was letting her continue to be an artist even though they both knew that making it in this world was, at best, a long shot. In return, she had figured that she needed to support him all the way, in any field he chose. Unfortunately, that had meant moving to this one-horse town.

Tori was beginning to think that she was losing her own identity. She had become Lucas's wife. She had taken his name. She had left all her friends behind and, since she was an only child, she had no one else in her life. The art scene here was nonexistent.

She was nobody.

It was this that had given her the drive to become a foster mother. She had firmly believed that if she had someone to care for, she could reclaim a life for herself. At the very least, she wouldn't only be living for Lucas. She wanted to be her own person once more.

The front door creaked open and she was upset. Couldn't she be left alone? She needed time to herself to reassess her life. Most of all, she didn't want anyone to see her in this state. Boyd took careful steps toward her. She swiftly wiped her eyes, but she couldn't keep up with the tears.

She forced a smile. "Aren't you supposed to be in bed, sweetie?"

He was wearing his cartoon baseball players pajamas. He sat on the edge of the chair next to her.

"Are you sad?"

"You should go back to bed, okay?"

"Tori, are you sad?" She wiped her eyes again, this time using the cuff of her blouse. "I don't like to see you when you're sad."

"It happens to everybody, you know. Even grown-ups."

"I like you a lot," he said. "Living here with you, it's the only thing good in my life. I want you to know that I appreciate it very much."

His words made her cry again, though this time it was out of joy. Feeling wanted and loved and useful gave her a major dopamine rush, something that hadn't happened in a long time. Without thinking, she stretched her arms to the side and took him in her arms. He didn't recoil, and even hugged her back, though not vigorously.

"Thank you, sweetie. What you just said, it really means a lot to me."

She was aware that he wasn't comfortable with physical contact, so she let go of him. He remained on the edge of his chair and she looked at him quizzically. Dr. Curnutt had to be wrong about him. He was the most gentle boy she had ever encountered.

"Are you crying because of Lucas? Did he make you sad?"

"It's nothing for you to worry about," Tori said dismissively.

"I heard the fight before."

"I'm sorry, Boyd. You never should've heard that. Grown-ups have arguments sometimes."

"He shouldn't have thrown those plates. That's not right, is it?"

She shook her head. "No, it's not."

"Is Lucas... Is he ever violent with you?"

She began to shake her head. Nevertheless, she

couldn't forget that time. It had only happened once and she could still feel his hard knuckles against her cheekbone. But that didn't count, did it? He had lost his job and had been drunk out of his mind. It had never happened again.

So did it count? She had told herself for years that it didn't. But what about the other kind of pain she had suffered?

"No," Tori replied, her voice barely a whisper. "He's not violent."

"He's not nice to you. Husbands and wives should be nice to each other."

"You're very wise for your age."

"I'm very wise for any age," he shot back with a grin, which made her laugh. "Why aren't you and Lucas happy?"

"Well…"

"Is it because of me?"

"No!" Tori countered, not wanting to add guilt to his already long list of issues. "Of course, it's not about you. Don't ever think that."

"Then what is it? You can tell me."

She spun toward the darkness again. She knew that she couldn't unload her burden on a child, but she couldn't help herself. She needed to talk to someone. He was the only person with whom she could talk, she realized.

"We stopped being happy about a year ago," she said without thinking. "I discovered that Lucas was having an affair."

She couldn't hold back from telling him everything. It was as if she needed it, even though she was talking to an eight-year-old who undoubtedly didn't need to hear any of this.

"I know what an affair means."

"It's that same old story: I came home when I wasn't supposed to and he was with another woman."

She didn't give him the sordid details about how they had both been naked in the living room, Lucas on top of her, barely managing to stop thrusting as Tori caught them. She had felt sick to her stomach, which had been mostly normal for her at that stage in her pregnancy, but it was worse than ever that night.

"I was so angry and shocked that, instead of staying put and throwing plates like Lucas would do, I ran to my car and drove off."

"Where did you go?"

"I don't know. I don't remember if I even knew where I was going. I just wanted to get away. My vision became blurry and I drove faster and faster. It was night, very dark. It was a lot like tonight. The fog was thick. After a few miles, I lost control of the car."

Boyd frowned. "You got into an accident?"

"Yes," she answered, still able to feel the impact, the sudden searing pain. "I didn't turn fast enough and rammed straight into this big oak tree. The entire front of the car got smashed in, flattened like a pancake."

"Were you hurt, Tori?"

"Cuts and bruises. The worst part is that I had a miscarriage. Do you know what a miscarriage means?"

"You were pregnant? You lost the little baby?"

She nodded, her tears coming up stronger. "Yes. She was nineteen weeks. The doctors couldn't save her."

She kept her eyes shut, stupidly thinking it could keep her from crying. Tears ran down her cheeks like a waterfall. She could still smell the antiseptic chemicals from the hospital.

She could still see the intern telling her that she had lost her precious Maggie, not even bothering with empathy. To him, it had just been another piece of late-night bad news. Nevertheless, it didn't begin to compare to the pain of learning that she'd never be able to have another child.

A few minutes went by and Tori composed herself. She sniffled and wiped her eyes, straightening up to let Boyd know that she was all right.

"After that, Lucas apologized and promised he would never cheat on me again. We moved to Steep Gorge to start over. We wanted a fresh start in a fresh place."

Boyd put his right hand on hers. It was so compassionate, she thought.

"I'm sorry I told you that, sweetie. I've never told anyone any of that. Not even Felicia."

"Thank you for telling me. Can I do anything?"

She laughed through the remnants of her tears. "That's very gentlemanly of you. Sometimes I think you're the most mature person I know."

"I'm serious, Tori. If you need me to do something about Lucas, all you have to do is ask."

"You're so sweet." She leaned sideways and kissed his forehead. "It's time to go back to bed now, okay?"

"Okay. Good night."

"Good night, Boyd."

She watched him get off the chair and go back into the house. Her heart felt lighter. Maybe she should have told that to someone a year ago. She shouldn't have told all that to him, it was unfair, but she couldn't shake the feeling that it was beneficial.

Then something creepy occurred to her. What had Boyd meant when he said he could *do something* about Lucas?

# CHAPTER 24

Texas Willie was the name of the bar. Aside from a longhorn skull on the wall—a cheap plastic knockoff—there wasn't much Texas spirit. And as far as Lucas knew, nobody named Willie had ever worked here.

In any case, he hadn't come here for the atmosphere. He had driven just out of town to the first place he could think of where he could get a decent drink at a decent price. Most of all, this was an establishment where he was unlikely to run into anybody he knew.

"Can I get another over here?" he shouted at the bartender after swallowing a shot of Wild Turkey.

The barman was pushing seventy. Despite his bushy beard—just like Lucas used to have, he thought with regret—he realized that the man was cringing. Judging. Lucas stared hard at him and he got the hint, coming over to refill his glass.

The bottle wasn't quite out of the way that Lucas had already downed the shot.

"Another."

"You might want to slow down, buddy."

"I'm not your buddy. I'm a goddamn customer. Now pour the shot."

There was hesitation. "Can I see some money first?"

Lucas sighed heavily to show his annoyance. He rummaged through his pockets and pulled out a few bills. He counted through them twice and then placed twenty dollars in assorted small bills on the countertop.

"Now pour."

"We have a house brand, if you want. More affordable."

That was depressing, Lucas thought. Wild Turkey wasn't exactly twelve-year-old single malt. Yet he wasn't desperate enough to go one peg lower.

"Pour. Please."

The bartender struggled not to criticize and finally complied. Lucas drank swiftly and, as he swallowed, he motioned for the man to refill his glass. When he didn't go fast enough, he pulled out more money. That did the trick.

It occurred to him that it would've been cheaper to drive to a liquor store to get himself a bottle. There was one just across the county line that was opened late and catered to desperate people like him.

That was the operative word: *desperate.*

He didn't want to be desperate. He didn't want to be one of those hopeless sons of bitches sitting in their car and drinking from a paper bag. His life was already going down the tubes and that would've been just another sad reminder.

When had everything turned to shit anyway? Before, he had told Tori that it was when the kid had shown up. He had said that in anger. However, it was true. If you were honest about it, he mused, that was when his troubles had started.

In the beginning, he had actually thought it was a good thing. It kept his wife happy and busy with her little things. It meant that government money was coming in. And, hell, he couldn't deny that it turned him into a family man.

In a small town like this, it was great for business. In New York City or Los Angeles or Miami, you buy real estate from a successful young professional with no attachments and you're fine with it. In Steep Gorge, people only trusted a family man with deep roots.

But his life had skidded off the rails. Chad Muhlenburg pulled his investment out. The project burned to the ground. Tori was becoming more and more of a bitch. He had nothing left. And the kid. *Jesus*, there was something about him that felt wrong.

He raised his glass and swallowed the whiskey in one gulp. It wasn't even burning his throat anymore. It felt like water. He slammed the glass down.

"Give me another."

"You've already had six, buddy."

"And I'll have six more. Come on, come on!"

"I don't think so."

"What?" Lucas spat, puzzled by the man's reaction.

"You've had enough. I'm cutting you off."

"You can't cut me off. I am a paying customer."

The bartender shook his head, staying put. "I've got the right to refuse service to anyone, especially when they're half in the bag."

"Okay, real funny. Now fill it up." Lucas slid his glass closer to the old man who remained impassive. "Come on!"

"I'll give you a coffee if you want. Or water. No more whiskey."

"What the hell are you talking about?! This is a goddamn bar, isn't it? Give me some goddamn whiskey!"

"Buddy, it's time for you to go."

"You're throwing me out?"

"I'm telling you it's time for bed, buddy," the bartender said. "Go home."

"I'm not going home!"

"You sure as hell ain't staying here. Please…"

Lucas stood up from his stool and stumbled. He grabbed the bar as to not lose his balance. Maybe he was a little tipsy after all. Still, that didn't give this geezer the right to decide what was good for him.

"I want another drink!"

"You won't get it from me, buddy."

"What?! This place sucks! No wonder your bar is empty, asshole. Client satisfaction, that's the first lesson in business."

Lucas spun around. The place was practically empty. There was a table in the back where a middle-aged couple was sharing a pitcher of pale beer, but otherwise it was deserted. He'd been hoping to rally people to his cause. The middle-aged couple didn't give a crap about him.

"You find that acceptable?" he shouted at them.

They didn't reply. Insulted, he kicked the stool next to his. It was heavier than he'd estimated and it just landed flatly on its side.

"It's time for you to leave," the bartender said, his voice firm.

"You're going to make me?"

The old man put down his rag and walked out from behind the bar. He was coming toward the customer. Lucas grabbed the shot glass from the counter and threw it on the floor. The glass was second-rate and shattered on impact.

"That's it, come on…"

The bartender seemed a lot more spry up close. He grabbed Lucas's wrist and twisted his body around, pulling his arm behind his back.

"Hey!"

"Let's go."

He marched Lucas toward the exit. No matter how much Lucas tried to resist, he discovered that he couldn't. His head was swimming and he couldn't mount an adequate defense. The guy was also far stronger than he looked. He probably had a lot of experience throwing regulars out.

The front door had a panic bar. Lucas was thrust forward, hitting it, and the door swung open. The man pushed Lucas out. He staggered off the porch, missed a step, and landed in the wet gravel. It was raining lightly.

"You stay right there, buddy. I'm calling you a cab."

"I don't want your cab! I'm taking my car and driving away from this shithole!"

"It makes no nevermind to me. Just don't come back."

The bartender walked back into the building, leaving Lucas by himself.

"What a dump," he whispered.

He pushed himself up, found his keys, and went to his truck. He settled behind the wheel and swore about soiling his seat with mud. He took a few deep breaths to make sure he was okay and drove out of the parking lot. Yeah, he was fine. The bartender had it all wrong. He wasn't drunk. He was perfectly fine to drive.

His destination was crystal clear. He was thirsty and he hadn't drunk enough Wild Turkey to fix this particular problem. Some issues required sleep or rest. Others required whiskey. Lots of it.

He had gone half a mile before he realized he couldn't see anything. He turned on the windshield wipers and he needed three attempts to find the right setting. He didn't bother with the radio. He wanted to hear himself think. He wanted to wallow.

He went faster and the jolt of adrenaline gave him something to feel good about. He pushed on the pedal further, the roar of the engine offering satisfaction. At least that was something he could control. For once.

"Where's that liquor store again?"

He started to doubt that he was taking the correct road. The last thing he needed right now was to take the long way around. He accelerated some more in spite of the rain, which was coming down harder.

That was a mistake.

As the truck drifted off the pavement, Lucas was slow to steer back. He also forgot to ease his foot off the gas. The Chevy slid down into the ditch.

"No, no, no!"

He gave it some gas, turned to the left, but the truck slid down further into the ditch until he stopped completely. The vehicle leaned sideways. The angle wasn't dangerous, he wasn't about to tip over, but Lucas couldn't get any traction as he pushed on the pedal. His wheels were spinning in mud.

Shit.

He got out of the truck to inspect the damage. The rain was coming down in sheets and he was wet from head to toe almost immediately. He held himself up against the vehicle, his feet sinking into the mud. He gave it a halfhearted push, but that only ever worked when someone was behind the wheel to drive forward. Wedging a piece of wood under the wheel did nothing either.

There was only one solution since he wasn't a triple-A member. He called Jasper, asking him to come with his own four-by-four since he knew it was equipped with a winch. It was almost thirty minutes before he showed up.

"What the hell happened to you?" he said after Lucas rolled his window down.

"I'm stuck."

"You look wasted."

"Not enough, man. Can you get me out or not?"

Jasper shrugged and returned to his truck. For his part, Lucas wasn't drunk enough to be a complete asshole, so he got out to lend a hand. At least he had something to focus on. Manual labor was his strength, anyway. Maybe that's why his business was failing. Maybe he should have stuck with being a carpenter, leaving the thinking to those with fancy degrees.

Considering that pissed him off even more.

They made quick work of unspooling the cable, hooking it up to the Chevy, and winching it out of the ditch as Lucas sobered up long enough to steer. They managed it on the first try. Jasper unhooked the cable and parked his vehicle on the curb. He joined Lucas inside his truck.

"You're good, Lucas?"

"I'm good. The truck runs fine."

"But are you good to drive? You look like shit."

"I feel like shit, man."

"Why don't you let me drive you home, dude? We can come back tomorrow to get your Chevy."

As he said that, Jasper gently reached for the keys, but Lucas swatted his hand away.

"Mind your business. I'm fine."

"Okay," Jasper said softly. "Okay. Anything going on to make you drink that much?"

"Thirst."

"I don't doubt it. But besides that?"

Lucas stayed silent for a moment. He stared through

the windshield. There was nothing out there but rain and trees lost in darkness.

"I had a fight with Tori."

"About what? I mean, I don't want to pry or anything. Sometimes it helps to talk about things."

Luke shook his head. "We're not the happy couple everybody sees. A whole lot of shit went down between us over the years. I screwed around."

"You cheated on her?"

"Couldn't help it. Christ, I still can't. I'm seeing another broad."

"Jesus, man…"

He could tell that Jasper had trouble taking it all in. It was the white picket fence myth where no one really knew what went on in their neighbor's home.

"I'm blaming the kid for everything," Lucas muttered. "Something isn't right with him. Something isn't right and it's making everything wrong for us."

Jasper nodded. "I agree."

"You do?"

"He's a little psycho. I still can't forget what he was doing to that fish. He wasn't playing. It was torture. It was mean. And Evan told me that he threatened him."

"What?"

"Boyd threatened my son. Hell, he threatened *me*."

"What do you mean?"

Jasper told him about the encounter in front of his

house. Lucas was surprised and, at the same time, not that surprised.

"I told him to stay away from Evan because he said he threatened him. Evan said he thinks that Boyd made him fall off his bike and break his arm. He told me to keep quiet. It was, I don't know, chilling."

"That boy's not right."

"You have to do something, dude."

Lucas nodded, his head clearer than ever. He really did need to act. He had to get that kid out of his life.

# CHAPTER 25

"You can't go in there," the secretary shrieked. "I have to announce you first!"

Gannon winked at her. "You just did."

She continued to panic, waving him to stay back while trying to make up her mind about picking up the phone and calling her boss about the visitor. She wasn't fast enough. Gannon walked past her desk and entered Captain Vail's office, allowing himself the briefest of knocks as a compromise in civility.

The captain had a mouthful of blueberry muffin and a cup of coffee in his hand. There was a paper napkin tucked into his shirt and he was halfway bent over his desk. He launched an objection about the intrusion. It came out garbled because the makeshift breakfast mostly blocked his vocal cords.

"I need to see the kid," the senior detective said, closing the door behind him.

Vail put the coffee down, swallowed his bite, and pushed the muffin away. He yanked off the napkin as if the thing was a national embarrassment to law enforcement everywhere.

"Damn it, Detective! Don't you know it's common courtesy to have yourself announced first?"

Gannon ignored him and came as close to the desk as possible, while remaining outside of punching range. He was standing tall against the sitting captain and that was exactly the point. Intimidation wasn't sexy, but it worked more often than not.

"Cap, you're on my back day and night about closing this Begum case. There's a chance to do this. I need to talk to the kid, Boyd. He lied."

"What?"

"The Begums didn't have a kid. I searched high and low. I talked to Larissa Begum's best friend. The lady couldn't have children and there are no records of the couple ever adopting any. This means two things. First, the kid lied to us about who he is."

"And second?"

"He lied to us about what went on. All we have to go on is a sketch of a bearded African-American, which doesn't jibe with anything we've been able to find out. Since his entire story is bullshit, I have reason to believe he lied to us about that, too."

"Christ…"

Vail pushed his muffin farther away, like it was the reason his day had suddenly turned to crap.

"At this point, it's necessary to revise our entire strategy," Gannon said in a much more reasonable tone. "In my opinion, that starts with interviewing the kid again."

The captain stared at his desk, his eyes shifting constantly. This went on for several seconds.

"Cap?

"No."

Gannon was taken aback. "Excuse me?"

"No. You're not meeting the child again."

"Why? This is our best shot at getting to the bottom of this. I mean, that's what you want, right? You've been on my ass since day one about it. I ask you—as a courtesy—and you turn me down?"

"Listen to me, Gannon. Do you know why I made captain while you're still detective?"

*Because I'm not a suck-up and I work for a living*, the older man wanted to reply, although he wisely kept his mouth shut. "Enlighten me, sir."

"Big picture. It's because I can see the big picture, Gannon. You're focused on the kid, but you're not seeing the implications. We live in a twenty-four hour news cycle world. People are literally paid to wait until we screw up so we can become their story."

"What? Cap, I don't see how that has any bearing on the situation."

"Okay, maybe the kid lied to you. If you say so, I believe you. But you know what the problem is with that whole scenario? He's a kid. He's an eight-year-old child. I want you to close your eyes and picture what it'll look like when the big bad detective with suspicion on his face demands to interrogate a vulnerable eight-year-old child."

"You're damn right, I'm suspicious."

"Then I want you to picture the reaction. His foster parents, or CPS, or the goddamn Rotary Club, they're bound to make a fuss. Can you picture it, Gannon? Try to see the headlines. *State Police harasses helpless child. Boy, eight, traumatized by State Police*. Can you see it?"

"The kid pointed to the scene of the crime. There was blood on him. He has some information about what really happened, Captain."

"You won't be there two minutes that your presence will already be announced on Twitter and Facebook and freaking CNN. That alone could derail the entire case. You don't need this and I don't need the chief to give me a hard time about it. Do you understand, Gannon?"

"But…"

"Did I make myself clear?" Vail asked with eerie calmness.

"Yes, sir."

~ ~ ~ ~

When Gannon walked through the bullpen, he saw Mobley waiting for him next to his cubicle. She was leaning against the partition. It wasn't like she was being cool and debonair. It was more like the partition was holding her up.

"And?" she asked.

"Request denied."

She was dejected, fixing her gaze to the floor. "What's the next step?"

"I'm not sure yet," he said, joining her at last. "But I have an idea until I think of something better. Go grab some coffee for the road."

"We have to drive somewhere?"

He shrugged. "I didn't say it was a *good* idea. Come on."

Five minutes later, they were in the car, each sipping subpar coffee as they merged with traffic. Morning rush hour was waning, so it wasn't completely terrible. They drove twenty minutes, the last ten spent mostly on red lights.

Three blocks from City Hall was an industrial district that had once won a statewide landscaping award. The developer had created the space to avoid the usual derelict scenery associated with this type of venue. As such, each building was surrounded by rolling lawns and flowerbeds, mature trees and decorative rocks.

The developer's real goal had been to justify charging more rent and higher sale fees. In the end though, it remained an industrial district and the real estate company never got its money back. It still looked nice, however.

Gannon explained that the warehouse they were going to was owned by the state. He wasn't sure, but he believed that they had come to own it as part of asset forfeiture procedures. Now the state used it to store whatever didn't fit elsewhere, including nonessential police evidence.

There was no security when they got there, certainly not any barbed wire or fences. The building was covered in gray brick with stylish pillars in front. They parked in the small lot on the side.

"As far as I know," Gannon began, "the Begum house is currently in limbo."

"Limbo?"

"No next of kin, right? Lawyers are undoubtedly going

back and forth over what to do with it. The county probably wants to own it, same for the state. Then I'm sure some do-gooder at CPS wants to have the house auctioned off so that the proceeds are put in a trust for the kid."

"Except the kid may not be *their* kid," Mobley said.

"Like I said, limbo. In the meantime, everything in the house was boxed up and stored here."

They entered the warehouse and a chirpy clerk had them sign in. She was visibly excited to have visitors for once. She guided them to the seventh aisle.

Mobley leaned against a steel shelf after she left. "What are we looking for exactly?"

"I'll tell you when I see it."

And with that, Gannon got to work. It was a monumental task to go through every single Begum belonging, but there was only one way to do it: start somewhere, anywhere. He pulled down a box, lifted the lid, and rummaged through it. Dishes. He pulled down a second box: glassware and silverware.

This was going to be fun.

Mobley joined in and the next hour and forty-five minutes passed surprisingly fast. They weren't getting anywhere, but at least they had something to do, which was a small measure of progress. Boxes of clothes. Boxes of books. Boxes of gardening tools. Boxes of dresses and underwear.

Catching her breath, Mobley leaned against the shelves again. She was panting hard and rubbing her leg. Gannon noticed and pushed away a box of collectible coins.

"You okay, partner?" he said cautiously.

She nodded and then shrugged.

"You sure?"

"I told you the other day about MS, right? Good days and bad days."

"And today is a bad day?" Gannon ventured.

"It's not the best day."

"How do you feel? I mean, if you don't mind me asking."

She slid down the steel column and sat on the ground, still massaging her leg.

"It's not the same for everyone. For me, at the moment, it's fatigue. I'm so tired, you have no idea. And I get these spasms in my legs. I could have trouble walking in a couple years. I try not to think about it."

She closed her eyes, leaning back.

"You want to take the rest of the day off?" Gannon asked.

"No, it's fine."

"It's no problem. I can cover for you."

"Thanks, but I want to stay. It's bad enough that in the near future I won't be able to do this job. I want to work while I still can."

He nodded to her, respecting her choice. He couldn't imagine what he would do in the circumstances. Then again, he was a couple of decades older than she was. Their perspectives were different. What he knew for sure, though, was that she was a tough kid.

"You got it, partner."

"What are we even searching for?" she asked.

Gannon looked at all the boxes on the concrete floor. They had gone through most of them so far.

"The question is, what *haven't* we found?"

"What?"

"Tell me, Mobley, have you seen any toys?"

She sat up straighter. "No."

"Videogames? Basketballs, baseballs, soccer balls?"

"No."

"We've gone through all the clothes, right?"

"I've never seen so many neckties," she said.

"Exactly. We went through everything and didn't find anything related to kids. No toys, no baby pictures, no children's clothes."

Gannon had to consider the possibility that CPS had packed his clothes when he was moved into foster care. They may have taken a few toys, too, but certainly not all of it. Most importantly, there would've been pictures. Parents always had pictures. They hadn't even found any, either physical or on the computers and phones.

"So what are you saying, Gannon?"

"The kid wasn't living in the Begum house."

He was even more frustrated now about not being allowed to interrogate the child. Nevertheless, that didn't mean they couldn't take the long way around to find the information they were searching for.

If he wasn't the son of John and Larissa Begum, and he hadn't been adopted, then…

"We're going to start looking for missing children."

"What?"

"We're going back to the station, loading up on coffee, and you and me are going to settle in to scroll through missing children reports. Kids just don't spontaneously appear. He has to be in the system somewhere."

# CHAPTER 26

His name was Younce and he looked like a younger version of Mr. Rogers. He was even wearing a cardigan even though it was over eighty outside. He shifted on his seat at the kitchen table. It took Lucas vast amounts of willpower not to push the table forward and crush him to death.

"What?" he said at a barely audible volume. "I don't understand."

"I'm sorry to be putting you in this less than enviable position, Mr. Ramsdale."

Lucas blinked like a cheap marionette. Everything had gone quite well so far today. He hadn't slept at home after drinking himself into a stupor. He had remained away, mostly in his truck. He was still groggy and hung over.

In the morning, he had returned to the house and it was with surprising serenity that Tori had let him inside. Things were still tense between them, but they both understood the importance of today's meeting with Younce. He was an insurance claims adjuster.

Tori had agreed that they should do as if everything was normal during the meeting. Even though she wasn't sitting at the table with them, she stood just outside the kitchen to listen in.

"We regret to inform you that we won't be issuing benefits on your policy, Mr. Ramsdale."

"Why? My property burned to the ground. You've seen the damages. You've seen how there's nothing that can be salvaged."

Younce nodded, twirling a pencil between his fingers. "I appreciate your frustration, sir. However, what you need to understand is that everything so far in our investigation points to arson."

"No way," Lucas muttered, shaking his head.

"We have reports from Fire Chief Dugan, from Sheriff McKenzie, and preliminary findings from our independent lab."

"I don't know what happened, but I sure as hell didn't set the fire!"

"Evidence indicates a deliberate act."

"Bullshit!"

"If your policy had been subscribed more than two years ago, you might have a case. But it hasn't been two years, Mr. Ramsdale, and you aren't covered under the arson provisions. And if I may speak frankly…"

He leaned forward and Lucas instinctively did the same.

"What?"

"Conjecture isn't your friend, sir. We've been able to uncover the fact that your business is struggling. Your main investor pulled out. Zoning is still an issue. You had to lay off employees because you couldn't pay them. This is what we call aggravating circumstances."

Lucas was fuming. "You can't prove anything!"

"You're right, we can't. And we don't have to. We're not a court of law. We're an insurance company. Since we have reason to believe arson was involved and that your profile doesn't meet the proper requirements, it is our decision that your claim be rejected."

No longer possessing the same comforting demeanor as Mr. Rogers, Younce put his paperwork inside his briefcase, although he left his report on the table. He stood up.

"I'm goddamn innocent! I was never late on a single premium. You can't get away with this. I'm gonna sue your ass!"

"That is your prerogative, Mr. Ramsdale. From experience, I doubt it will change anything for you, though. But my work here is done. Good luck to you."

He stretched his hand toward Lucas. He didn't take it. Younce then turned around and nodded to Tori. She nodded back. Before she could accompany him to the exit, he was already walking away.

A second after Younce left, Lucas stood up. His chair tumbled back. He turned, looking at it as if it was a mysterious artifact. He was zoning out.

"Lucas?"

By way of answering, he kicked the chair. It bounced loudly against the cupboards. He kicked it again and broke off one of the legs.

"Lucas, stop it!"

"I'm bankrupt!" he shouted. "Can you see that? Word of arson is going to spread. There's no way in hell I'll get any new investors now."

His face went rigid with anger before softening as he was on the brink of tears. Then it was back to anger. His skin was blood red. He was foaming at the mouth.

Tori came forward although she stayed on the other side of the table. "We need to talk about last night."

"Now? You want to talk about your precious feelings now?!"

"No, not our feelings. We need to talk about the things you said to me. It was unacceptable. After all the years and all the support I gave you…"

"Spare me!" he shouted. "You never supported me. You only ever cared about yourself."

She was flabbergasted. "What?! I moved halfway across the country for you."

"If you had really wanted to support me, you would've gotten a real job instead of living in your fantasy art world. I mean, you have to know that this is bullshit, right? Who ever makes it as an artist, uh? Who has ever made a dime with painting, aside from a few foreign fags? Uh, tell me!"

Tori simply stood there, immobile. Her jaw was hanging open, reeling back at the harshest words she had ever heard him say. Then she almost smiled.

It had taken her all this time to realize that there was no love between them anymore. She had understood that his feelings for her weren't as strong as hers, but now she saw that she didn't have any either.

It was time that she stood up for herself.

"You're an asshole," she said.

"Oh, I'm an asshole? You're the lazy bitch who won't get a job to help your family, and *you* call me an asshole? You're the one who invited that creepy kid into our lives."

She ignored his attack, something she should've done a long time ago.

"Where were you last night?"

"What does that have to do with anything?"

"You're having an affair again," she said, matter-of-factly.

That made him laugh in a cruel, soulless way. He shrugged and rolled his eyes. "Okay, fine. Yes, I'm having an affair. You're happy now? That's what you wanted to hear? I've been seeing someone else. I've been plowing your friend Felicia for the last six months."

Tori stopped breathing. *Felicia*?!

Could this be true? Was he just making this up to cause her pain? Then a hundred memories came flooding back. No, they weren't memories; they were pieces of evidence.

She would call Felicia after Lucas left, and she wasn't there. Lucas would be away while she was with Felicia, and suddenly she had somewhere to be. They were finding excuses to be together. It all made sense.

Being betrayed by her husband wasn't as horrific as being stabbed in the back by her only friend.

Lucas found amusement in that. He grinned.

He headed to the front door, but turned before

leaving. "Now you know what it's like to have your life destroyed, just like mine."

# CHAPTER 27

Gannon didn't dare rub his eyes even though he could barely see straight.

He had spent the last five hours staring at a computer monitor, scrolling through picture after picture of missing children. He feared that he would skip the one he was looking for if he blinked. He couldn't afford that, so he binged on coffee and desperately craved a cigarette.

According to recent statistics, there were about eight hundred thousand children reported missing each year. A quarter of those were kidnapped by family members, usually as part of custody battles. Another sixty thousand were abducted by strangers, although most cases were quickly resolved. Only about a hundred or so were taken by deranged criminals.

This meant that roughly half a million of those missing children were runways or unexplained disappearances. It was a huge pool to sift through for Gannon and Mobley.

"Got anything?" she asked him.

She was sitting next to him, a computer of her own on the desk, angled toward her.

"Yes, I found him an hour ago, but I'm continuing to search because I love looking at low quality pictures."

She groaned and shook her head. Her expression was the only moment of levity in his entire day, so he enjoyed it.

The saving grace was that they knew Boyd's gender, race, and age range. This narrowed down the pool significantly. Searching by his name yielded no result though, so they resorted to good old-fashioned browsing, starting with this state and slowly expanding.

And so they scrolled. The computer had thousands of results and all the two detectives had to do was look at the picture which took up the left-hand side of the screen, see if it could possibly match their target, and then hit a key to move on to the next candidate.

Click, squint, click again.

Judge. Click.

Judge. Click.

Judge. Click.

Some of the kids had a passing resemblance and Gannon wrote down the reference number in case he needed to return to it later, but for the most part they both went through the process of elimination in a very fast and methodological way.

At three o'clock, Gannon began to wonder when Captain Vail would show up. No doubt, he would consider this whole endeavor futile and make them stop. Maybe it would be for the best. Maybe Vail would see that talking to the kid was the right thing to do after all.

For the time being though, Gannon was prepared to stay here until after his shift ended. He had to.

"Wait, wait, wait!" Mobley said excitedly.

"You found him?"

Gannon propelled his swivel chair closer to hers and craned his neck to look at her computer.

"That's not him," he said. "They got the birthday wrong."

Then again, that wouldn't be the first time. Data entry was a notoriously unreliable field. Also, they couldn't trust the posted height and weight since children changed so fast as they grew up.

"Look at his face, Gannon. Look at the features."

They had a reference image of Boyd taken the day after he had been found. The two cops went back and forth looking at it, comparing their picture to the one on the screen. Both had a round face with soft skin. The features blended into each other. The hair was the same color, although shorter on the computer.

"Look at those eyes," Mobley said, pointing with a pen. "That's him. That's a hundred percent him."

"You're right," the older man replied after a beat.

The name on the report was listed as Cody Irwin Aten. He had been reported missing from Lynnwood, Washington.

"That's across the country," Mobley breathed incredulously.

Gannon didn't feel tired anymore. If anything, he felt energized. He felt twenty years old again. He stood up, struggling not to jump to any conclusion, and had his partner find him a number for the Seattle Police Department.

With the time zones, most people on the West Coast had to be on their lunch break. Gannon didn't want to delay any further, so he called right away.

The mention that this was related to a missing child case didn't make hearts go aflutter. Most calls were probably dead ends, so there was very little enthusiasm. Gannon talked to a receptionist who passed him on to a civilian secretary.

She said she was new here and wasn't sure how it worked, so she switched the call to a beat officer who was manning a desk. He was as useful as a thick steak in a vegan restaurant and called his sergeant over to take over. The man had a mouth full of corned beef sandwich and Gannon could only understand half of what he said. Still, the guy was an old pro and he knew how to search his files.

"It says Barrera handled this case. That's who you probably want to talk to."

"That would be great," Gannon replied, hoping that he wasn't about to be informed that this Barrera guy was now retired, or worse, dead.

"Hold on, I'll patch you through to the cell."

"Thank you, Sergeant."

The phone rang six times. Gannon was depressed all over again. He didn't have time to play games and he was certain that this would lead to another day being wasted. He was going over what kind of message he would leave on the man's inbox when someone answered.

"Barrera."

The voice belonged to a woman. She sounded older.

Her voice was hoarse. She was a smoker, which made him like her immediately.

"Yeah, hi. I'm Detective Gannon," he said, giving her his credentials with the State Police. "Listen, I'm inquiring about a missing person you handled and I think it's related to a case I'm working on. The name is Cody Irwin Aten."

There was a brief pause before the woman spoke. "Hold on, I'm pulling over."

There was a rustling sound on the line. Barrera was obviously in her car and, because of that, Gannon decided not to put the phone on speaker. Mobley understood and came closer to eavesdrop.

"Okay, talk to me."

"It's a strange case," Gannon began. "There was a double homicide in this sleepy town called Hillford. A couple was found dead in their home after a child named Boyd was picked up walking down the road at night. He said the couple were his folks. No next of kin, the kid went into foster care, and I'm the poor schmuck who has to solve the case."

"Right," Barrera said, followed by sound of a lighter flicking on.

"All my leads hit a brick wall until I learned that Mrs. Begum, our vic, couldn't have children. There are no adoption records either. Me and my partner started to dig, figure we would look at missing persons, and we stumbled upon this one who looks an awful lot like ours. Cody Irwin Aten. So I'm sure you can see how puzzled I am. A Little Leaguer with a false identity, it's not something you see every day."

Gannon's mind was already working different hypotheses. Could this be some sort of federal protection case? The kid had seen something he shouldn't have before being placed in the witness relocation program? He was feeling very much out of his depth.

"Are you absolutely sure that it's Cody Irwin Aten?"

"All I have to go on is a picture, but I'm confident." Gannon glanced at Mobley who was nodding emphatically. "We're very confident."

"Christ…"

"Is that a good thing or a bad thing, Detective? The missing report doesn't have any details. It just says to contact Seattle PD."

"What I'm about to tell you is in strict confidence, do you understand? Until we have confirmation that we're dealing with the same minor, it has to stay between us."

"And my partner," Gannon added. "She's listening in right now."

"Okay, sure."

"What's the deal?"

Detective Barrera took a long drag off her cigarette, making Gannon jealous.

"Two years ago, Cody Irwin Aten was found with two corpses next to him. His parents. He had killed them using a razor blade. Slashed the jugulars, the wrists, the femoral arteries. It was a bloodbath."

Jesus…

"And before you start doubting my story, let me assure you that the whole thing was recorded by the nanny cam. A cute little stuffed animal on a shelf in the living room. It caught everything, HD quality. The case was a slam dunk. But what do you do when it's a little kid, right?"

"What happened?" Gannon inquired, his mouth dry.

"He was committed to a children's psychiatric facility. Only the place wasn't equipped to handle serious offenders, you know? They're kids. Security was crap."

"And?"

"The boy escaped seven months ago."

# CHAPTER 28

Dr. Curnutt's fingers tightened around her pen. She looked at her patient, Zola. She was fidgeting on the couch in front of her, avoiding her eyes.

"Go on, Zola. What happened next?"

The little girl was not quite ten and she looked even smaller for her age. She was delicate, as if she was made of fine bone china. And yet, even though this session was their most difficult so far, there was inner strength in her.

"He made me sit on his lap," she said. "I told him I didn't want to."

"And he ignored you?"

Zola nodded. "He held me down by the waist. His hands were really strong, squishing me. His breath smelled bad when he kissed my cheek. He made me do multiplications, the table of seven, and he put his hand on my leg."

Even though she was staring at the floor and wringing her hands, her voice remained solid.

"His hand went up under my skirt."

"Did that make you feel afraid, Zola?"

"Yes. And angry. His fingers were rough. The longer

he did it, the more rough he became. It hurt. I told him to stop. He called it our special game."

Dr. Curnutt struggled to keep her temper out of her voice. "And did he stop?"

"No. He said that all math teachers did this with their favorite students. It's to make sure we learn correctly."

As far as she was concerned, Dr. Curnutt had a very clear definition of doctor-patient privilege. Her first order of business once this session was over would be to call the police.

She had been in trouble before because it turned out a patient had confounded fantasy and reality. It had led to an innocent man getting arrested. However, Dr. Curnutt had decided long ago that she would never hesitate to take the side of her patients, especially when they were children.

First, she needed more details. She needed to prod Zola about the specifics of the situation. This was obviously a job for the police, but Dr. Curnutt also saw a therapeutic benefit to it. By making the child's memories concrete, she would be able to address the root of the event and, most importantly, make sure that Zola wouldn't ferment guilt.

She opened her mouth to ask a question—always difficult to do when dealing with sexual abuse—when there was a knock at the door. She was instantly enraged. She had no other appointment this afternoon and there was still twenty minutes until this session was over. Zola's mother wasn't scheduled to come back until then.

The knocking continued, becoming more insistent.

"Excuse me for a moment, okay, Zola?"

Dr. Curnutt stood up from her chair and opened the door a crack. Standing before her was the foster father of one of her other patients.

"Mr. Ramsdale?"

"I need to talk to you, Doc."

"I see. I'm with a patient at the moment. Can you come back in twenty minutes?"

He shook his head. "No, this can't wait. Please, I need to talk to you."

"Is Boyd all right?"

"That's what I need to talk to you about. It's important and I can't wait."

With a conflicted sigh, Dr. Curnutt glanced at her watch and then at Zola who was staring into the distance. Frankly, she wondered how much more she would be able to tell her this afternoon. These cases tended to evolve very sluggishly.

"All right, give me a moment."

~ ~ ~ ~

It took a couple of minutes for Dr. Curnutt to cut her session short with Zola. The girl didn't seem disappointed that it was over. If anything, she appeared to be relieved that she didn't have to talk about her gruesome experience again today.

The sun was shining and Zola said she would wait for her mother outside. She had brought her jump rope, as she always did, and waiting wasn't a problem for her. Dr. Curnutt peeked from behind a curtain and saw that she was safely in front of the house.

The mature woman turned around and faced Lucas Ramsdale. He was definitely not as serene as the child.

"What's wrong with Boyd?" she asked. "What is it that couldn't wait?"

"I want to know about the kid."

"Boyd?" She felt a strange detachment from him as he referred to Boyd as *the kid*. "What do you want to know?"

"Do you think he could have committed arson?"

Frowning, she walked to her desk, going around it. She didn't sit down since she could tell that Ramsdale was too restless to do so himself.

"You're talking about the fire at your real estate project?"

"The cops, the fire department—hell, the goddamn insurance company!—they think it was arson."

"And why are you asking me about Boyd?"

"Because he's creepy, okay? The way he talks… He hinted that he knows how insurance money works. I think he had something to do with the fire."

"Mr. Ramsdale…"

"Lucas."

"Lucas. I'm a therapist, not a police officer."

He ran a hand through his hair and scratched his face where a beard was slowly growing back. "It's just… Everything is piling up, you know? There's the fire, there's the time when he tortured a fish. He didn't play with it; he tortured it. He threatened my buddy Jasper's son."

"Threatened him?" Dr. Curnutt asked, her interest growing.

"Yes. And Jasper believes that Boyd made his kid fall off his bike. I'm talking intentionally. He made him get into an accident. He broke his arm. He's pretty banged up. So between that and everything else… And you told my wife that the kid might be a psychopath. You did tell her that, right?"

Dr. Curnutt winced, not too comfortable at having her diagnoses repeated, analyzed, and twisted around.

"I also told your wife that it was too soon for a proper diagnosis. I think Boyd requires many more therapy sessions. I'm talking years. I also mentioned that he should meet with a neuropsychiatrist. There's an outstanding one I trust at Johns Hopkins and…"

"Is he a psycho or not, Doc?"

"I can't answer that, Lucas. I truly can't."

"I'm… I'm scared of him. I'm scared of what he could do."

At that, Dr. Curnutt offered a soothing smile. "I understand your concerns, but I assure you that you have nothing to fear from Boyd. He may be troubled, given his past, but you have nothing to fear from him. He's just a little boy. What I suggest is that you decompress."

"What? I'm not making this up!"

"I know, Lucas. What I mean is that, sometimes, stressful situations can make us take issues out of proportion. My professional opinion is that you should go home and relax. If you want, I could write you a prescription for Xanax."

Lucas was hurt by that. "I'm not crazy. That little kid is, and I want him out of my house!"

He walked away, slamming the door behind him.

She understood his reaction. It wasn't rare among parents. No one wanted to believe that their children suffered from an abnormal condition. Most of the time, the frustration came from the knowledge that they were helpless, they couldn't make their kids feel better, which was counterintuitive to the quintessence of being a parent.

While she didn't blame Lucas Ramsdale for the way he had confronted her, it made her second guess her own judgment. She opened the bottom drawer and pulled out Boyd's file.

She sat down and reviewed her notes. Page by page, she read it all, wishing her handwriting had improved over the years. She was still convinced that there was no clear pathology with the child. He was too young to be diagnosed as a psychopath or sociopath.

But there were clear signs that something was wrong with him.

She started to wonder if perhaps he needed more than therapy. He needed to be medicated. In fact, she started evaluating whether he would be better treated if he was committed to a psychiatric ward. It would be a shock to him at such a young age, but it was because he was so young that there was hope that his condition would improve.

Torture. Arson.

He may have hurt another child.

Those were tangible signs that he was a danger to others. Dr. Curnutt hated being in this position. She had to make a decision that would change not only a child's life, but the lives of the people around him as well. Nevertheless, they weren't her concern. Her duty was to look after her patients' well-being.

She flipped through the folder until she reached the last page. There were several contact numbers. One of them was for a Detective Gannon. Wasn't it her role to inform the police if she had suspicions of any wrongdoing? After all, she was about to do just that in Zola's case.

She reached for the phone and started to dial the number.

Was she going too fast? Shouldn't she give Boyd the benefit of the doubt? Calling the police so soon in his therapy might drive him away. Perhaps she needed more time to get him to open up. Perhaps she could comfort him. Perhaps she could heal him.

She put the phone down.

~ ~ ~ ~

The girl was jumping her rope in the driveway of the Victorian house. She mumbled a rhyme to herself, but was otherwise quiet. She stopped when a boy approached, holding his bicycle upright. He hadn't come from the street. It seemed like he had come from around the house.

"Hi," he said.

She hesitated. "Hi."

"I'm Boyd. What's your name?"

"Zola."

"Are you waiting for your mom to pick you up?"

"Yeah."

"I like Dr. Talia. She's nice. Do you like her?"

"She's your doctor too?" Zola asked, suddenly warming up to him.

"Yeah. She's helping me understand some stuff."

They stared at each other. Boyd liked that she didn't look at him with disdain like Evan and his friends did. He came a little closer.

"I was near the window before," he said.

"What?"

"I just happened to overhear what you said. You shouldn't let your teacher get away with what he did. If he touched you, you should hurt him."

She was transfixed by his words, visibly mortified that he knew her secret.

"Zola," he continued. "You always have to punish those who hurt you. You wouldn't be doing anything wrong."

Boyd nodded to drive home his point. He got on his bike and pedaled away.

# CHAPTER 29

Boyd slowed down and took his feet off the pedals as he approached the Harbuck house. Felicia was out front, sitting in the grass next to a flowerbed. She was wearing cut-off jeans and an old flannel shirt tied around her waist. She was barefoot.

She plucked out weeds here and there, but she was far more interested in what was on her phone. She scrolled with her thumb and only ever returned to the gardening when there was a lull in whatever she was watching. Next to her, a plastic wine glass sat on the grass, surprisingly stable.

A loud mechanical noise came and went. It originated from behind the house, the distinctive sound of a lawnmower. There was a fence around the backyard and a gate kept it out a view from the street. However, Jasper was visible through the slats as he walked from left to right.

Taking his time, Boyd approached, staying on the curb. Felicia took a sip of her drink. She was sluggish and Boyd knew immediately that it wasn't lemonade in the glass. It really was white wine. What was strange to him was that it wasn't even lunchtime yet. Adults clearly could do anything they wanted.

Well, that didn't have to apply *only* to adults...

Felicia noticed him as she drank. Her eyes were glazed over. She kept the glass in her hand, the rim below her lips.

"Oh. Hi, Boyd."

"Hi, Felicia." He set his bike down on the curb and crossed the lawn toward her. "You're gardening?"

She snorted as if she herself believed that what she was doing could barely be described as gardening. "Yeah. Evan isn't home."

"I see," Boyd replied.

"And honestly? Even if he was here, I don't think he would want to see you." The kid nodded, clearly dejected. "I'm sorry, Boyd. I'm sure you'll make lots of new friends when school starts. There'll be plenty of children your age to play with."

"That's okay, Felicia. I know not everybody likes me. But I'm sure one day I'll get a best friend. Like you and Tori."

She perked up at that. "Oh?"

"Yes, she tells me all the time that you're her best friend. She says she's happy to have you in her life."

Felicia didn't know how to respond to that. She smiled, but looked away from Boyd. She drank and didn't stop until there was almost nothing left.

"She is your best friend too, isn't she?"

"Yes, of course," Felicia said. "Tell her I say hi. I'll call her later."

"Okay. Bye, Felicia."

"Bye, Boyd."

He turned around, heading for his bike. Suddenly, he spun on his heels.

"Hey, can I use the bathroom please?"

That caught her off guard. "Uh, sure. You know where it is, right?"

"Yes, thank you."

Boyd gave her a wide, grateful grin and went into the house. Even here, the engine was deafening. He saw the backyard through the kitchen window and Jasper was bare-chested, pushing that lawnmower back and forth.

The bathroom was on the left, but what held Boyd's attention was what was on the kitchen table. It was a cell phone. He grabbed it, turned it on, and Boyd saw a dozens of icons.

He took the phone with him to the bathroom and, four minutes later, he came out. The phone returned to the kitchen table and Boyd left the house.

He waved at Felicia who was still juggling drinking, weeding, and playing with her phone. "Thanks. Bye!"

"Bye, Boyd."

He got on his bike and headed to town. He took the long way around. He wanted to avoid the schools, any place he was liable to run into other kids.

He turned onto the sloping street where Evan had gotten into an accident and focused his attention on the Candy Shop. The neon sign was on and there were no other bicycles out front. He slowed down and eventually stopped.

He looked through the window. There was no fancy display; just corporate stickers from the various candy manufacturers. He couldn't see kids inside. He went in.

A bell chimed over the door, exactly like in an old movie. Almost immediately, Mr. Larsen appeared out of nowhere. He stood behind the counter and smiled broadly.

"Hi! Welcome!"

"Hello," Boyd said timidly, realizing that cheery music was piped in from the ceiling. It was Radio Disney.

The store smelled wonderful, a mixture of chocolate and fruity flavors. On the left, the lower part of the wall was nothing but shelves which contained standard candy bars, the kind you found at the supermarket. Some were in packages, but most were single bars.

The shelves were no higher than four feet. It was probably so that kids could access everything, Boyd thought. On top was a display of balloons and party decorations. On another wall was a rack of glass jars. Inside were gummy bears, jellybeans, Milk Duds, malt balls, bubblegum, and dozens of other candies.

In the middle of the store, there was a circular table with drawer bins from which you could scoop out entire bags of individually wrapped candy. Boyd had never encountered so many sweets.

"See anything that strikes your fancy, young man?"

Boyd didn't reply right away. He looked at a jar of red Twizzlers. He looked at a jar of Tootsie Rolls.

"You're the boy who's staying with the Ramsdales, aren't you?" He nodded to the old man. "You sure got a raw deal, son. I'm sorry."

"Thank you," Boyd said as he continued roaming through the store.

He inspected a bag of jawbreakers and then looked past the checkout counter. There was a narrow corridor that led to the storeroom. There was also another door before the hallway hooked left.

The reason he had come here.

"Say, are the kids still giving you a hard time? I remember when they practically ran you off the road."

"No, it's fine. We had a conversation and they stopped. Thank you for caring, sir."

Mr. Larsen beamed. "What a well-behaved young man you are! Tell me, what are you in the mood for? I just had this new order come in, four-flavored lollipops from this little company out of Denver. They're delicious!"

"Sir, do you think I could use the bathroom?"

"Sure thing, son. It's this way, down the hall and to the right."

He pointed at the hallway Boyd had noticed before.

"Thank you."

Boyd walked past the counter and went down the hallway. He put his hand on the bathroom door and glanced over his shoulder. The elderly man wasn't looking at him. He was bent over a ledger. Boyd walked further back, going around the corner, and found what he was looking for. It was the office and the door was already partly open.

It was small, mostly just a desk with a computer and

some gray metal filing cabinets. Boyd walked in and gently closed the door behind him. Without hesitation, he went to the phone.

Just over a minute later, he tiptoed out, saw that the owner was still busy with his work, and he went into the bathroom so he could flush, therefore announcing that he was done here.

Mr. Larsen smiled when he came back out.

"I took the liberty of preparing something for you. Here." He handed Boyd a small paper bag. "I saw you looking at the Twizzlers before. I also added a few Sour Patch Kids and Jelly Tots."

"Thanks!"

Boyd reached inside his pocket for change. Tori was giving him an allowance because she said he should learn about money. Mr. Larsen stopped him with a wave.

"Don't bother, son. This is on me. I want to welcome you to Steep Gorge."

Just as he was walking out, a few older kids he'd never seen before came into the store. He was beginning to like this town after all.

~ ~ ~ ~

An hour later, Boyd rode his bike by the Harbuck house again. Only the scene had changed.

Felicia was nowhere to be seen on the front lawn. Her wine glass was next to the flowerbed, tipped over. More importantly was the crowd which had gathered on the street. They were chatting amongst each other, their gaze fixed on the house as if a show was about to start.

A police car was parked on the curb.

Boyd got off his bike and pushed it closer to the crowd. Tori was right in the middle, standing with her arms crossed. He joined her.

"Hey, Tori. I went home for lunch, but you weren't there. I came here to see if Felicia knew where you were. What's going on?"

"I don't know, sweetie," she replied, beginning to chew on her fingernails. "I tried to ask Deputy Gonzales, but he wouldn't say anything."

Around them, the neighbors were gossiping. Someone hypothesized that there had been a robbery. Another wondered if it was drugs, because it was always about drugs, they said.

The front door opened and the crowd went quiet. The show was truly beginning. It took a moment, but Sheriff McKenzie came out. Next to him was Deputy Gonzales who was leading Jasper out.

He was handcuffed and looking down, avoiding the spectators. He was evidently under arrest. They put him in the back of the police cruiser.

Felicia appeared in the doorframe and remained on the porch. Her face was white. Tori looked at her. What she had learned about her and Lucas still made her sick to her stomach, and yet her first instinct was to offer comfort. She hated herself for that. She hurried forward, not caring that Boyd was following her.

"What's happening? Why was Jasper arrested?"

Felicia was on the brink of tears. Her lower lip

trembled. "I can't believe it, Tori. I just cannot believe it."

"What?"

"The police came over because they received an anonymous tip. They found something on Jasper's phone."

"What *something* are you talking about?"

"Pictures. They found pictures, Tori. Disgusting pictures."

Tears were running down her cheeks and she turned away from the crowd, although she didn't walk into the house. It was as if the place reminded her of a nightmare and she wanted to distance herself from it.

"Calm down. Tell me what's going on. What kind of pictures?"

At last, Felicia's features hardened. "There were pictures of a little boy on my husband's phone. I saw it over the Sheriff's shoulder. He was naked! There was no face in the images, but it was a young boy and he was completely naked!"

"Oh my God…" Tori whispered.

"All these years we've been married and I never suspected my husband was a pedophile. Our life is ruined. Ruined!"

Felicia buried her face in her hands and wept. The right thing for Tori to do would be to take her into her arms, to get her into the house, out of view from the neighbors. The fact was that she didn't want to do the right thing. This woman was sleeping with her husband. She had betrayed her.

As awful as the situation was, Tori couldn't help feeling a little satisfied at Felicia suffering. She hated herself for it, it was petty, but revenge was thrilling.

The two of them remained there for several minutes, neither noticing Boyd getting back on his bike and leaving the scene.

Neither noticing the smirk on his face.

# CHAPTER 30

Captain Vail sighed and gestured for his two guests to shut the door.

"Tell me all this again very slowly," he said.

Gannon spun around and closed the door, careful not to drop his beverage. He returned to the desk where Mobley was already sitting down. She hadn't been invited to sit, but he had known her long enough now that he could tell her legs were tired.

"Detective, get rid of that, please. No soft drinks are allowed in my office."

"Oh, come on, Cap…"

Gannon held on to his can of Cherry Coke as if it was the Holy Grail. He had scheduled it earlier than usual this week. He needed it more than ever because of the stress.

"Toss it."

After two seconds of hesitation, Gannon committed a cardinal sin: he guzzled the soda until he couldn't take it anymore. There was barely anything left when he stopped. He smiled smugly at Mobley and his superior before setting the can down on top of a cabinet across the room. He figured a man like Vail would get his panties up in a bunch if he didn't recycle, too.

"Happy?"

"You'll always be a smartass, uh?"

"As long as the *smart* part applies."

Vail chose not to respond and sat down in his executive chair. Gannon sat next to Mobley.

"From the top, Detective."

Gannon produced his notepad even though he knew the case by heart.

"The kid who directed us to the Hillford murders may not actually be Boyd Begum. By all accounts, John and Larissa had no children. This was confirmed by checking with her gynecologist and a fertility clinic."

He glanced at Mobley so she could endorse this. "That's right. Then we located Larissa Begum's best friend and she stated that the victims had no plans to ever adopt. We verified. There are no records, either here, or in North Carolina, that the Begums ever went through the adoption process, or even foster care procedures."

"So obviously, we had a problem on our hands," Gannon picked up. "Who's the damn kid? CPS took him in without any records, taking his word that he was this Boyd Begum character. Someone who doesn't exist. The Begum house had no toys or children's clothes either. We took it upon ourselves to search through missing persons. Took a while and we finally got a match."

"Who?" Captain Vail asked.

Mobley checked her own notepad to make sure all the facts were right. "Cody Irwin Aten, from the state of Washington. It's hard to tell because the only thing we have to go on is the picture. We are pretty sure it's him though, Boyd Begum."

"How sure, Detective?"

"Rather sure."

"Anyway," Gannon interrupted. "We called Seattle and talked to this Detective Barrera who handled the case. This is where things get interesting. Little Cody escaped from a children's psychiatric facility."

"What?!"

"That was pretty much our reaction too, Cap. The boy killed both his parents with a razor blade. Remind you of anything?"

"Jesus…" the captain whispered.

"So we want to be clear on the procedure going forward," Gannon said, his tone more serious now, his Cherry Coke long forgotten. "My police blood wants to haul in the kid, at the very least for questioning, but I have a feeling you might have a different opinion."

Vail stared at the blotter on his desk, lost in thought.

"Captain, shouldn't we bring in the child?" Mobley asked. "The facts are strange, yes, but there's essentially a killer on the loose. An escaped murderer."

The superior officer looked up, doubt no longer in his features. "No."

"Excuse me?"

"We have to tread carefully, Detective Mobley."

"But…"

"I hate when that happens, but he's right," Gannon added, puzzling his partner even more.

"I don't understand."

"Detective, try to think two moves ahead. Look at different possible outcomes. We are dealing with a minor."

"A murderer."

"Allegedly," Vail corrected. "You said you're *rather* sure we're dealing with this Cody…"

"Cody Irwin Aten."

"Right. You don't have absolute confirmation that it's him. Think of the consequences. We bring in a poor helpless child in foster care, the press gets wind of this, and we're wrong. We would be crucified, Detective."

Gannon nodded reluctantly. "It's true. At this level, we can't afford to be wrong."

"The entire department would suffer," Vail said, jabbing his desk with his finger. "We would never recover. Can you imagine the lawsuits on top of the bad press? I'd lose my career and the two of you would wind up in dead-end assignments. Nobody has anything to gain by rushing this."

"But sir, at the risk of repeating myself, there is a killer on the loose and we might know who it is!"

"All I'm saying is that we can't rush this, okay? Let me submit some questions to the state attorney's office, see what they have to say."

"Yes, Captain," Mobley said, suitably chastised.

Gannon shifted in his chair, one of the most uncomfortable he had ever experienced. "So what's the next step?"

"We wait for legal advice. I'll ask the state attorney's office about the feasibility of DNA tests. Maybe we can find a way of doing some tests without arousing suspicions. If we match Begum with Cody…"

"Cody Irwin Aten."

"Right, Cody Irwin Aten. If they turn out to be the same person, then we move in and we'll all look like heroes."

"Sir, DNA testing can take weeks."

"Police work is about patience, Detective. Stick to that. Don't cut corners or you'll end up like your partner over here."

Gannon figured he was being dismissed and he left his seat. He grabbed his Cherry Coke on the way out and made a show of finishing it before leaving the office. Mobley joined him in the bullpen.

"God…" she muttered in frustration.

"Vail can be a world-class dick, but he knows procedure. Police work is not always about swooping in and saving the day in the nick of time."

"Yes, but we're *riiiight there*. I hate the thought of having to wait weeks to get DNA results and close this case."

"I know," Gannon shrugged. "That doesn't mean we have to stay idle, though."

She perked up. "What do you have in mind?"

"Let's try to understand this kid better. Now that we know who he is—that *we think* we know who he is—let's see if there's anyone who can tell us about him. Come on."

They headed to his cubicle and Gannon gave serious thought to getting himself a second Cherry Coke. It was against his rules, but the previous one didn't feel as if it counted.

# CHAPTER 31

The sun was going down fast and with it came a brisk wind. Talia Curnutt looked out the window. Branches were swaying, but the leaves hadn't flipped over. She didn't think they were in for another storm.

"I think your water is boiling."

The voice came from the iPad propped up on the kitchen island. The FaceTime app was on and the entire screen was taken up by the face of a woman in her early thirties, Debra. She had long blond hair which was currently tucked behind the ears. She had glasses, a dark frame, which gave her a very scholarly appearance.

Dr. Curnutt turned toward the gas stove and, sure enough, a cloud of steam was rising, the water underneath bubbling.

"What would I do without you, my darling?"

"Are you being sarcastic, Talia?"

"Who, me?"

The two women laughed as Dr. Curnutt measured a small fistful of fettuccine, which she then dropped into the boiling water. Then, she turned to the saucepan next to it and stirred it. It smelled delicious, garlic and herbs slowly filling the room with the fresh fragrance.

Okay, it wasn't actually fresh. Dr. Curnutt and Debra cooked in batches. Sometimes they made sauces, which they froze in individual zip bags. Sometimes they made several pans of shepherd's pie.

On the first Sunday of every month, it was cookies. That was Dr. Curnutt's favorite day. It was playful, romantic. She loved how Debra always *accidentally* smeared cookie dough on her cheek which, of course, required her to lick it up.

"Will you save me a plate?" Debra asked.

"I can't make any promises, you know that. Cheers."

Dr. Curnutt poured herself a second glass of Merlot and toasted in front of the tablet. Debra was in New York City, in her hotel room. She herself lifted vodka tonic in a plastic cup. They drank silently for a moment, each enjoying the sip as they always did. It was better when they were together, but the Internet connection made it bearable.

Besides, Debra would only be gone for a few more days before coming home. She was at a conference on geriatric psychology. Incidentally, that was how they had met, geriatric psychology.

Dr. Curnutt had attended a seminar at Princeton where Debra was finishing her post-doctorate work. Love at first sight was an ugly cliché, but neither of them could find a better term for what had happened between them. A month later, they were moving in together.

"I can't wait to come home, Talia. People here are so boring."

Dr. Curnutt chuckled and took a long swallow of wine. "I take it you're not finding anyone to replace me over there?"

"Don't even joke about that. You know I love you."

"I love you too, but that doesn't mean that I'm not old enough to be your mother."

"Who cares about that? Besides, senior discounts could come in very handy, especially with our upcoming nuptials."

Dr. Curnutt groaned and drank again. "Debra, please…"

"I just don't see what the big deal is? We're not in the fifties anymore? This is the twenty-first century. People in love are actually allowed to spend their lives together, to get married."

"Steep Gorge is a small town, Debra. I have a practice to think about."

"Your patients are children. Children don't care if their therapist is out of the closet or not."

"Please, you have to give me time to wrap my head around this, my darling."

Debra sighed. "I know. I know. Go check on your pasta."

Turning around, Dr. Curnutt went to the stove and gave a stir to both the fettuccine and the sauce. How fortunate was she to have this young woman in her life. She even managed to check on the food from her hotel in Manhattan. Sometimes she wondered if she really deserved her.

When she returned to the island, she didn't go straight back to her Merlot. Instead, she grabbed the pill bottle next to it, pulling a tablet from it. She swallowed it with three mouthfuls of wine.

"Talia, is that a Valium?"

"It's just to take the edge off," the older woman replied, closing her eyes as if it was going to kick in at any moment.

"You should be careful about mixing that and the wine."

"What are you, my mother?"

"It feels like it sometimes," Debra said. "I don't want anything bad to happen to you."

Instead of firing back a flippant remark, Dr. Curnutt winked at her and gave her a silent kiss. She was well aware that self-medicating was wrong, and a serious problem among the medical community, but she knew her limits.

"What's stressing you, sweetheart?"

"Just one of my patients, that's all."

"I know you care, but you need to detach yourself. We talked about this, Talia."

"It can be hard. You don't have a practice, Debra. You don't know what it's like to interact with people so intimately."

Debra leaned closer to her camera. "But that doesn't mean you have to take on their problems yourself. You're there for guidance, to offer advice. You listen to their issues, but you leave them at the office."

"It doesn't always work that way, my darling."

Dr. Curnutt emptied the rest of the wine into her glass and took a sip. Already she felt the buzz. It was the alcohol, yes, but also the Valium working its way into her bloodstream. Her limbs felt much lighter.

"I'm fine," she said.

"Is it the same patient that's been giving you difficulty sleeping?"

"Now you're just fishing for details."

Debra shrugged and winked. "Can you blame me? I love you. I want to help you."

"You can't help me with this particular case. I don't think anyone can, unfortunately."

She had spent the last day going over her notes about Boyd Begum. She had tried to sound as professional and reassuring as possible when speaking to the Ramsdales. In reality, she was worried. The child did show signs of being very troubled. Maybe it had been a mistake not to call the police.

"Talk to me, Talia. I know that look. I know when something is bothering you."

"Stop worrying about me, my darling."

"Is it the boy who's in foster care?"

"You know I can't say anything."

"You haven't told me anything about him, but I know you've been taking a particular interest in his case. You stay up some nights and I know you're reading his file."

Dr. Curnutt's eyes welled up. Her girlfriend knew her better than anyone she had ever met. She was beautiful and smart and incredibly perceptive. She truly didn't deserve her. What's more, she wanted to tell her everything. She had a need to share her burden with her. Debra might even be in a position to offer helpful advice.

On the other hand, she was bound by her oath. She couldn't divulge any information, as much as she wanted to. She had to remain professional.

This gave her a moment to clear her head, to sort through her feelings. She made a decision about what she would do next. In the morning, she would call Detective Gannon and share her suspicions about her young, disturbed patient.

"Thank you, my darling."

"Okay, you're welcome," Debra said dubiously. "What are you thanking me for exactly?"

"I think I know what to do about this patient."

"Good, then. Go check on your pasta. My room service is about to get here any minute now. Then we can have a quiet romantic dinner."

The older woman snorted and rolled her eyes, covertly wiping them. "A romantic dinner over the Internet, ha!"

"It's the wave of the future."

They shared a laugh and drank some more. And then there was a rattling noise.

"What was that?"

"What?" Debra asked.

"I think I heard something. Hold on."

"Talia, wait…"

It was too late. Dr. Curnutt was already leaving the

kitchen. She went past the living room where everything was quiet. She walked beyond the playroom she kept for her young patients and walked toward her office.

She was on pins and needles, wondering if she should have brought a knife along. She padded into her office. It was dark and she held her breath.

The noise was louder.

She reached with her left hand and flicked on the switch. The recessed lights came on. The office was empty, just as she had left it. Then she saw it, the source of the noise. The window was unlocked and open, swinging back and forth against the wall.

With a sigh of relief, she marched forward to close it. That's when she asked herself a hard question: had she even opened the window?

She couldn't remember. Panic gripped her once again. If she hadn't done so, that meant someone else had. That meant there was an intruder in the house.

A hundred different scenarios popped into her head before she settled down. Her girlfriend had wondered about this, hadn't she? It was stupid to mix Valium and alcohol. That's what it was. She wasn't thinking straight.

She went to the window to close and lock it. Then she turned around, heading back to the kitchen. It was so silly, really.

"Debra," she began as she walked back into the kitchen. "You're not going to believe how ridiculous I was being–"

She stopped in her tracks. She had been wrong about everything. There was in fact an intruder in the house. He was standing in front of the stove.

It was Boyd.

# CHAPTER 32

Searching through Cody Irwin Aten's family tree turned out to be rather easy.

Mobley contacted Detective Barrera and she generously emailed scans of the most relevant information. From there, it was just a matter of sifting through the documents, which were unfortunately not thoroughly indexed. Gannon was happy to let his partner do the legwork on this.

The victims of this case were Joan Schott and Frank Aten, the kid's parents. Joan Schott had been adopted from an orphanage in Lithuania. Her lineage had never been known beyond that, and her adoption hadn't been a pleasant period in her life since she had left her family behind after high school.

Frank Aten had lost his own parents in a bush plane accident in the late nineties, during a fishing trip in Alaska. His only remaining family was a sister, Veronica. By all accounts, they had been close. She was a librarian and, for most of her life, she had worked for the city of Seattle.

When Mobley called, she discovered that the woman didn't work there anymore. That's when things got tricky.

Throughout the afternoon, the two detectives opened

a missing person case of a different nature. It seemed like Veronica Aten had not only left the state of Washington, but the United States altogether.

The former employer and landlord had no real clue where she had moved to. It finally took several calls to the IRS and the State Department—not to mention getting Captain Vail's green light to do so—in order to get a real answer. The woman had relocated to the United Kingdom.

In midafternoon, they found her new address. She lived in some place called Wivenhoe. Arranging a phone call took more time. She was at work and they left messages. The time zones didn't work in anyone's favor. She was too busy for a quick conversation and mentioned that her daughter had a piano recital tonight that she couldn't miss. They finally made an appointment for a Skype call.

"It's almost time," Mobley said, poking her head out of the station toward her partner.

Gannon accelerated the puffing on his cigarette and still had to stub it out before it was entirely consumed. He went inside the station and the atmosphere was almost serene. It was dinnertime and the day shift was gone. Only a skeleton crew remained, mostly people in uniform, on duty to handle emergencies.

"You sure I don't have time for a snack?"

Mobley shook her head. "I set it up in the interrogation room. We should be comfortable there. And private."

They went into the interview room. The younger woman had set up a computer on the table, with two chairs side by side in front of it. She had been careful to angle it so that the two-way mirror wouldn't face the camera. She'd thought of everything, Gannon realized, impressed. They sat down.

Checking her watch, Mobley decided it was time. She consulted her notepad for the appropriate contact information and typed it in. A second later, the familiar Skype melody resounded through the cramped interrogation room.

It went on and on.

"You sure you have the right number, Mobley?"

It continued to chime and finally ended up as a missed call.

"Please don't tell me we wasted our afternoon on this lady."

Mobley didn't say anything. She clenched her jaw and typed the username once more. The little song started from the beginning.

And continued, looping over and over again.

"Two will get you ten that we hit another wall," Gannon said.

Mobley glared at her partner, taking this as a personal affront. They both continued to stare at the black screen.

And then a face appeared. It was a woman in her late thirties. She had curly black hair and bags under her eyes. The lighting quality was poor and gave the image a yellow tint.

"Hello."

"Ms. Aten, hi!" Mobley exclaimed, caught off guard.

"I'm Detective Gannon. This is Detective Mobley. Can you see us okay?"

"Yes, it's fine."

The older man looked at his watch. "I'm sorry about the time. It's midnight in England right now?"

"Just about. Listen, I want to help you, but I have to get up early for work in the morning."

"Right, absolutely. So you're a librarian over there in Wavy Hoe?"

"Wivenhoe. Well, I have a Master of Library Science, but I'm not a librarian anymore. I do research and database analysis for an IT firm."

Gannon's eyebrows shot up. They were a long way from the typical image of the stern old lady in glasses who told you to keep your voice down. He let it go.

"Thank you for giving us a few moments of your time. The reason we contacted you today is that we'd like for you to tell us about your nephew, Cody."

This stunned her. She actually recoiled in front of her computer.

"Why? Why would you ever want to ask me about that… child? I've done my best to forget about him."

"We're very sorry," Mobley began. "I know this is hard."

"Hard? You have no idea what *hard* is, Detective. You don't know how hard it is to be called into the city morgue and asked to identify the bodies of your brother and sister-in-law. *Hard* is squinting because they've been slashed so much that you're not even sure if it's them anymore. Cody did that."

"I'm terribly sorry, ma'am," Gannon said, still feeling some hope since the woman hadn't hung up yet.

"It's one of the reasons why I moved halfway across the world. I needed to put my past behind me. I hope he rots in jail for the rest of his life. In any case, he's been convicted and he can't do that to anyone else."

"Yeah, about that…" Gannon couldn't help muttering.

"What?"

"There has been a new case, a couple killed with what seemed to be a razor blade. An individual on the scene matches the description of Cody and…"

"Wait, what?" Veronica interrupted. "I don't understand. Cody is locked up in a psych ward."

The two police officers shared a glance. They had gone over their questions beforehand, but had somehow neglected to address this particular fact.

Mobley leaned forward, squaring her shoulders. "I regret to inform you that Cody escaped from custody."

"Oh my God," the woman cried, covering her mouth. "No, this can't be happening."

"Rest assured that we are doing everything in our power to capture him."

Gannon felt this was a lie, but she needed to hear this. Only she didn't hear, or at least didn't seem to. She was looking away, rubbing her cheeks and chin. She was rocking back and forth.

"From what we can tell, he assumed a new identity

and is currently living with a foster family."

Veronica was still avoiding looking at the camera. Her eyes shifted from left to right as if her brain was on overdrive. She was chilled to the bone.

"Ms. Aten, what can you tell us about Cody?"

This caught her attention again and she nodded, realizing she had an important duty to perform.

"I always had a bad vibe about him."

"Bad how?"

"He was smart, you know? He started to speak in complete sentences almost from the start. Then, when I would see him, I'm talking when he was three or four, he would ask these weird questions. Like, what's it like to die? What happens if you drink bleach? We all thought it was cute at first, you know? Funny. But then it got real."

"What do you mean?" Mobley asked.

"It was his birthday, I remember like it was yesterday. It was his eighth birthday. He received a guppy, with a fishbowl and all that crap. After we had cake, he went to his room. My brother went up to check on him and he had the fish on his little desk. He was using a spoon to saw its head off."

Gannon and Mobley were speechless yet remained impassive.

"Go on."

"A few months later, they caught him in the woods out back. He was using snares to catch kittens. He had already killed two of them and a third was impaled on a pike. It wasn't dead yet. Its little legs were still moving. It was all so horrible. Cody was just grinning with pride."

"My God…" Mobley whispered.

"And he lied about everything. Lying came easy to him. He would make up stories about his parents drinking and neglecting him. The school wanted to meet them once. It was tense. I know for a fact my brother and his wife never would've laid a hand on him. You could never be sure what the truth was with that kid."

"Geez…" Mobley sighed.

Gannon was thinking the same before a lightbulb went up in his head. "Wait a minute… You said he did the fish thing on his eighth birthday. Are you sure about that?"

"Believe me, Detective. You can't forget something like that. I have nightmares about it sometimes. It was the day he turned eight years old."

Mobley finally got it and she turned toward her partner. "That can't be."

"So Cody would be how old now?" Gannon asked.

"Ten. He's ten years old now. He did always look small for his age, though."

Gannon was agape. That explained so much. That was why the date of birth on the missing persons report didn't match the data they had on Boyd Begum.

"Be careful, okay? Veronica said, leaning closer and speaking lower. "That child is a genius. He's smart and manipulative. That's the real reason I moved to the UK. I was terrified of him. Cody is evil, Detectives. You can't trust him. He is pure evil."

# CHAPTER 33

"What are you doing here, Boyd?" Dr. Curnutt asked in what passed for a genial voice even though she had trouble faking it.

The child was standing between the kitchen island and the stove. He was upright, his arms hanging down alongside his small body. The room was filled with steam from the cooking pasta and the water rumbled softly behind him.

"Hello, Dr. Talia."

The elderly woman hated herself for having taking a Valium on top of drinking the bottle of Merlot almost completely. She felt as if her synapses weren't firing as quickly as they should.

Still, she had to remain professional. She was about to tell her girlfriend that she would call her back when she noticed that the screen of the iPad was already black. The device was off. Had Debra terminated the call?

It didn't matter. She looked at her young patient. "Boyd, you can't be here. You know how it works, don't you? You're old enough to understand. There's a difference between personal life and professional life for grown-ups."

He didn't even blink.

"Just because my office is in my home, that doesn't mean you can come anytime you choose. You coming here tonight, it's unprofessional. I'll be happy to meet you at our next appointment."

"Is it about the money?"

She nearly chuckled at that. "Mostly it's about keeping boundaries in our relationship. How did you come in the house anyway?"

"I knocked and no one answered. The door was unlocked."

"It's not right to come into someone's house without being invited, even if the door is unlocked."

"I thought you couldn't hear me. I came here because I need help."

This softened her. Her desire to assist her patients was what drove her. It always had. To hear a child like this ask for help made her priorities straight. She dismissed her misgivings about him at once.

"What's going on, Boyd? Is it Tori and Lucas?"

"No. Well, maybe a little. Lucas isn't nice."

"Has he done anything to you?"

Boyd nodded. "Yes."

"What did he do?"

"He called me names. Bad stuff."

"What sort of bad stuff?"

"He called me a psycho."

Dr. Curnutt offered a warm smile. "Sometimes grown-ups use words even when they don't know their real meaning."

"The thing is, though, *you* know the meaning and you weren't that reluctant to call me that either."

"What?"

"I think you believe that I'm a psychopath, Dr. Talia. Why do you think that?"

Her mouth went dry as she realized it was no longer a little boy standing in front of her.

"Boyd... uh... I... There are multiple stages in establishing a diagnosis. Sometimes you have to think through different scenarios before you land on the right one. I'm doing this just to help you."

"By calling me a psychopath?"

"I never said that. How do you even know this, Boyd?"

"I overheard you talking with Lucas."

"Then you also heard that I said it was too early to tell what your..." She caught herself before saying *your problem*, which would sound accusatory. "What your condition is."

"Don't play games with me," Boyd said. "You're just like all the others. You think you know what's best for me."

"It's my job."

"You think you know what's going on inside my head. Well, let me tell you what's going on inside my head, Dr. Talia. I'm always thinking. I see everything. I'm perfectly aware that everyone around me thinks I'm a freak."

"Boyd, I don't…"

"But I'm not freak. I'm operating ten levels above all of you ordinary creatures. I can tell what everybody thinks. I can see everybody judging one another. It's so pathetic. This disgusting sentimentality, this desire to help, to please, to be accepted. That's not how the world works, Dr. Talia."

"It isn't?"

"No," Boyd said, his voice as even as ever. "We were put on this earth to do what *we* want. Nobody seems to understand that. Except me. I do what I want. I'm the only one who knows how to take care of myself. And this brings me to the real reason I came to see you tonight."

The psychologist had never been so frightened by someone's words before. It was even worse since it came from a young boy.

"Why did you come?" she asked.

"I've come to let you know that no one is going to have me committed again. It's not where I belong. I'm not crazy. I'm insightful. I know how to deal with tricky situations."

"You do?"

"No one should ever underestimate me. And Dr. Talia? No one should ever hurt me in any way."

"I'm not here to hurt you, Boyd. I've always been here to protect you."

"Calling me a psychopath and considering having me sent to a psychiatric hospital is hurting me. We can't have that, now can we?"

She stopped breathing. She had been right all along.

He truly was dangerous.

"What do you want, Boyd?"

"I want you to be punished."

Before she could ask what he was talking about, he grabbed the dishtowel which was lying on the corner of the kitchen island. Swiftly, he turned around and threw it on the stove.

What the…

The cloth landed square in the blue gas flame under the saucepan. It caught fire.

"No!" Dr. Curnutt shouted.

Instinctively, she ran forward to put out the fire. He was just messing with her and the worst part was that it was working. It was psychological warfare. Torture. He wanted to scare her.

Only there was something much more terrible that she didn't comprehend until it was too late.

As she ran the fifteen feet that separated her from the stove, she lost her footing. It was weird, unexpected. She had never known the ceramic floor to be this slippery before. Between her speed and her running start, her body was thrown forward.

She fell straight down, the momentum making had slam into the oven door head-on.

"Ah!"

The pain was excruciating, as if her head had been split open. Irrationally, she continued to fret about the flaming dishtowel on the stove. She didn't want her house to burn down.

Boyd looked at the old woman on the floor next to him. His plan had worked. Squeezing liquid dish soap on the floor had worked like a charm to make her slip. Now she was helpless, writhing in confusion.

He snatched the dishtowel from the stove and tossed it in the wet sink so the smoke alarm didn't go off. Next, he took hold of the empty wine bottle from the counter, tightening his fingers around its neck.

Dr. Curnutt hazily turned on her back, her eyes half closed from shock.

"Boyd, wait…"

He had no intention of waiting.

With strength incompatible with his age, Boyd swung the bottle down on her head. The heavy green glass hit her straight on the temple. The temporal bone cracked and blood gushed out.

The old woman lost consciousness immediately. That didn't stop Boyd from continuing to hit her.

The bottle came down again and again and again as he bashed her head in. Blood exploded against the oven door as well as on Boyd's face, arms, and chest.

He continued to hit her in the face and behind the head, well past the point where she was dead.

He was exhausted when he straightened up. Exhausted, yes, but also satisfied. The water on the stove boiled over in a piercing hiss. He used his knuckles to turn off the gas. The last thing he wanted was a catastrophe before he was ready to leave.

He opened the cupboard and used it as a stepping stool to reach the sink. He rinsed his prints off the bottle and blood from his skin. There wasn't much he could do about his shirt. He would have to wear it inside out until he could change. It had worked once or twice before.

He was about to leave when he noticed something on the kitchen island. It was a small orange bottle. Pills. He cocked his head to the side to read the prescription. He didn't know that Dr. Curnutt took Valium.

He smiled and pocketed the bottle.

# CHAPTER 34

Lucas walked into the house. He didn't wipe his feet and he didn't gently close the door behind him. He felt the relationship was beyond the need for civility.

He found Tori standing in the middle of the kitchen. Her arms were crossed. Behind her were pots and pans, some vegetables that had been abandoned in the middle of chopping. There was an open can of tomato sauce. Overall, it was very disorganized and very unlike his wife.

He was about to bring up the subject, to ask what was happening, but in reality he just didn't give a shit. Spending the day away had made him come to the realization that he couldn't bring himself to care either way. He felt guilty about their last dustup, but maybe it was what they both needed. It was the catalyst to send them both their separate ways.

"You don't have to say anything," he began, stopping in the den. He was keeping his distance. "I want to gather some things. I'll spend the night downstairs and tomorrow I'll move into my office."

The words tasted bitter coming out of his mouth. With his investment gone and the project at a standstill, he had no clue how long he would be able to afford his office. The rent wasn't that high, but it was a monthly expenditure that would quickly become superfluous.

"Next Saturday, I'll come by and we can talk about financials."

Tori turned to him, as if noticing his presence for the first time. "What?"

"I'm not stupid. It's over between us. We have to start thinking about divvying stuff up. We could put the house on the market this weekend. I know some real estate guys. We need liquidity."

This might be his saving grace, he thought. He could see it unfold from here and it was hard not to smile. They naturally owed a big chunk on the house, but a share could be reinvested in his development, or in starting a new one. Getting rid of his wife might be the best business decision he'd made in months.

"Whatever," she said, looking away again. "I don't care about any of that."

"I was hoping you wouldn't be such a bitch about it, but fine." He regretted his words instantly. He was the one having an affair and she could put this on him. "We can talk through lawyers if that's what you want."

She didn't reply, instead choosing to pace around the kitchen.

"What?" he asked.

"Have you seen Boyd, Lucas?"

"He's not here?"

"Do you think I would be standing here, chewing my nails, if he was?"

"He's not in his room?"

She shot him daggers. "You don't think I've checked

everywhere?"

"Maybe that's a good thing," Lucas muttered.

"You're such an asshole!"

"Look, that creep running away is the best thing that could happen. We're lucky. *You're* lucky. He's someone else's problem now."

Lucas allowed himself a grin. That was the sole bright spot in his day. After he had told Felicia this morning that Tori knew about the affair, she had insisted on ending things. She was embarrassed, remorseful. He was fairly confident that she would come around on that subject, although it meant he was on his own for the time being.

Tori didn't see the humor like he did. She spun toward him and pointed a finger.

"You do realize that if Boyd leaves, that's a thousand dollars you're not getting. That's all you ever cared about anyway, right? Money. It's always about money with you."

He snorted a laugh. "You know? A thousand bucks a month isn't worth it for that little psycho. Let somebody else handle him."

"You're horrible, Lucas."

"I'm a realist. So I'll get my things and then I'm going downstairs to drink and sleep. I'll be out of your hair by morning."

Lucas turned, heading to the stairs. He stopped cold. Boyd was coming down the steps one by one. He was wearing pajamas, the one with the cows on it.

"Boyd!" Tori shouted when she saw him.

He rubbed his eyes, shaking the cobwebs away.

"What's happening? Why are you shouting?"

Tori hurried to him and gave him a hug, utterly relieved. "Where were you?"

"I was here."

"No, you weren't. I searched everywhere, Boyd."

"My bike got a flat tire and the chain fell off. I had to walk home. My clothes were all greasy, so I changed into my pajamas. I didn't want you to be mad, so I tried to do laundry in the basement. I didn't know how to work the machine though. Then I fell asleep."

"I was so worried!"

"I'm sorry."

Tori pulled back, holding him by the shoulders. Her face was a mask of anger.

"Don't ever do that again. Do you hear me? Don't ever disappear without letting me know. It's dangerous out there. Understood?"

"Yes."

"Now go up to your room."

"But… I didn't eat dinner," Boyd said.

"You should have thought of that before running off. Go upstairs. Now."

She pointed to the second floor. The kid hesitated for a moment and finally turned around.

"He's gonna think you're a bitch, too," Lucas said once Boyd was gone.

"He has to learn not to disobey."

Lucas rolled his eyes. "You can't see it, can you? Those little puppy dog eyes. He's messing with you. He's making you eat right out of the palm of his hand. He's pretending to go along with what you say because, that way, you feel in control and you lose sight of what he's doing."

"No..."

"Yes, Tori. He's a master manipulator. You're just too dumb to realize that."

"Lucas, grab your shit and get out of my sight."

She returned to the kitchen and began flinging vegetables into the garbage. For a moment, he remembered why he'd been attracted to her in the first place. If only she hadn't changed...

~ ~ ~ ~

On Boyd's nightstand was an alarm clock shaped like a small football. The blue digital readout displayed 1:57. Initially, Boyd had wanted to wait for two o'clock because it was a nice, round number. However, he couldn't wait to do what was next on his list.

He got out of bed and put on socks. Then he took something from under his bed and placed it in his waistband.

He tiptoed out of his room and headed to the master suite. He pushed the door in carefully so it wouldn't make any noise. He peered inside. There was enough light to make out Tori. She was on her side, the sheet down to her waist. One of her breasts almost completely spilled out of her top, which told him she was sound asleep.

He entered the bathroom and didn't bother to turn on the light. There was a chair in the corner and he dragged it in front of the sink. He climbed on it, opened the medicine cabinet, and took what he had come here for.

Then he left and headed for the stairs. He didn't stop on the ground floor, instead going all the way down to the basement. The light was on in Lucas's home office. There was noise as well. Music which played softly.

As he came closer, he saw Lucas sitting behind his desk. He was swigging whiskey, shot after shot. His entire body was sluggish, as if he was doing it underwater. He was more than drunk.

Without hesitation, Boyd entered the office and closed the door behind him.

"You? What the hell do you want?"

He filled his tumbler. There was virtually nothing left in the bottle. He put it back on the desk but it slipped, landing sideways. Barely any liquid spilled out. He glared at Boyd, defiantly, and struggled to bring the glass to his lips. He sipped slowly.

"Goddamn kid. It's all your fault. You know that?"

Boyd came closer still, unhurriedly going around the desk.

"All my problems, they're because of you. Boyd." He spat his name facetiously, pronouncing every letter. "Such a stupid name for such a stupid boy."

"You're right, Lucas. It's not the best name, but I like it."

"I hate kids, all kids. All you do is ruin good people's lives."

Lucas finished his glass and took deep breaths as he considered whether or not to refill it.

"You enjoy Wild Turkey, don't you? You're the only one who drinks it."

"Little Miss Perfect upstairs is too good for whiskey."

Boyd walked until he was inches away from the man's chair. "My mother used to drink Wild Turkey. I always hated the smell. Tell me, Lucas. How does it taste?"

"What?"

For the first time, Lucas noticed how cool the child was. He was stranger than normal.

"Do you think it tastes stronger than usual? Does it taste different?"

Lucas couldn't remain upright, even in his chair, and he leaned back into it. His breathing was deep and slow.

"What's going on?" he asked. He tried lifting his arms and it was as if cinderblocks were tied to them. "What did you do to me?"

"I have to say, I'm very impressed with Valium. I wasn't sure of the effect." Boyd placed the orange pill bottle on the desk after pulling it from his waistband. "I crushed twenty-eight pills into your Wild Turkey."

"What?"

Lucas was drooling, he couldn't keep his eyes open even though he was attempting to do so at any cost. He managed to grab the bottle, but the prescription printout had been removed from it. The bottle slipped from his fingers and fell to the floor.

"I've been reading a lot this week. Apparently, people

going through bankruptcy often commit suicide. Did you know that?"

"You…" Lucas was slurring, fighting to stay awake. "You l-little…"

Boyd opened his hand, revealing the razor blade he had taken from the medicine cabinet.

"I'm going to tell you a secret," he whispered. "This was the only reason why I wanted you to shave your beard."

In a flash, Boyd pulled the man's hand open, pushing it down. Lucas had no strength to resist as his eyes squinted, burning with fear, something the kid enjoyed. Boyd didn't waste time slashing the blade down, starting in the middle of the forearm and going all the way to the wrist.

"No…" Lucas whispered, his strength fading away as pain seared.

Without missing a beat, Boyd went to the other side and repeated the gesture, opening his other artery. Blood poured out as if he had opened a faucet.

"No!" Lucas's shout came out as a mumble.

Boyd pressed the blade between his foster dad's right fingers to get his prints on it and let it fall to the ground. Next, he returned behind Lucas and covered his mouth with his small hands.

"Shhh, let it happen. Your problems are going away." Boyd approached his lips to his ear. "*My* problems are going away."

Lucas did his best to struggle, but he didn't have the strength. Boyd kept his hands in place over his mouth and he watched raptly as blood continued to drip onto the basement floor.

It was such a beautiful sight. It was art.

# CHAPTER 35

The two brothers were arguing again on HGTV, only this time it wasn't with each other. They were trying to convince a homeowner that it was better to have three nice bedrooms than four small ones.

That was usually Gannon's favorite moment, when they put down some know-it-all couple. There was one of those every week, it seemed. It was nice to see competent people get the upper hand. If it didn't happen in real life, at least it happened on TV.

Unfortunately, he couldn't enjoy it at the moment. He was stressing out. He couldn't sleep. It was the middle of the night and he had finished all the Cherry Coke he had in the house. He was on his last cigarette.

He was sure that he would've fallen asleep by now. He was getting on with age and sometimes he nodded off after dinner. Now it was late at night and he was wide awake.

*Jesus*, when was the last time that a case had kept him from going to bed? When had he started caring? This was a young man's game and he should've been past that. He was obsessed.

He thought about going to the liquor cabinet and getting something potent to drink. With luck, it would knock him out. He decided against it. He wanted a clear head since he was going over his notes for the thousandth time.

Was it useful? Probably not. He knew everything by heart already. But there had to be something, no? There had to be more than just waiting for the state attorney's office to come back with their recommendations. He had thirty years' experience with those clowns. They were budding politicians. They played it safe.

Even though the right thing to do was to issue a court order and have the kid brought in, to have his DNA tested, they would dither. They would look for the path of least resistance. They would look for what was best for their careers, and that usually meant avoiding bad press.

Which meant doing nothing.

Gannon inhaled the last bit of smoke. The tobacco was gone and only the filter remained. It tasted like it, too. He was being too harsh on the lawyers. They were looking for justice; it was just that they took the scenic route in order to avoid hurdles. He just had to wait.

"There has to be something..." he muttered to himself as he crushed the butt into the ashtray.

He grabbed his phone, flicked through his contacts, and called Mobley. It rang six times.

"Hello?" The voice was sleepy.

It also wasn't Mobley. It was a woman, just not his partner.

"Uh, hi. I'm looking for Detective Mobley?"

"Mister, do you know what time it is?"

Gannon glanced at his watch and winced. It was two o'clock in the morning.

"Yeah, I'm sorry about that. But it's very important."

"I'm sure it is, but my daughter needs her sleep. I don't know if she told you about her condition—God knows I told her that police work wasn't for her—but the last thing she needs is to be kept up in the middle of the night."

There was rustling on the other end of the line and the woman's voice faded away.

"Mom, it's fine," Mobley said, obviously in the process of grabbing the phone from her.

"No, it's not fine! You need your rest, Ghislaine. You promised me that you were going to keep this job strictly nine-to-five. That was the deal, honey. That was the bargain we struck. Do you remember?"

"It's okay, mom. Just go back to bed, okay?"

There was more arguing, but the woman was walking away and Gannon couldn't make out her words. A door closed.

"Gannon?"

"Right here."

"Sorry about my mother. She means well but, you know, she's a mother."

Mobley's voice was faint, weak. It was more than simply being groggy from having been woken up.

"It's all right. Say, are you okay? You sound like you should still be in bed. I'm an asshole for calling you this late."

"Good days and bad days, remember? I'm the one who was dumb for thinking I could have a regular career with this disease. MS is quite the unpredictable bitch."

"Take it one day at a time, right?"

"That's what they say," she replied with resignation. "What's up?"

"It was stupid to call. I'll see you tomorrow at the station."

"No, tell me. You got me out of bed already. The least you can do is not having me wait until tomorrow. You find anything?"

"I wish," Gannon said as he dropped his heavy body on the couch. He sank several inches and felt the springs digging into his flesh. "I just wanted to recap with you, see if there's something we haven't considered before."

"Let's do it. I'm awake now."

"If I didn't know any better, I'd say this is an accusation, partner."

"Hey, you're the one who called me at two AM!"

They both shared a chuckle though it was strained for her. She wasn't in good shape. He didn't say anything about it.

"All right," he began with a sigh. "What do we know? Cody Aten killed his parents for no apparent reason, not that it matters. Killed them with a razor blade. It was caught on the nanny cam. He's arrested and committed. Then he escaped."

"He didn't just escape. He crossed the country. That's a major achievement for a kid."

"He's smart, remember? His aunt said he was a troubled kid and also a genius. Then, he murders this other couple in Hillford. Complete strangers. From the looks of it, they were thrill kills."

"It's sick," Mobley spat. "He's sick."

"You're preaching to the choir. Now he's in foster care in the middle of Bumhole, Nowhere. He has to be seeing a shrink. We should get in touch with him, see if he has any insight."

"He probably won't speak to us, doctor-patient privilege and all."

He shrugged even though she couldn't see it. "It's worth a shot anyway. What's certain is that we can't ignore this any longer. It's more than just a homicide investigation now. We're dealing with a fugitive."

"You're forgetting one thing, Gannon."

"What?"

"This is all conjecture. We don't even know if we're dealing with the same kid. This Boyd Begum could be someone else entirely."

"Yeah," the older man replied as hope hissed out of him. "We just have to wait for the damn lawyers to have their say, and they work at typical lawyer speed."

Neither of them said anything else. The implications were plain enough. If this was the same kid and if these were indeed thrill kills, he would undoubtedly do it again.

Waiting for legal advice and the captain to give the go-ahead was a matter of life and death. Gannon prayed he wasn't too late.

# CHAPTER 36

"I am the resurrection and the life, says the Lord. Those who believe in me shall live, even though they die, and whoever lives and believes in me shall never die."

The church was packed and the pastor's voice carried. He didn't need a microphone even though there was one inches away from his mouth.

"I am the Alpha and the Omega, the beginning and the end, the first and the last. I died and behold I am alive for evermore; and I have the keys of Death and Hades."

Tori was done with crying and she felt guilty about it. In fact, she had only cried in the beginning, after she had discovered Lucas in his office. She had kept Boyd upstairs so he wouldn't witness this. She couldn't imagine how he would react if he saw the body. After he had seen his own slaughtered parents, this would probably send him into a catatonic state.

She had called nine-one-one right away and the paramedics confirmed that Lucas was dead. Sheriff McKenzie himself led the investigation and concluded it was a suicide.

Tori refused to believe it at first. Lucas was combative, not suicidal. Nevertheless, she had to face the facts. Their marriage had fallen apart. His business deal was dead.

They were facing bankruptcy. His drinking had increased exponentially. There had been no intruders. He had died peacefully at his desk.

The autopsy had revealed that Lucas had had vast quantities of diazepam—Valium—in his body. She had been shocked because she didn't know he had a prescription for that. Indeed, he didn't. However, the sheriff assured her that it was common for people to get anxiety medication on the black market, especially with depressed people. He had really taken his own life.

The pastor looked up from the Bible and spun toward Tori. "Because I live, you too will also live."

She thought about Boyd again. Even if she had shielded him from the dreadful events, he had still been smart enough to figure things out. You couldn't hide police officers and humorless people from the coroner's office traipsing through the house.

He had spent the next two days locked in his room. Whenever she checked on him, he was rocking back and forth. After she'd realized that she couldn't handle this by herself, she had called Dr. Curnutt, only to find out that she was dead.

It had been a home invasion. Rumors going around town spoke of a crazed former patient. After all, that had been her stock in trade. The guy had apparently broken in and killed her with a wine bottle. Her iPad had been taken, along with all the cash in the house.

People in town wanted action. They wanted security cameras everywhere. Gun sales were spiking. This sort of thing couldn't happen in sleepy Steep Gorge.

Tori was too much in shock about her husband to give

it consideration. It was tragic, and unfortunate that Dr. Curnutt wasn't there anymore to help Boyd cope with this new catastrophe, but ultimately she blocked it from her mind.

"The Lord works in mysterious ways," the pastor said, no longer working from a script. "That's what pastors like to say, isn't it?"

The crowd gave a polite chuckle.

"Yet, it's true. The Lord does work in mysterious ways. As difficult as it is for us to accept the hardships He puts in our path, we must accept that there is always a reason. Is it to test us? Is it to make us stronger? Is it to make us realize that it's only through faith that we can overcome? It is because of all these reasons."

A neighborhood teenager was keeping an eye on Boyd. She was a good kid and she'd given her a few drawing lessons in the past. She'd figured she could be a good, regular babysitter. It was just awful that she hadn't needed her until Lucas's funeral. They had never gone out on a date since they'd become foster parents.

This was a testament to their failing marriage, she thought. Their relationship had been destined for failure. She should have seen that a year ago when she discovered that he was cheating. She should have left him after losing the baby.

She shook her head, dismissing the notion. It was too late now. She had followed her heart, choosing to give him a second chance when he never really deserved it. She had gone down the wrong path. It was the story of her life.

She looked around, no longer listening to the pastor.

There were many people, but she knew practically no one. It was more like a social event for them. It was something to do. Or maybe they wanted to be congratulated for caring about their community members.

The service ended and people filed out, very few heading to the cemetery. Lucas's parents and two brothers had flown in. They hadn't been close to him or Tori, but they insisted on holding a small reception after the burial. Tori had agreed to go, although she was now reconsidering.

She didn't want to pretend to be in mourning. She was angry. She felt very little sadness. It felt wrong to accept condolences. It was hypocrisy.

They came over to her, saying that they would head straight to the restaurant where they had rented a small reception room. They would make sure everything was fine before going to the cemetery. Tori said that instead she would go home to be with Boyd.

She would attend the burial because she didn't have a choice, but then she was going home. They obviously knew she was bailing on them and they didn't try to change her mind.

Most likely, they were glad that she wouldn't be a part of the family any longer. It gave them the moral high ground, as if they were the only ones justified in their grief. She was happy to let them think that. They weren't exactly wrong either.

A few other people came to shake her hand, saying how sorry they were. She recognized Mr. Larsen from the candy store. She recognized the lady from the post office. She wondered if they blamed her for his suicide. Had she been a bad wife? Had she driven Lucas to drinking? Had she made him so desperate that the only way out had been to kill himself?

Tori decided that she didn't care what people thought of her. What mattered was the truth.

She took her time leaving the church. She didn't want to speak to more people. She figured that if she stayed back, they would all avoid her. It worked, for the most part. As she walked past the last pew, someone was waiting for her.

"Hey, Tori."

It was Felicia. Her eyes were red from crying although her cheeks were currently dry.

"I'm so sorry," she said.

Tori shrugged and said, "Thanks. I suppose I should say it back to you."

They hadn't spoken since Jasper had been arrested. It was clear that they both knew that the affair was in the open now.

"I caused you so much pain. There's no way I can apologize enough for what I did."

Tori looked at her, unsure what to say. In a soap opera, she would have slapped her, hoping for an audience so that everyone knew that Felicia had wrecked her marriage. In reality, the marriage had been crumbling for years. The betrayal from her friend still hurt, but she felt very little resentment.

"Did you love him?"

"I thought I did," Felicia replied. "He was so…"

"Charming."

"Yes, that's it!"

"That was his signature move," Tori said, remembering when they first met. "He could be very charming in the beginning."

"I had never cheated on Jasper before. I never wanted to. It just happened with Lucas. I never saw it coming."

Tori shook her head, closing her eyes. "You can stop making excuses, okay? If you think I'm blaming you for Lucas killing himself, you're wrong."

She felt like a bitch for saying that, because now Felicia was bound to blame herself. It was petty, beneath her, and she didn't actually believe that. However, it did feel good to get in at least one good punch as her life disintegrated around her.

"Thank you, Tori. I realized I wasn't in love with him when Jasper was arrested. That's when all my priorities became clear-cut, you know?"

"So what's happening with him?" Tori asked, glad to change the subject.

Felicia became teary again. "He's been indicted. We're just waiting for the trial now. He says he's innocent and, honestly, I never had any suspicions about him being into kids. I talked to Evan and he swears Jasper never touched him. Same with his friends. But the evidence they have on him… It's just so damning. I mean, I saw the pictures."

"The pictures on his phone?"

"I saw them when they arrested Jasper. A little boy, completely nude. I saw all the details. Let me tell you, I'll never see another appendectomy scar without thinking of child abuse again. It's all I can see now."

"I'm sorry, Felicia."

The woman nodded and produced a tissue. She dabbed her eyes, smearing her mascara. They were silent for several seconds and it became uncomfortable.

Tori opened her mouth to say goodbye, ready to leave. Felicia straightened up, her sadness gone. Instead, it was replaced by rage.

"I think Jasper is right," she said.

"Right about what?"

"I didn't want to believe it at first, I swear. But now I can't deny it. Everything that's been happening in this town, it started when Boyd came to live with you."

"Felicia..."

"I'm serious, girl. Evan getting into an accident, the fire, Jasper getting arrested, the shrink getting killed in a home invasion, Lucas. I don't want to believe in curses, but I don't believe in coincidences either."

She stared at Tori in silence for a moment, letting it sink in, and then she left the church.

As much as Tori wanted to offer a rebuttal, she couldn't. Lucas had been telling her the same thing and she had ignored it.

What if he'd been right all along?

# CHAPTER 37

Gannon couldn't take it anymore. Waiting was killing him.

Which meant it could actually get someone else killed.

He had barely slept for the past several days. No decision had been made regarding what to do about the kid. It was like no one was realizing that there was a ticking clock. Sure, he understood that they needed not to make waves.

All it took was one of the foster parents to make a fuss, to tweet something about how cruel the state was to harass a child. If by some miracle it went viral, they would all be out of a job.

The attorneys weren't making things easier by taking their time. He had been calling every day for updates, and every time he was told to be patient. Maybe that was a good thing since he remembered that Boyd—Cody—was supposed to be a genius.

If he was smart, he would lay low. That was in his best interest. Don't rock the boat, try not to stick out, that's how most serial killers had managed to evade capture for so long. Commit a crime and then go to ground until the urge becomes unbearable. Eventually though, the urge always made them do it again. The more they did it, the more liable they were to make a mistake.

Gannon exhaled loudly as he looked at the Reuben sandwich in front of him, on the counter. It made him ill that his only strategy was to wait for another crime to be committed. He couldn't take the chance.

He had to do something.

He paid, leaving his food untouched, and left the diner. Any other day, he would have considered the act blasphemous. To walk away from such a delicious meal was heartbreaking and just plain wrong. It was replaced by some sort of euphoria which he hadn't felt in over two decades.

Against all odds, he loved his job again. Maybe he was making a difference. Maybe his entire career hadn't been a waste. *Hell of a time to get an epiphany*, he thought.

The moment he was out of the restaurant, he wedged a cigarette between his lips, although he didn't light it. The adrenaline coursing through his veins was all he needed.

He pulled his phone out and called the station. He wouldn't ask permission. No, he would just inform his boss of his intentions. It seemed like a good compromise. He had given Vail and the lawyers enough time to get their thumbs out of their asses. They had to realize that he had a job to do as well.

"I'm sorry, Detective," his secretary said. "He's out for the day. He had a tee time at noon."

"Can't you patch me through to his cell?" Gannon asked evenly, doing his best to hide his irritation.

"Captain Vail shuts down his phone when he's out

golfing with the mayor, always does. I'm sorry."

He resisted the urge to give her crap about that. It wasn't her fault. There was even a chance that the captain was avoiding him. In any case, he thanked her and hung up. He had done his best to go by the book. Now it was time to do things his way.

Mobley hadn't come into the station today. She hadn't called in sick, but this had to be one of her bad days. He called her house.

"Yes?" The voice was different. It was her mother again.

"Hi, Mrs. Mobley. Could I speak to your daughter, please? This is Gannon, her partner."

"No, you can't. She's asleep at the moment."

"This is important, ma'am."

"And so is Ghislaine's health. She was so weak today that she couldn't even sit up in bed. Don't you understand how fragile she is at the moment, Detective Gannon?"

Arguing with her would be a waste of time. He was hoping that Mobley would wrestle the phone away from her mom like the other night. She didn't.

"Is it okay if I ask you to pass on a message to her?"

The woman exhaled as if that was asking a lot from her, costing her undue amounts of money and energy. "Fine. Let me get a piece of paper."

It was several seconds until she said she was ready.

"Tell her to call me as soon as possible with the foster parents' address. The name is Ramsdale, I think. They live in a town called Steep something. I need the exact location and she knows all of this by heart."

Mobley had brought several files with her the day before. The information was probably still in the computer somewhere, but Gannon knew it would be faster for his partner to give him the information than to rummage through the system himself.

"I'll give her the message, but don't count on her calling you back, Detective. My daughter is in a much poorer condition than she lets on. She needs her rest."

The woman hung up before he could thank her. Was it true? Was Mobley that weak? He felt sad for her. She was so young. She was too young to retire on disability. What's more, she was good at her job and it would be a shame if she couldn't be a cop anymore.

Gannon got into his car and reached for the accordion folder on the backseat. He had brought some files with him to study while he ate, but had decided at the last second to focus on his sandwich instead. That plan had gone sideways fast.

He hadn't been idle these past few days and he had discovered that the child was indeed seeing a therapist. He hadn't contacted her though. He'd been waiting for the go-ahead from Vail and the lawyers. He was done with waiting.

He turned the car on to get the air-conditioning going and dialed the number. He saw in the file that the town was actually called Steep Gorge.

"Hello?"

"Hi, this is Detective Gannon from the State Police. Can I speak to Dr. Talia Curnutt please?"

There was a pause. The woman on the other end of the line sniffled.

"I'm afraid she has passed away," she said.

"Excuse me? How did it happen? If you don't mind my asking."

"There was a home invasion. It makes no sense. Talia was always so careful."

Gannon was speechless yet felt like he should say something. "She was your boss?"

"She was my fiancée."

"Oh. I'm sorry for your loss." The woman was breathing erratically. She was sobbing. "Did the police catch the perpetrator?"

"No. They think it might have been one of her former patients. Doesn't make much sense since she only treated children. I don't know what I'll do without her. She was my life, Detective."

He barely heard her. Gannon didn't believe in coincidences. This kid might've been a genius, but he wasn't lying low after all.

He started the car, maneuvered toward the highway, and sped up north toward the mountains.

Toward Steep Gorge.

# CHAPTER 38

Tori had planned on spending the afternoon feeling sorry for herself, mostly feeling guilty about skipping the reception. People were bound to talk about her.

They would judge her and absolutely call her a shrew. What kind of wife doesn't attend the reception after her husband's funeral? She obviously didn't love him. It was clear that Lucas had killed himself because she had made his life miserable.

She didn't care. In fact, the minute she returned home she stopped thinking about Lucas. She paid the babysitter and it was just her and Boyd in the house.

He stood in the foyer as the teenage girl walked away. He looked at Tori with interest, as if he expected her to tell him about the funeral or ask how things had gone with his babysitter. She did neither.

No, the feeling that overwhelmed her as she got home was disgust. She couldn't forget Felicia's words. Worse, she believed her. Boyd wasn't normal, and being in his presence gave her chills.

She didn't want him in the house anymore.

Admitting this to herself was revolting, but also a relief. She had believed herself stronger than that. She had thought that as a woman, her maternal instinct would make her the best candidate to help the child. It was love he needed and she had it in spades.

Nevertheless, the coincidences were piling up in a terrifying way. She saw it now. Boyd could be highly manipulative. The way he talked to her, constantly asking her if everything was all right. He was angelic with her. Too perfect.

He had been playing her.

"Do you want me to help make dinner tonight?" he offered with a delicate smile she would've considered genuine until this morning.

She couldn't stand to look at him. She wanted him out of the house as soon as possible.

"Maybe later," she replied dismissively.

She went up to her room and changed out of her black dress. She got into jeans, a T-shirt, and sneakers. It did nothing to change her mood.

Next, she fetched the foster care paperwork and found the number for Ruth Zakrzewski at the Department of Children and Families. She hit her voicemail.

"You have reached Ruth Zakrzewski. Please be aware that I am on vacation until September third. For any urgent matter, please visit our website or call the emergency hotline."

The woman had the courtesy of spelling out the number and Tori called it immediately. She went through seven separate options and was ultimately transferred to a case officer named Dorthy Holmes.

After some niceties and explaining that Ruth Zakrzewski was her usual contact, Tori dove right in.

"I'm looking for information on how to give up the child in my care."

"Give up?"

"I…" Tori was appalled by what she needed to say. "I don't want him anymore."

"I see. Is there a medical condition?"

"No."

"Has he been violent or involved in an incident with law enforcement?"

Tori winced, evaluating whether she should lie or not. "I'm not sure."

"Mrs. Ramsdale, I'll be honest with you. I haven't been working here for long and I don't quite know how to handle your situation. My best advice is for you to wait until Monday. Ruth is a pro. She will know what to do."

After hanging up, Tori wondered how she'd expected any other answer. It had been foolish to hope that the state would send someone right over to pick Boyd up. In the meantime, she had to keep living with him.

That in itself was torture.

Simply thinking about him, picturing his soft features, it made her want to scream. She thought of Lucas who had warned her about him. She thought of Jasper.

"Jasper…" she whispered as this triggered a memory.

She returned to the folder lying on her bed and rifled through it. There was the official foster care paperwork, brochures and information pamphlets, but also Boyd's medical record. After he'd been taken by CPS, he had undergone a medical checkup and this was the report.

She held her breath as she read the report. Blood type, vaccines. Then she saw it, under *Past Surgical Procedures*.

Appendectomy.

~ ~ ~ ~

Gannon turned off the radio. He'd been listening to music to keep himself distracted, but it wasn't working. Worse, he had the eerie feeling that it would keep him from hearing his phone ring. That was the most important part.

Mobley still hadn't called. Had her mother given her his message? He could see how she would have crumpled the paper and thrown it away. What mattered most for her was her daughter's well-being and, visibly, it didn't involve police work.

He fished out a cigarette as he thought about what to do next. Keeping his eyes on the road, he produced his lighter and flicked the wheel. There were sparks, but no flame.

"Come on…"

Sparks again. And again.

"Shit."

What was it with modern cars not having lighters anymore? What idiot thought that was a good idea? He yanked the cigarette away and tossed it on the seat next to him, along with the empty Zippo.

He wondered if he should call Mobley once more. If her mother answered, she would really be pissed off now and his opportunity of finally getting his message to her daughter would be gone for good. She was that type of woman.

A sign by the side of the road read *Steep Gorge 10 miles.*

He still had a few minutes before requiring the precise address. Then he could figure out what to do. Maybe he'd stop at a supermarket and ask about the Ramsdales. It was a small town and he figured everybody here knew each other.

That seemed like an awful long shot. But it was all he had.

He went faster, pushing away his nicotine craving.

~ ~ ~ ~

Tori was winded, realizing that she was still holding her breath.

Felicia had said that the child, Jasper's alleged victim, had had an appendectomy scar. She had seen the images. Pieces of the puzzle fell into place.

Boyd was the kid in the pictures, but Tori didn't believe for a moment that Jasper had abused him. It was too neat. More likely, it was the other way around. Jasper had been framed. It all made sense now. Lucas had been right!

Boyd had manipulated the whole thing. He was smart and he always had his way. He was some sort of criminal mastermind.

What else had he done?

She wanted the kid out of her house as soon as possible. She felt trapped, as if the walls were caving in.

She grabbed her phone and thought of only one way to get rid of Boyd. She was about to call when claustrophobia set in.

She took several deep breaths and peeked out of her room. The coast was clear. Clutching the phone like a lifeline, she made her way out and hurried downstairs. She didn't see Boyd anywhere.

She practically ran out of the house, toward the workshop. It had always been a safe haven, the only place where she felt at ease. She walked in and relaxed for the first time, although she wasn't out of the woods yet. She called the Sheriff's Department.

"Could I speak to Sheriff McKenzie, please?"

"I'm sorry, there's this eighteen wheeler that flipped over in West Gorge. I'm afraid Sheriff McKenzie won't be back for at least an hour. Is this an emergency? Do you want me to send a deputy?"

Tori desperately wanted to say yes, but the facts were against her. If she said that she was afraid of her eight-year-old foster child, she would be laughed at. If anything, she would be the one suspected of wrongdoing.

She was on her own.

She hung up and put the phone down on her workbench, willing herself to unwind. Then she heard the door screech behind her. She turned around, gasping.

Boyd was coming in, that innocent little smile across his lips. How could she have been so clueless? His expression wasn't innocent. It was taunting.

"What's going on, Tori?"

"Nothing."

“Oh yeah? What are you doing here? Aren’t you going to prepare dinner?”

“In a little bit, okay? I just want to paint for now. I need to clear my head.”

Boyd took a step closer. He shook his head. “You shouldn’t do that, Tori.”

“Do what, paint?”

“Lie. You’re not good at it.”

“What are you talking about?” she said, intending to sound affable yet knowing that she was coming off nervous and terrified.

“There is one thing I hate above everything else, Tori. I hate adults who lie to me. I just hate it.”

He took another step toward her.

# CHAPTER 39

What a shitty town this was, Gannon thought.

Every house looked the same to him. Green lawn, single-family homes, very few sidewalks. Franklin was by no means a metropolis, but it was alive. Steep Gorge was the complete opposite.

And the opposite of alive was dead. That only contributed to his developing sense of dread. With each passing minute, he had the feeling that something bad was happening, that he was too late.

*Christ*, he shouldn't have listened to his captain. That man had no instinct for police work. He was a politician. All he cared about was his own ambition, which meant doing anything in his power to avoid getting his hands dirty. Meanwhile, the public wasn't being served as they should be.

There was a supermarket up ahead. It was small by anybody's standards. Since he still didn't know where the foster family lived, he had to resort to the plan of asking around.

Gannon was pulling into the parking lot when his phone vibrated. He stopped breathing, petrified that hoping it was his partner would only disappoint him. With his luck, it was Vail ordering him back to the station.

He pulled the phone out. It was Mobley.

"I'm so glad to hear from you."

"You sure know how to speak to a woman," she said.

Her voice was just above a whisper.

"Are you all right?"

"Yeah, I'm fine. I managed to escape my overprotective mother and I saw your message. Sorry it took so long to get back to you."

"Don't sweat it, Mobley. You have the address?"

"The Ramsdales live at 1730 Meadow. You think something's wrong?"

"I have a bad feeling. Take care of yourself. I'll call you later."

He hung up and opened the map app on his phone. He had never typed so fast before. He made three mistakes and hated his sausage fingers.

He swung out of the parking lot and followed the indications on the screen. It was a mile away.

~ ~ ~ ~

Without knowing she was doing it, Tori curled her fingers into fists.

She was determined not to let her fear show. That was what they recommended when you came across a wild animal, wasn't it? You had to project dominance. She squared her shoulders and lifted her chin.

It had no effect on Boyd. He took another step toward her, still as cool as ever. Her heart was about to burst out of her chest.

And that's when she remembered she was the adult here. That was her secret weapon. She didn't have to be afraid of a prepubescent boy. She was his foster mom. She was the grown-up.

"Go back to the house," she ordered, her voice as authoritative as she could make it.

"I heard you on the phone, Tori."

"Stop talking back and go back to the house right this minute."

He took another step in her direction. Without knowing she was doing it, she took a step back. They were circling each other, she realized.

"Why do you want to get rid of me?" he asked. "Don't you like me?"

"Boyd, I just came here to paint for a while. Please leave me alone, okay?" She hated herself for pleading. She had already lost the strength in her voice. "Go to your room."

He shook his head. "There you go again with the lying. I told you I hate when adults lie to me. They think they're so superior. It's the opposite, in fact."

He was next to the easel and gave it a casual glance. He traced her brushes and tubes of paint with his fingertips. His hand stopped above the palette knife. He took it.

"Why did you call the government woman and ask her how to take me back?"

Tori was mortified that he knew. She felt shame. "I…"

"Did I do something to offend you, Tori? Is it because I'm not yours? You would love me if I had come out of you, but, since I didn't, it gives you the right to throw me away? Is that it?"

"I don't know what you heard, Boyd, but you're wrong. Go back to the house now."

"No, I think I want to stay here and paint, too." He lifted the palette knife to eye level, inspecting it. It was pointy and sharp. She couldn't escape the feeling that he was menacing her. "You want to paint with me, Tori?"

Why hadn't she kept her phone in her pocket? It was on the workbench, out of reach. She had to change strategies.

"Why don't you give me some answers, Boyd? I have questions."

He snorted back a chuckle. "I'm sure you do."

"Did you break Evan's arm?"

"That was fun. Do you know the pleasure you get when getting back at someone? I was nothing but nice to Evan. I only wanted to be friends, but he mocked me. He made his friends laugh at me and call me names."

"So you broke his arm?" Tori replied, fascinated by how lightly he was taking this.

"Evan broke his own arm. The only thing I did was prove to him that riding a bike is dangerous. If he had slowed down, he would've seen the rope. It's his fault, really."

*Geez,* Tori thought. He was so casual about all this. He

was talking like an adult.

"What about the fire? Did you have anything to do with that?"

"Once again, I'm being blamed for someone else's incompetence. There were so many flammable materials lying around that the construction site should've been shut down. I'm surprised it didn't go up in flames before I showed up. Please, I'm disappointed in you."

That stunned Tori. "What?"

"The only reason I snuck out of the county fair and set the fire was to help you and Lucas. Money was tight and that was a wonderful solution. It's not my fault if you guys couldn't play along. Lucas was especially ungrateful."

"What have you done?" Tori asked, her voice coming out as a murmur.

That made him laugh. "You remind me of Dr. Talia."

"What about Dr. Talia?"

"Oh, come on! You really believe that story about a home invasion? That house was never locked. The windows could be opened from the outside without difficulty. Walking in could hardly be described as home invasion."

"What about her, Boyd?"

"She was like you, you know. She thought she was a saint. She thought she knew me better than anyone. She thought she knew what was wrong with me. But here's the thing, there's nothing wrong with me. I'm a little different, sure. I'm smarter, definitely. But there's nothing *wrong* with me. She wouldn't understand that."

Tori's blood ran cold. "What did you do to her?"

"She hit her head," he said with a shrug. "It wasn't really my fault. I just made her stop suffering."

"Oh God…"

"She thought I was a psychopath, did you know that? Did she tell you? I hate being called names. People call you names behind your back and smile to your face. Bunch of hypocrites."

Tori focused on her breathing because she had trouble wrapping her mind around the fact that this eight-year-old had basically just confessed to murder. She couldn't process that.

"What about Jasper? It was you in the pictures, right?"

He chuckled at his own cleverness. "My first day of school—like, four, five years ago?—I was taught about Stranger Danger. Tell someone if an adult touches you in an inappropriate way. You grown-ups freak out about that stuff. All it took was two minutes in a bathroom with Jasper's phone. Just two minutes. Do you understand now how powerful I am?"

*Batshit crazy* was more like it, she concluded, although she couldn't say that.

She was scared of him. He was a deranged little boy. Nevertheless, he seemed to be happy to talk. He enjoyed boasting. She needed to keep him at it because as long as he did that, he wasn't doing anything to her.

"And was it your first time?"

"Having someone arrested for being a pedophile? Yes."

"And the rest?"

"What rest, Tori?"

"K-Killing people."

He smirked, running a finger along the blade of the knife. He shook his head.

"My parents wanted to have me committed. I had to do something about that, didn't I? And then there was that nice couple, the Begums. I stayed with them for a few days, until they got it into their heads to call the authorities about me. Honestly, though, they were boring me."

"So you killed them?"

"It's not like they're going to be missed or anything, don't worry."

Everything having fallen into place, Tori's mind went elsewhere. "What about Lucas? He didn't commit suicide, did he?"

"He would have, eventually. He was the type."

"Oh Boyd…" Tori wailed, the truth dawning on her.

"I did it for you, Tori. You can see that, yes? He wasn't nice to you. He cheated. He was violent. He couldn't support you. You should be thanking me. You know why? Because I think the two of us would get along if we didn't have any of those obstacles around us. I always liked you."

She didn't speak. What was there to say anyway? There was no reasoning with him and she was afraid that he would misconstrue her words. Her eyes welled up and she couldn't think. She wanted to get away from him, only she didn't know how.

"Let's go to the house, Tori."

# CHAPTER 40

"What?"

Boyd made a show of setting down the palette knife on the windowsill next to the door.

"We can make dinner together and start over as a family. Just you and me. What do you think?"

He walked out of the workshop and took a few steps. He turned back toward her and beamed.

Tori had no choice, she decided. She had to play along, at least for a little while, until she could think of a way to escape. In all fairness, she could get her phone, but who would she call? Who would take her seriously?

She realized that she was an adult and that she could outrun him. However, he had killed at least six people, all adults. What made her think that she was better than they'd been? They hadn't been able to get away from him.

Slowly, she headed out of the workshop. That's when her eyes caught the glimmer from the palette knife. That could be her salvation. As discreetly as she could, she grabbed it and walked out onto the lawn.

Boyd spun toward her again. He winced, his gaze on the weapon in her hand.

"Oh Tori. I'm disappointed. You shouldn't have done

that."

He produced a razor blade from the pocket of his jeans. It caught the sunlight, its sharpness unmistakable.

"Boyd, I…"

"You're just like the others after all, Tori."

He placed the blade between his thumb and index finger as if he'd done that a thousand times. His expression turned into a rabid snarl and he leapt on her.

~ ~ ~ ~

Gannon found himself in another residential neighborhood. All the houses were at least thirty feet from the road. He slowed down and squinted to look at the addresses.

2250.

2376.

2732.

What kind of system did they have here? That's another thing a city had on this damn town; addresses were sequential.

There was an elderly woman walking a tiny dog on the left. He swerved across the road, pulling alongside her. He buzzed his window down.

"Excuse me? Do you know where the Ramsdales live? I've been going up and down the street and can't find the address."

"Lucas Ramsdale?"

"That's right."

The woman frowned and shook her head. "Such a shame what happened to that nice young man."

"Uh? What happened to him?" Gannon asked, his heart sinking.

"He committed suicide. They found him at home with his wrists slashed."

*Oh God…* Wrists slashed often meant a razor blade. Just like the Begums. Just like the Atens.

He really was too late.

"Which one is their house?"

"They're over on Meadow *Drive*. This is Meadow Lane. It's just around the corner."

He didn't bother thanking her and peeled off, making his tires squeal.

~ ~ ~ ~

"Wait, stop!" Tori screamed.

Boyd ignored her and jumped. He was on her immediately, making her lose her balance.

There were a hundred things she could've done, she knew. She could have gotten into a defensive stance. She could have hit him. She could have run away. The truth was that she was paralyzed by how unreal the situation was. She was being attacked by *a child.*

He swung his hand from left to right. She felt the microscopic edge of the razor blade break the skin of her forearm. It burned more than it hurt, but the shock couldn't be escaped. She automatically let go of the knife and tumbled backwards.

"Ah!"

Without hesitation, Boyd got on top of her and finally her instincts kicked in. She pushed on his small body, doing her best to keep him at bay. But he was strong, much stronger than she would've thought.

He was also ferocious. He was virtually foaming at the mouth. His eyes had turned black as if there wasn't a trace of life left in him. He was a beast. A machine.

A killing machine.

"Stop!" she ordered.

It didn't matter how much she pushed back—he kept coming. She squirmed against the grass. There was nowhere to go. He was fast and agile. He slashed the blade at her face, connecting once more.

The pain was intense now. She felt the heat of the blood pouring out under her eyes. He was going to murder her, just as he had done to Dr. Curnutt, to his parents. To Lucas.

"No!" she shouted, gritting her teeth.

"You're just like all the others, Tori."

She tried to roll away, but he still held on. He slashed again, this time even higher on the right cheek. Blood gushed out and, as her head tilted back in the struggle, it pooled into her eyes. It burned and she started to panic. She couldn't see.

That's when she understood how this kid could have killed all these people. He had a gift for violence. No matter what she did, Boyd would get his way. She would wind up as just another one of his victims.

Even worse, the kid knew it. He was smiling at her, saliva dripping from the corners of his mouth. He was readying for the kill.

"No!"

The bloodied razor came down to her throat.

~ ~ ~ ~

It occurred to Gannon that he might have been panicking.

This situation had evolved for weeks. Maybe he should have followed the captain's orders after all and he wouldn't have to live with the consequences of his actions. He wouldn't get fired before his pension kicked in. If the kid was dangerous, it wasn't like a few minutes or a few days would matter.

This made him feel better as he found the address on Meadow Drive and hopped out of his car. There was a Subaru and a pickup truck in the driveway. At least he hadn't driven up here for nothing.

He was heading for the front door when he heard a scream coming from the backyard. It was a woman.

A woman scared to death.

Panic had been a good thing, he figured. He ran around the house, out of breath after four steps. He hadn't so much as jogged since the nineties. What he saw was simultaneously satisfying and terrifying. He had been right, but he may have been too late.

The kid was holding down a woman and he had some sort of blade in his hand. No matter how much she wriggled, she couldn't shake him off. He was good.

Gannon ran closer and drew his sidearm, aiming at the child.

"Stop, police!"

The kid was taken aback and looked up, although he didn't loosen his grip on the Ramsdale woman.

"You're not going to shoot me."

"Let go of her now, Cody!"

"Have you seen what happens to a cop's career when he shoots a child?"

Gannon narrowed his eyes, his pistol still aimed at the boy's head. He wavered for the moment.

"You're right, Cody."

Lowering the weapon, Gannon finally dropped it on the grass. The woman was stunned, all hope draining from her. The opposite happened with the kid. He was smiling from ear to ear.

He cocked his shoulder back, getting ready to slash her windpipe open.

In the same fluid movement in which Gannon had let go of his gun, he reached under his jacket for something clipped to his belt. He came up again with a black and yellow device. A Taser.

He pointed it forward, took half a second to get a bead on the kid, and pulled the trigger.

The two probes flew out at a hundred and eighty feet

per second, hitting the kid square in the chest with fifty thousand volts. The discharge lasted ten seconds.

"Aaaarrrggghh!"

The kid was thrown backwards, landing hard on the ground. He didn't pass out, but he was immobile from pain, his muscles seizing up.

Without wasting a moment, Gannon ran forward. He dropped the Taser and produced handcuffs. It felt wrong to restrain a child until he remembered everything that he had done. Hell, he'd just been in the process of murdering a woman.

He removed the razor blade from his hand and tossed it away. He did a cursory search and found no other weapons. He swiveled toward the woman.

"It's okay, Mrs. Ramsdale. I'm State Police. Detective Gannon."

He fell to his knees next to her, pulling out a packet of paper tissues from inside his jacket. He inspected her injuries. She had cuts on her face, on her arms and hands.

"You're fine," he said. "The cuts aren't deep. I don't think you'll need sutures."

He wiped the blood from her eyes and she had difficulty keeping her emotions under control. She glanced at the kid, at him, at herself. She cried and the remaining blood gave her red tears.

Gannon congratulated himself for having finally listened to Vail and signing out a Taser. On the other hand, remembering the child's past deeds, he wondered if it wouldn't have been better to put him down permanently. Then he decided that no, it wasn't his place to pass judgment. The justice system would take care of him from here on out.

"Thank you," she whispered as he helped her sit up. "Thank you so much! How did you know to come here?"

"Some things didn't add up and I figured Cody would act up again. The investigation has been going on for a while."

"Cody?"

"Meet Cody Irwin Aten, ten-year-old murderer on the lam."

They both turned to the child. He was breathing heavily, lying on his side away from them. The woman began sobbing in earnest. Gannon couldn't imagine everything she had been through and figured that, if anything, she was relieved.

"Thank you," she repeated.

# CHAPTER 41

The applause was deafening. Everywhere Tori looked, people were smiling at her and clapping even louder.

"The woman of the hour, ladies and gentlemen!"

She couldn't keep from blushing as she turned toward the gallery owner, Savely Artemiev. He was the most enthusiastic about the applause and encouraged the others to do the same.

She gave a little wave, feeling self-conscious, and eventually Artemiev took pity on her. He stopped clapping. The hundred or so attendees soon did the same, returning to their champagne, hors d'oeuvres, and conversations.

The Artemiev Exhibit wasn't the most exclusive art gallery in Los Angeles, but it was getting there. It had featured several painters and sculptors who were now the toast of the scene. Artemiev had a lot to do with that, being a natural showman with a gift for sales.

The official story was that he had escaped the Soviet Union by being smuggled over the Berlin Wall, all because Communists stifled the artistic spirit, but Tori had her doubts. It was the sort of narrative only he would come up with, just to make his stock rise. He had toiled in galleries in New York and London before opening his own, here in LA.

He grabbed two flutes of champagne from a passing waiter and headed over to her, handing her one of the glasses. She didn't feel like drinking, but took it anyway.

"This show is a success, my dear!"

"You really think so?"

She was impressed by the turnout. There were expensive cars outside. The women wore beautiful gowns and jewelry. One of the guests she recognized from the original *90210* TV series.

"Tori," the man whispered into her ear. "All your paintings have been sold."

"All?"

"Every single one. So I want more, my dear! How soon can you paint and deliver a dozen or more?"

"Uh, I…"

"Your cut from tonight's sales is over a hundred thousand dollars. Next time, I think we can bump this up to half a million. Easy."

Her jaw was on the floor and, of course, that's when an admirer chose to introduce himself.

"I just love your work! I'm a fan for life."

That was the template for the rest of the evening. Art collectors came over to shake her hand, letting her know how much they admired her postmodern landscapes. It was overwhelming and she took it in stride.

It had been six months since the episode that had changed her life.

She had wanted to put it behind her as fast as possible and her cuts had healed quickly. She had moved back to California, eager for a fresh start, reverting to her maiden name. She had devoted herself to painting again.

She was well aware that most of the interest people showed had something to do with her relationship with Boyd. Cody, or whatever the hell his name was. There was a morbid fascination with someone who had been involved with a murderer, especially a child who'd turned out to be a wanted fugitive.

She had been in the news, most of the time against her will, and the way she had made peace with it was by embracing it. If people could use her to sell newspapers and online ad space, then she might as well use them to sell her art.

She had sold a few pieces here and there at first and received glowing reviews. Obviously, the critics never failed to refer to her as The Foster Mother, yet they also recognized the strengths of her paintings. All this had led to Savely Artemiev offering to put on a show for her.

She couldn't believe that she owed a part of this success to Lucas. He had told her to stop painting dainty landscapes, that it would never make her rich and famous. After moving to Los Angeles, she had decided to follow his advice. Well, partly. Her subjects were still landscapes, mostly mountains, but her approach was Cubist, using shapes and textures to convey her vision.

She went even further. All her paintings nowadays were created using nothing but a palette knife. This was her solution to make the nightmares stop. It allowed her to own the terror Boyd had made her feel, the way he had destroyed her life.

In a crazy way, she was grateful for the entire experience. The tragic losses notwithstanding, that's what it had taken for Tori to realize that her life had been broken for years already. Her career, her marriage, it had been a sham. It was only by taking a step back and seeing how the events had unfolded that she could see it now.

She kept in touch with Detective Gannon, the man who had saved her life. In fact, he had called her this morning to wish her luck. He was retiring soon and opening a private investigations firm with his partner, Detective Mobley.

Gannon had told her everything about Boyd, and Tori had trouble believing what a twisted story this was. Killing his parents, traveling across the country and massacring another couple. There was talk of trying him for the murders of Lucas and Dr. Curnutt, but the evidence was circumstantial at best.

For the time being, he had been sent back to the Pacific Northwest. The state accepted that no one knew how to handle a child murderer, so he was committed to a place called Deercove. Once he turned eighteen, his case would be reevaluated and he would most likely be sent to a state penitentiary.

Tori cleared her mind of all that. She had nothing to do with it anymore. Her future relied on focusing on the present. It worked, too. She was doing what she loved for the first time in her life. She felt happier and stronger than she ever had.

~ ~ ~ ~

A light winter rain was falling on the Deercove

Psychiatric Institute.

It officially consisted of several buildings, but the main pavilion had once been the mansion of a man who had been a lumber baron before the Great Depression.

The family was long forgotten, but the home remained, its Gothic influence inescapable. The gray stonework had darkened with time and the vaulted windows cast spooky shadows on the expansive lawn dotted by spruce trees.

"I'm sure you're gonna love it here," Nurse Soto said.

He was a middle-aged man who was beginning to get paunchy. His uniform was getting tight around his midsection and he was the only one who hadn't noticed.

"I'm sure," the young woman next to him said.

She was in her early twenties, blonde and cheerful. First day on the job.

"It's Madeleine, right? We don't like to be too formal around here."

"Everybody calls me Maddie."

"Maddie. I like that."

His smile was lecherous. He probably thought he was flirting.

He continued to give her a tour of the facility. The patients' wing, the break room, the doctors' quarters, the important stuff.

"It's pretty laid-back around here, honestly."

"Is it?" she said with wavering conviction. "I heard some rumors. Some of the inmates here…"

Nurse Soto leaned toward her, getting into her personal space. "Never inmates. We say patients. Makes everybody feel better. As long as you have your pass with you, you'll be fine."

And with that, he unclipped his pass, scanning it on a wall-mounted unit. There was a soft buzz and he opened the door.

They walked into a pleasantly decorated den. There were chairs and couches, a television which currently displayed cartoons. Tall, barred windows made the space seem more open. There was only one person in the room.

"This is The Haven, as we call it. It's kind of a playroom for the patients. They get to come here if they behave. Frankly, it keeps them calm and that makes all our jobs easier."

A boy was kneeling in the middle of the room, on a pastel rug. He was wearing sweatpants and a *LEGO Batman* shirt. He was playing with wooden blocks, arranging them in no discernible order.

Nurse Soto's phone chimed and he fished it out of his pocket with annoyance. He read the screen.

"Shit. They're having problems with Patient Seven. She's a biter."

"A biter, really?"

"Don't worry. She's about to go on a primo Thorazine nap. Always does the trick. Anyway, I have to go. Are you okay by yourself for a minute?"

The young nurse wasn't certain, but she wasn't about to admit it. She smiled tightly and nodded. "Sure."

"I'll be back soon."

Nurse Soto turned around and jogged away. The woman inspected the room. Overall, it was a much nicer facility than she'd been led to believe. She would like it here, she decided.

The little boy was looking at her now. He seemed so nice. Peaceful. What was he doing in a place like this? She approached and bent forward to address him.

"Hi. I'm Nurse Maddie."

"Hello. I'm Cody, but I prefer to be called Boyd. It kind of grew on me recently. I hope we can have fun together."

As he said that, he tightened his grip on one of the wooden blocks. He could feel the sharp corner and he rotated it until it protruded between his knuckles.

"It's nice to meet you, Cody. I mean, Boyd."

Continuing to smile at her, he glanced at the ID badge clipped to her shirt. Then he looked at the door beyond. A plan began to form.

She was leaning toward him, within arm's reach. He twisted his hand so the block would connect with her left temple, if he decided to act. She would take no more than two blows. Then he could snatch her pass and make a run for the exit. His chances of making a clean getaway were fifty-fifty, he estimated.

Those were good odds.

THE END

# ABOUT THE AUTHOR

Steve Richer is the international bestselling author of the thrillers *The President Killed His Wife* and *The Pope's Suicide.* He went to law school and film school before considering becoming a sherpa, though he abandoned the idea upon discovering what a sherpa really was. Now he spends his days writing books.

He specializes in fun, over the top thrillers that read like action movies. He splits his time between Montreal and Miami.

You can Like Steve on Facebook for all the latest news.

Like Steve on Facebook for all the latest news at

facebook.com/OfficialSteveRicher

Sign up for the newsletter now and receive a free novel and exclusive short story!

SteveRicherBooks.com

Turn the page for more exciting books by Steve Richer!

# ALSO BY STEVE RICHER

The President Killed His Wife (Rogan Bricks 1)

Counterblow (Rogan Bricks 2)

Murder Island (Rogan Bricks 3)

The Pope's Suicide

Critical Salvage

Terror Bounty

Park Avenue Blackmail

The Kennedy Secret

The Gilded Treachery

Never Bloodless

The Atomic Eagle

Sigma Division

First Thrill

Innocent Games

Intense Past: Historical Thriller Collection

Eyes Only: Spy Thriller Collection

Made in the USA
Middletown, DE
04 May 2019